TERMINATOR SALVATION
FROM THE ASHES

TERMINATOR SALVATION
FROM THE ASHES

TIMOTHY ZAHN

TITAN BOOKS

Terminator Salvation: From the Ashes
ISBN: 9781848560864

Published by
Titan Books
A division of
Titan Publishing Group Ltd
144 Southwark St
London
SE1 0UP

First edition March 2009
10 9 8 7 6 5 4 3 2 1

Terminator Salvation: From the Ashes is a work of fiction. Names, places and incidents either are products of the author's imagination or are used fictitiously.

Visit our website:
www.titanbooks.com

Did you enjoy this book? We love to hear from our readers. Please email us at readerfeedback@titanemail.com or write to us at Reader Feedback at the above address.

To receive advance information, news, competitions, and exclusive Titan offers online, please register as a member by clicking the "sign up" button on our website: www.titanbooks.com

A CIP catalogue record for this title is available from the British Library.

Printed and bound in the United States.

As always,
For always,
For Anna.

PROLOGUE

The last day of his life, he remembered thinking afterward, had been hell on earth.

It wasn't just the heat of the Baja desert. That was awesomely intense, shimmering across the dirt and scrub, and he knew some of his fellow Marines were suffering in it. But U.S. Marine Sergeant Justo Orozco had grown up in East Los Angeles, and he had no problem with heat.

It wasn't just the job, either. The Eleventh Marine Expeditionary Unit prided itself on its ability to fight anywhere on the planet, and there wasn't any particular reason why Orozco's platoon shouldn't be here running a drug-interdiction exercise with their Mexican Army counterparts. Never mind that the theory underlying the exercise was bogus. Never mind that the Mexicans probably saw this as a slap at their own capabilities. The logic and politics of the situation weren't Orozco's concern, and he wasn't being paid by the hour.

No, what made this particular mission hell was the way every single damn Mexican insisted on calling all the Americans "gringo."

Including Orozco.

It irritated the hell out of him, which was probably

why they kept doing it. He was an American, yes, but he was also full-blooded Hispanic, and he was damn proud of both. Why some people seemed to think those two identities had to be mutually exclusive was something he had never understood. He'd never put up with that nonsense before, and it galled the grit out of him to have to put up with it now.

But he was under orders to be cooperative. More than that, he was a professional, and he was damned if he would let a few resentful locals get the best of him.

It was getting on toward evening, and the team was just wrapping up a search-and-corral exercise, when out of the corner of his eye Orozco saw the flash.

His first reflexive assumption was that the Mexicans had sneaked an aircraft into the exercise, just to shake things up a little, and that he'd caught a flicker of sunlight off one of its windows. He turned that direction, opening his mouth to warn the rest of the team.

The words died in his throat. In the hazy distance far to the north, right where he'd seen the flash, a tiny, red-edged cloud had appeared.

And as he watched, its top boiled over into the shape of a mushroom.

He was trying to wrap his brain around the sight when there was another small flicker, slightly brighter this time. He waited, still staring at the mushroom cloud, when a second fiery pillar boiled up from the earth a little ways to the east of the first.

"My God," someone whispered beside him. "Is that...? Oh, *God*!"

"It's San Diego," Orozco said, the sheer unnatural calmness in his voice as frightening as the mushroom clouds themselves. "San Diego."

"Maybe Mexicali, too," someone else muttered.

"Or Twentynine Palms," Orozco said, marveling at the strange disconnect that had severed the link between his intellect and emotions. "Who the hell would want to take out Mexicali?"

"I just thought—"

"*Oh, Dios mio!*"

With an effort, Orozco tore his eyes away from the twin pillars of death. One of the Mexicans was staring past Orozco's shoulder, his eyes wide and horrified, his face as pale as any of the gringos he derided. Moving like a man slogging through a nightmare, Orozco turned to look.

In the distance to the southeast, another tiny mushroom had appeared, clawing its way toward the sky.

"What the *hell*?" someone gasped. "That can't be—"

"Hermosillo," one of the other Mexicans said in a quavering voice. The man had tears shimmering in his eyes, and Orozco remembered him talking about his family in Hermosillo.

Orozco stared at the third mushroom cloud, his mind reeling with the utter insanity of it. San Diego, yes. Twentynine Palms, maybe. But Hermosillo? The place didn't have a single shred of military or political significance that Orozco could think of. Why would anyone waste a nuke taking it out?

Unless someone had decided to take out everything.

Slowly, he turned to look at the rest of his team, their faces etched with varying degrees of terror, anger, or disbelief. They'd figured it out, too. Or they would soon enough.

Their lives were over. Everyone's life was now over.

Orozco took a deep breath.

"I think," he said, "we can safely say the exercise is over."

"What do we do now?" someone asked.

Orozco took another look around the group…and this time, he saw something he hadn't noticed before. All the Marines were looking at him. Even Lieutenant Raeder, whose face was as frozen as anyone else's. They were all looking at Orozco.

Waiting for their sergeant to tell them what to do.

He took another deep breath. One of these deep breaths, he thought distantly, would be his last. He wondered if he would even know at the time which breath that would be.

"We'll be all right," he said. "We'll survive, because we're Marines, and that's what Marines do. We'll start by going back to camp and figuring out what we've got to work with."

For a moment no one moved. Then the lieutenant stirred.

"You heard the man," he called. "Gather up the gear and head back to camp."

Slowly, the clustered knots broke up as the men finally began to move. Orozco took one last look to the north, noting that the mushroom clouds, too, were starting to break up.

And as he began helping the others collect the gear, he realized he'd been wrong. This day hadn't been hell on earth. This day had been paradise.

Hell on earth had just begun.

CHAPTER ONE

It was after one in the morning by the time John Connor and his Resistance team made their way back through the rubble of Greater Los Angeles to the half-broken, half-burned-out building they'd called home for the past three months. He supervised the others as they stowed their gear, then sent them stumbling wearily to their bunks.

Then, alone in the small pool of light from his desk lamp, amid the outer darkness that pressed in against it, he sat down to make out his report.

In many ways, he reflected, this was one of the worst parts of the war against Skynet. In the heat of battle, with HK Hunter-Killers swooping past overhead and T-600 Terminators lumbering in from all sides, there was no time for deep thought or grand strategy or clever planning. You played it on the fly, running and shooting and running some more, hoping you could spot the openings and opportunities before Skynet could close them, trying to achieve your mission goal and still get as many of your people out alive as you could.

But sitting here alone, with a piece of crumpled paper laid out on top of a battered file cabinet, things were different. You had the quiet and the time and—worst of all—the hindsight to replay the battle over and over again.

You saw all the things you should have done faster, or smarter, or just different. You saw the mistakes, the lapses of judgment, the miscues.

And you relived the deaths. All of them.

But it was part of the job, and it had to be done. Every Resistance contact with the enemy—win, lose, or draw—was data that could be sifted, prodded, evaluated, and tucked away for possible future reference. With enough such data, maybe the strategists at Command would someday finally find a weakness or blind spot that could be used to bring down the whole Skynet system.

Or so the theory went. Connor, at least, didn't believe it for a minute. This was going to be a long, bloody war, and he had long since stopped hoping for silver bullets.

But you never knew. Besides, Skynet was certainly analyzing its side of each encounter. The Resistance might as well do the same.

It took him half an hour to write up the report and transmit it to Command. After that he spent a few minutes in the bathroom cleaning up as best he could, scrubbing other men's blood off his hands and clothing. Then, shutting off the last of the bunker's lights, he cracked the shutters to let in a bit of fresh air, and wearily headed down the darkened corridor to the tiny room he shared with his wife.

Kate was stretched out in bed, the blankets tucked up under her chin, her breathing slow and steady. Hopefully long since asleep, though Connor had no real illusions on that score. As one of their team's two genuine doctors, the hours she put in were nearly as long as Connor's own, and in some ways even bloodier.

For a minute he just stood inside the doorway, gazing at her with a mixture of love, pride, and guilt. Once upon a time she'd had the nice, simple job of a veterinarian, where the worst thing that could happen in a given day was a nervous horse or a lap dog with attitude.

Connor had taken her away from all that. Wrenched her out of it, more accurately, snatching her from the path of Skynet's last attempt to kill him before the devastation of Judgment Day.

Of course, if he *hadn't* taken her away, she would be dead now. There were all too many days when he wondered if that would have been a kinder fate than the one he'd bestowed on her.

There's no fate but what we make for ourselves. The old quote whispered through his mind. Kyle Reese's old quote, the words Connor himself would one day teach the boy—

"Good morning," Kate murmured from the bed.

Connor started.

"Sorry—didn't mean to wake you," he murmured back.

"You didn't," she assured him, pushing back the blankets and propping herself up on one elbow. "I only got to bed an hour or so ago. I heard everyone else come in, and I've just been dozing a little while I waited for you. How did it go?"

"About like usual," Connor said as he crossed to the bed and sat down. "We got the Riverside radar tower—not just taken down, but blown to splinters. If Olsen's team got the Pasadena tower like they were supposed to, that'll leave Skynet just the Capistrano one and no triangulation at all. That should take a lot of the pressure off our air support in any future operations. At least until Skynet gets around to rebuilding everything."

"Good—we can use a breather," Kate said. "How many did we lose?"

Connor grimaced.

"Three. Garcia, Smitty, and Rondo."

"I'm sorry," she said, and Connor could see some of his own pain flash across her eyes. "That's, what, ten including the ones Jericho lost when his team took out the Thousand Oaks tower?"

"Eleven," Connor corrected. "Those towers come expensive, don't they?"

"They sure do," Kate said soberly. Abruptly, she brightened. "By the way, I have a surprise for you." Reaching to the far side of the bed, she came up with a small bag. "Merry Christmas."

Connor stared at the bag in her hand, a surge of husbandly panic flashing through him. How could he possibly have forgotten—?

"Wait a minute," he said, frowning. "This is *March*."

"Well, yes, technically," Kate conceded innocently. "But we were all kind of busy on the official Christmas."

Connor searched his memory, trying to pick the specifics out of the long, blended-together nightmare that life on earth had become.

"Was that the day we raided the air reserve base for parts?"

"No, that was Christmas Eve," Kate corrected. "Christmas Day we were mostly playing hide-and-seek with those three T-1s that wanted the stuff back. Anyway, I didn't have anything for you back then." She jiggled the bag enticingly. "Now, I do. Go ahead—take it."

"But I didn't get anything for you," Connor protested as he took the bag.

"Sure you did," Kate said quietly. "You came home alive. That's all I want."

Connor braced himself.

"Kate, we've been through this," he reminded her gently. "You're too valuable as a surgeon to risk having you go out in the field."

"Yes, I remember all the arguments," Kate said. "And up to now, I've mostly agreed with them."

"Mostly?"

She sighed.

"You're the most important thing in my life, John. In fact, you're the most important thing in *everyone's* life, even if they don't know it yet. Whatever I can do to keep you focused, that's what I'll do. Whether I personally like it or not. If having me stay behind helps that focus, well, I've been content to do that."

Connor had to turn away from the intensity in her eyes.

"Until now?"

"Until now." She reached up and put her hand on his cheek, gently but firmly turning him back to look at her. "People are dying out there. Far too many people, far too quickly. We need every gun and every set of hands in the field that we can get. You know that as well as I do."

"But you're more valuable to us right here," Connor tried again.

"Am I?" Kate asked. "Even if we grant for the sake of argument that I'm any safer hiding in a makeshift bunker than I am out in the field, is this really where I can do the most good? Patching up the wounded after you get them back is all well and good, but I can't help but think it would be better if you had me right there with you where I could do the preliminary work on the spot."

"You could teach some of the others."

"I *have* taught them," Kate reminded him. "I've taught you and them and everyone everything I can about first aid. But there's nothing I can do to give you my experience, and that's what you need out there. You need a field medic, pure and simple. So you've got Campollo and me, and Campollo is seventy-one with arthritic knees. This is one of those decisions that really kind of makes itself, don't you think?"

Connor closed his eyes.

"I don't want to lose you, Kate."

"I don't want to lose you, either," she said quietly. "That's why we need to be together. So that neither of us loses the other."

With her hand still on his cheek, she leaned forward and gave him a lingering kiss. Connor kissed her back, hungrily, craving the love and closeness and peace that had all but died so many years ago, when the missiles began falling to the earth.

They held the kiss for a long minute, and then Kate gently disengaged.

"Meanwhile," she said, giving him an impish smile, "you still have a Christmas present to open."

Connor smiled back.

"What in the world would I do without you?"

"Well, for one thing, you could have been asleep fifteen minutes ago," Kate said dryly. "Come on—open it."

Connor focused on the bag in his hand. It was one of the drawstring bags Kate packed emergency first-aid supplies in, turned inside out so that the smoother, silkier side was outward.

"I see you've been shopping at Macy's again," he commented as he carefully pulled it open.

"Actually, I just keep reusing their bags," Kate said. "Adds class to all my gift-giving. For heaven's sake— were you this slow on Christmas when you were a boy?"

Connor shrugged.

"Given that my mother's typical Christmas presents were new Browning semi-autos or C4 detonators, it didn't pay to open packages too quickly."

Kate's eyes widened.

"You *are* joking, aren't you?"

"Of course," Connor said with a straight face. "Christmas was survival gear; Fourth of *July* was munitions. Okay, here goes." He reached into the bag.

And to his surprise, pulled out a badly cracked jewel case with a slightly battered compact disc inside.

"What's this?" he asked, peering at it in the dim light.

"A little memory from your childhood," Kate said. "Or at least from simpler days. An album called *Use Your Illusion II.*"

Connor felt his eyes open. A memory from his childhood, indeed. "Thank you," he said. "Where on earth did you find it?"

"One of Olsen's men had it with him last month when they came by to swap munitions," Kate said. "I remembered you talking about listening to it when you were younger, so I traded him a couple of extra bandage packs for it. You know, those packs we dug out of the treatment room at the Orange County Zoo."

"I just hope Tunney was able to get that CD player working," Connor commented, cradling the disk carefully in his hands. "I miss music. That and Italian food, I think, are what I miss most."

"For me, it's definitely music," Kate mused. "Vocals, especially—I used to love listening to a live choir in full four-part harmony." She smiled faintly. "Just a *bit* different from your taste in music."

"Differences are the spice of life," Connor reminded her.

"And G'n'R is probably better music to kill machines by."

"Probably." Kate's smile faded. "Besides, nowadays what reason does anyone have to sing?"

"There's still life," Connor said, eyeing his wife closely. Kate didn't get depressed very often, but when she did it could be a deep and terrible pit. "And love, and friends."

"But mostly just life," Kate agreed. "I know. Sometimes we forget what's really important, don't we?"

"A constant problem throughout history," Connor said, breathing a quiet sigh of relief. So she wasn't going there, after all. Good. "Thanks again, Kate. This really makes my day. Probably even my *year*."

"You're welcome," she said. "Oh, and *rock on*. The man who gave me the disk told me to say that." She took a deep breath, and Connor could see her chasing the memories back to where they belonged. "Meanwhile, it's been a late night, and the world starts up again in about five hours. Come on, let's go to bed."

"Right." Standing up, Connor reached for his gunbelt. And paused. "Did you hear something?" he asked in a low voice.

"I don't know," Kate said, her head tilted in concentration.

Connor frowned, straining his ears. A whispery wind was blowing gently across the bunker roof, setting cat-purr vibrations through the piles of loose debris up there. Everything seemed all right.

But *something* had caught his attention. And something was still screaming wordlessly across his combat senses.

"Stay here," Connor told his wife, crossing back to the door. He listened at the panel for a moment, then cautiously opened it.

The earlier overcast sky had cleared somewhat, allowing a little starlight to filter in through the cracked shutters. Connor checked both directions down the empty
corridor, then headed left toward the rear of the bunker
and the sentry post situated between the living quarters
and storage room.

Piccerno was on duty, seated on a tall stepladder with
everything from his shoulders up snugged up inside the
observation dome. Like everything else these days, the
dome was a product of simplicity and ingenuity: an old
plastic office wastebasket that had been fastened to the
top of the bunker, equipped with a set of eye slits that
permitted 360-degree surveillance, then covered from
above with strategically placed rubble to disguise its
true purpose.

"Report," Connor murmured as he stepped to the foot
of the ladder.

There was no answer.

"Piccerno?" Connor murmured, the hair on the back
of his neck tingling. "Piccerno?"

Still no answer. Getting a one-handed grip on the ladder, Connor headed up. He reached the top and pushed
aside Piccerno's bunched-up parka collar.

One touch of the warm, sticky liquid that had soaked
the upper surface of the collar was all he needed to know
what had happened. He spent another precious second
anyway, peering up into the narrow space between
Piccerno's face and the rim of the dome, just to make
sure there was nothing he could do.

There wasn't. Piccerno's eyes were open but unseeing,
his forehead leaning against the dome, the blood from
the hole in his left temple still trickling down his face.

Skynet had found them.

Quickly, Connor climbed back down the ladder, a kaleidoscope of Piccerno's life with the team flashing through his mind. Ruthlessly, he forced back the memories.

This was not the time.

Grabbing the Heckler & Koch MP5 submachine gun that was propped against the wall, he hurried back to the living quarters.

Kate was already dressed, her gun belt in hand. "What is it?" she asked tensely.

"Piccerno's dead," Connor told her grimly. "Long-range sniper, or else one hell of a silencer."

"Terminators?"

"I didn't check," Connor said. "Skynet's obviously trying the sneaky approach, and I didn't want to do anything that might alert it that we were onto the game. Get back to supply—I'll go roust everyone and send them back there. Make a quick sort of the equipment and load them with as much as you think they can handle."

"Right," Kate said as she finished strapping on her gun belt.

"And keep everyone as quiet as you can," Connor added. "The longer Skynet thinks we're all still asleep, the longer we'll have before the fireworks start."

Kate nodded.

"Be careful."

"You, too."

He continued along the corridor, ducking into each room as he passed and nudging or whispering the occupants awake, giving them a set of terse instructions, then moving on as they grabbed their clothing and weapons.

Finally, he reached the bunker's main entrance. There, to his complete lack of surprise, he found Barnes waiting, standing beside the bunker door with his eye pressed to one of the eyeslits, a 9mm Steyr in his holster and one of the group's few remaining grenade launchers clutched to his chest. A few feet away stood the young man who was supposed to be on sentry duty tonight, his throat working as he nervously fingered his rifle.

"We got eight T-600s on the way," Barnes reported as Connor came up beside him. "What's goin' on in back?"

"They took out Piccerno," Connor told him. "Quietly, and at least several minutes ago. Probably means Skynet's about to send in the heavy stuff—T-1s or maybe a tank or two—and was hoping to sneak up on us."

Barnes grunted and straightened up from the peepholes. His bald head glistened with a week's worth of sweat, his clenched teeth glinting through two weeks' worth of beard stubble.

"So what's the plan?"

"We run on our timetable, not Skynet's," Connor replied. "If we can buy a few minutes, I can—"

Barnes nodded.

"Got just the thing."

With that he pulled open the door, and fired.

There was a soft *chuff* as the grenade shot skyward out of its tube. Biting down hard on his tongue—*I can get more men here before you engage*—Connor stepped quickly to the other side of the doorway and looked out.

In the faint starlight he could see eight towering, human-shaped figures picking their way carefully across the treacherous ground. One of the T-600s looked up at the sounds from the bunker, and Connor caught a glimpse of glowing red eyes.

And then, with a brilliant flash, Barnes's grenade exploded.

Not in the midst of the approaching Terminators, but

in the doorway of the half-collapsed four-story building immediately to their right. There was a stutter as the grenade's shockwave set off a line of smaller charges embedded in the pockmarked masonry.

And with a horrendous crunch, the entire wall gave way, raining blocks of concrete and rebar and broken glass across the street, toppling and burying all eight of the Terminators.

"That how you wanted it?" Barnes called to Connor over the echoing roar.

"Pretty much," Connor said. So much for giving the group as much time as possible to make their escape.

On the other hand, if Barnes hadn't blown the building when he did, the eight Terminators would soon have passed that particular trap, and Connor's fighters would have had that many more enemies to deal with.

"I'll send you some backup," he added, moving away from the doorway. "Hold for ten minutes, or as long as you can, then pull back to the tunnel."

"I don't need no one else," Barnes growled, throwing a contemptuous glance at the shaking sentry. "You just get the people and stuff out."

"I'll send you some backup," Connor repeated, making it clear it was an order, and headed back down the corridor. Barnes was probably one of the best ground fighters in the entire Resistance, but this wasn't the time for lone-wolf tactics. If indeed there ever was such a time.

If anyone had needed extra incentive to get moving, Barnes's wake-up explosion had apparently done the trick. The whole bunker was alive with people, many of them still scrambling into their clothing as they ran toward the supply room and the emergency exit beyond.

A few of the faster dressers had taken up positions in

doorways along the way, their weapons pointed toward the front of the bunker, ready to sacrifice themselves if necessary to slow down the machines once the outer defenses were breached. Connor grabbed two of them and sent them up to the entrance, gave everyone else the same ten-minute warning he'd given Barnes, then headed back to his room for anything he or Kate might have left behind.

He made especially sure that he grabbed his new G'n'R CD.

Most of the fifty-odd people of the team had made it to the supply room by the time he arrived, with only a few stragglers still coming in. Kate was in the center of the activity, coolly pointing each newcomer to the boxes, bags, and packs she'd selected for the must-save list.

"How are we doing?" Connor asked as he picked up two ammo satchels and slung one over each shoulder.

"Another ninety seconds and we'll have everything we can carry," Kate told him, threading a bungee cord between the satchels' straps and fastening them together across Connor's chest so that they wouldn't slip off his shoulders. "They took Piccerno's body down," she added more quietly.

Connor nodded. He'd noticed that on his way through.

"Have Blair and Yoshi been through? I didn't spot either of them, but it was pretty dark and I wasn't exactly taking roll."

"Blair's here," Kate said, waving to a pair of latecomers and pointing them to a stack of ration boxes. "She said she'll go out with the rest of us and make her way back to the hangar. Yoshi's already there, or at least he's supposed to be."

"We'll need to get the ground crew out, too," Connor

said, grimacing as a low vibration tickled at the soles of his feet. "Here comes our company."

The words were barely out of his mouth when one of the younger women dashed in from the direction of the sentry post, nearly running down an eight-year-old boy in the process.

"T-1s," she announced breathlessly. "Coming in from all directions."

"Are they heading for the main door?" Connor asked.

"No, toward here. I saw them through the—" she faltered a little "—where Piccerno was. Maybe a hundred meters out."

Connor nodded. T-1s were heavy, splay-armed fighting machines mounted on heavy treads, slower than the humanoid T-600s but more heavily armed and even harder to take down. The plan was probably to roll them up onto the roof near Piccerno's sentry post in hopes of collapsing it by sheer weight and trapping the group in a pincer.

"Go to the front and tell Barnes and the others I said to pull out now," Connor told her. "They're to collect the rest of the backstops along the way."

The girl nodded and took off down the corridor at a dead run.

"Tunney?" Connor called, looking around at the heavily laden men and women.

"Here, sir," Tunney called from the side wall. He and the other lieutenant, David, were standing beside the dark opening that led into the bunker's emergency exit. Like Connor, each man was loaded with two shoulder bags of ammo or grenades, but instead of just a sub-machine gun each of them also carried a grenade launcher and flame thrower. "Time to go?" he asked.

"Almost," Connor said, squeezing Kate's shoulder briefly and then crossing to join them. "Now it is," he said. "I'll take point; keep a three-meter spacing between us."

"I believe it's my turn for point, sir," Tunney said, his voice low but firm.

Connor shook his head.

"My team; my job. Stay alert—if Skynet's found the far end, we'll have some unpleasant surprises waiting."

He looked back at the group, to find them silently watching him. Watching, and trusting.

"Stay as quiet as you can, and don't stop moving," he said, keeping his voice as calm as if this was just another training exercise. "Once you're through the tunnel, depending on what's waiting out there, we may decide to split into small groups of two or three. Everyone knows where Fallback One is?"

The room bobbed briefly with nodding heads.

"Then I'll see you all there," Connor said. "Good luck." Nodding for Tunney and David to follow, he headed into the tunnel.

The group referred to the emergency exit as a tunnel, but a real, hand-dug tunnel would have taken far more time and manpower than the group had had to spare over the past few months. The route was instead a mostly natural pathway consisting of half-crushed hallways, basements, and service corridors. Connor's people had cleared out the blockages, propped up the ceilings, and dug short connecting shafts where necessary until they'd created an exit route that could take them invisibly a good three blocks from the bunker.

But there was always the chance that one of Skynet's endlessly roving machines had spotted the route, and

Connor felt his nerves tightening with each step as he made his way through the darkness.

There were dozens of places where the roof had eroded through to the outside world, allowing in some badly needed starlight but also precluding the use of any lights by the escapees. Worse, the longest straight-line segment anywhere in the tunnel was about six meters, with everything else being a collection of zigzags, right-angle turns, and occasional backtracks. A T-600 waiting in the darkness around any one of those corners could have Connor and his vanguard dead before they even knew what had hit them.

But each corner was clear, the starlight filtering through the fissures never blazed with HK floodlights, and he heard nothing of the telltale growl of T-1 treads. Gradually, Connor's hopes and pace began to pick up. They might make it. They just might make it.

He was about halfway through the tunnel when the sounds of distant explosions and gunfire began to echo through the passageway from behind him.

He swore feelingly under his breath. The blasts could be nothing more ominous than Barnes setting off the last string of the bunker's booby traps. But they could also be the rear guard fighting desperately against T-1s that had succeeded in crashing through the bunker roof.

And Kate would be one of the last of the group to leave, probably just a couple of steps ahead of Barnes. If the Terminators had cut through...

If they had, there was nothing Connor could do to help. He could only trust to hope, and to the destiny that linked him and Kate to humanity's ultimate salvation.

He'd gone twenty meters more when a blast rolled through the tunnel, sending a wave of warm air across the back of his neck. The final booby trap had been triggered, bringing down the bunker's ceiling and burying any Terminators that had made it inside as it sealed off the end of the tunnel. Connor and his people were committed now, with nowhere to go but forward.

Still no sign that Skynet had noticed them. Connor kept going, the drifting air currents from the overhead gaps slowly becoming a single steady breeze in his face. He rounded one final blind corner, and with a suddenness that for some reason never failed to surprise him, he was at the end.

Cautiously, he looked out between the carefully positioned rotting two-by-fours that blocked the exit. The street beyond was cleaner than some he'd seen, with much of the masonry and wood having been scavenged over the years by the handful of civilians who still scratched out a tenuous existence in the ruined city. More importantly, there was no sign of Terminators.

From the direction of the bunker came a short burst of gunfire from one of the remote-activated guns set up there and in nearby buildings. The burst was answered instantly by a longer, staccato roar from the T-600s' miniguns. Connor gestured Tunney forward, and the two men set to work clearing the exit.

The wooden barrier looked sturdier and more impassible than it actually was, and it took less than half a minute for them to silently move the boards out of the way. Connor started to step out.

And ducked back as an HK swooped past, just half a block away, heading toward the bunker. Connor waited a few seconds, then tried again.

Nothing jumped or swooped out at him, either metal or human. As the sporadic gunfire continued from the vicinity of the bunker, he did a quick three-sixty, then gestured to Tunney and David. The two men slipped past him, moved ten meters in opposite directions down the street, and did three-sixties of their own. They hand-signaled the all-clear, then hunkered down in the rubble with weapons ready.

Connor stepped back into the tunnel, went back around that final blind corner, and gestured to the line of people waiting tensely in the dark.

Blair Williams, her dark hair tied back in a ponytail, was the fifth one out. She spotted Connor and stepped out of line.

"I'm heading for the hangar," she announced softly. "Any special orders?"

"Yes; that you wait a minute," Connor told her, grabbing her arm and pulling her down into a crouch as another HK appeared to the west, weaving its way between the skeletal remains of two of the taller buildings.

"Why?" Blair countered.

"Just wait," Connor repeated.

Blair huffed something under her breath, but obediently moved over to the stubby remains of a fire hydrant and squatted beside it, drawing her big .44 caliber Desert Eagle from its holster.

Two more HKs had swooped in to join the party at the bunker before everyone made it out of the tunnel. But none of the machines came close, and there was no indication that they'd noticed anything amiss, especially with all the gunfire masking any sounds the group might make.

Kate, as Connor had expected, was the last one out before the rear guard. At the very end of the line, also as expected, was Barnes.

"You seen my brother?" he asked Connor, hefting his

grenade launcher as he looked around.

"Yes, he's already out," Connor assured him. Along with his launcher, Connor noted, Barnes had also picked up a Galil assault rifle somewhere along the way and had the weapon slung over his shoulder along with his gear bags. If all the extra weight was bothering him, it didn't show.

"Good," Barnes said. "We're splitting up, right? I'll get my squad and take point."

"David will handle your squad," Connor told him. "I want you to take Blair to the hangar."

Blair rose from her crouch, a look of outraged disbelief on her face.

"Is *that* why you made me wait?" she demanded. "For *him*?"

"I don't want you trying to get to the hangar alone," Connor told her.

"I don't need him," Blair insisted.

"Right—she doesn't need me," Barnes seconded.

"More importantly, Wince and Inji are still in there," Connor explained patiently. "Once the planes are out, someone has to get them to safety."

Barnes bared his teeth, but reluctantly nodded.

"Fine. Come on, flygirl. Try to keep up."

He set off down the street, his head moving back and forth as he watched for trouble. Blair paused long enough to roll her eyes, then followed.

"I'm sure they're secretly very fond of each other," Kate offered dryly.

"As long as they dislike Skynet more, I'm happy," Connor said. "Come on, let's get these people out of here."

CHAPTER TWO

The gunfire back at the abandoned bunker was starting to trail off as Blair flitted down the street like a ghost, her eyes automatically picking out the quietest route through the debris and rusting cars and occasional pieces of shattered human skeletons. She took advantage of every shadow, and since the main source of light was the HKs' spotlights three blocks away, the shadows were both plentiful and deep. She'd done this sort of thing a thousand times, and was very good at it.

Certainly better at it than Barnes. He wasn't bad at shadow-hopping, but the sheer bulk of the gear he habitually lugged around automatically made him noisier than she was. In addition, he had a habit of turning his whole upper body back and forth instead of just his head as he scanned the area, which tended to jingle his equipment belts and ammo bandoleer. Blair had pointed it out once or twice in the past, and had gotten a highly ungracious and extremely unoriginal expletive for her trouble.

She didn't trust Barnes. Not because she thought that he would ever betray them to the Terminators, but because he was a loose cannon who tended to act without thinking. Sometimes in the heat of combat that was what you had to do, and Blair had certainly done her share of such flailing. But Barnes not only did way too much of it, in Blair's opinion, but he also seemed perversely proud of his refusal to think things all the way through.

Besides that was the man himself. He was good to have on your side once the fighting began, but he had none of the idealistic courage that Blair could sense in both of the Connors, the commitment to the people whose lives had ended up in their hands. Barnes fought because he liked to fight, and because he hated Skynet.

Which wasn't, for Blair, a particularly durable motivation for this kind of long-term war. As far as she could make out, Barnes didn't particularly like people, had never gotten along with authority figures of any sort, and probably hadn't been a particularly outstanding citizen of the pre-Judgment Day world. In fact, she could easily envision him running along these same streets, in this same darkness, carrying a flat-screen TV from a broken store window instead of the grenade launcher he was currently clutching to his chest.

But he was hound-dog loyal to John Connor, and Blair was one of Connor's people, and for that reason alone she knew Barnes would get her to the hangar safely or die in the attempt. The big man might not be the best argument for saving humanity, but if humanity *was* to be saved, Barnes would probably be one of those who would make it happen.

Probably dying somewhere before it was all over.

Possibly while saving some flygirl's butt.

The hangar was just ahead, a broken remnant of an old air-space museum whose roof had caved in so far that it was obviously no longer able to conceal anything bigger than a Piper Cub. Barnes lifted up a closed fist in warning as they approached, trotting to a crouching halt beside a mangled sign just outside the grounds.

Blair crouched down beside him, adjusting her grip on her Desert Eagle as she studied the open space that lay between them and the hangar. A handgun, even one this powerful, wouldn't do much against T-600s except slow them down, and would be of even less use against a T-1, unless she got in a lucky shot. However, there were also human gangs still roaming the streets, scavenging for buried supplies or stealing from the people who'd gotten there first, and the Eagle's .44 magnum rounds were more than adequate for opening their guts to the cool night air.

But either it was past the gangs' bedtimes or else the ruckus a few blocks away had scared them back under their rocks. Nothing was moving out there, human or otherwise.

"Looks clear," Barnes murmured. "You want me to walk you in?"

"You just stay here," Blair murmured back. Did the man deliberately go out of his way to tick her off? Probably. "I'll send the crew out to you."

Barnes grunted. "Make it snappy."

Blair took a deep breath, and headed toward the hangar, taking the open ground in as fast a sprint as she could without risking a broken ankle. She spun halfway around as she reached the building, landing her back against the wall beside the door as she gave the area one last quick look.

Still nothing.

Panting a little, she slipped inside and pulled the door closed behind her.

And jerked back as a bright light exploded in her face. She had just enough time to slam her eyelids shut before the light disappeared.

"Sorry," Yoshi's voice came from behind the purple blob floating in front of her eyes. A hand reached out and took her arm. "Come on."

"Where's Wince?" Blair asked as she let Yoshi guide her across the broken floor.

"He and Inji are prepping your plane," Yoshi said. "I'm assuming Connor wants us to blow this popsicle stand?"

"Yeah, that's kind of a given," Blair said. "Why, were you thinking of staying?"

"Not if everyone else goes," Yoshi said, an odd wistfulness in his voice. "I just hate to see the place go, that's all."

Blair looked around. Actually, so did she. The purple blob was fading now, and behind it the familiar cramped area beneath the hangar's crushed roof was coming into view.

Or rather, now that the false floor had been rolled aside, the uncramped area of the basement storage room, a sublevel that Skynet's initial surveillance had missed. By removing the floor and installing a winch-equipped ramp, Connor's people had turned an expanse of otherwise useless space into a very cozy spot for stashing the team's two A-10 "Warthog" attack jets.

Blair ran a quick eye over her plane as she and Yoshi headed down the ramp. It was as banged-up as everything else in Connor's meager arsenal, though the wild flying-shark paint job she'd adorned it with hid a lot of the damage. But to her, the nicks and bullet holes were nothing to be ashamed of. They were marks of honor, wounds suffered in the cause of humanity's war for survival.

And scarred or otherwise, the plane was no more ready to give up the fight than Blair herself was. A pair of Sidewinder air-to-air missiles hung from two of the

A-10's four remaining under-wing pylons, while the seven-barrel GAU-8 Avenger Gatling gun nestled beneath its nose promised a hornets' nest of 30mm explosive and armor-piercing rounds to any HK or T-1 foolish enough to get in her way.

Her remaining two pylons, she noted, were sporting equipment nacelles, undoubtedly loaded with everything Wince and Inji could pry up and pack inside. That was going to play hell with the A-10's balance and maneuverability, but Blair would just have to deal with it. It wasn't like the two men could lug everything out on their backs. Not even with Barnes to help.

"Is everyone okay?" Wince's disembodied voice drifted out from somewhere behind the two planes. "It sounded pretty nasty there for awhile."

"It was," Blair said, deciding there was no point in burdening him with the news of Piccerno's death. He'd find out about that soon enough. "We need to get moving, too. If Skynet follows its usual post-raid pattern, the T-600s could be knocking on the door anytime now. We don't want to be here when they do."

"No argument there," Wince agreed, coming into sight around the rear of the plane, his white hair glistening in the starlight that filtered through the cracks in the roof. "You probably saw the cargo pods we strapped on. You going to be okay with that?"

"I'll be fine," Blair assured him. "Barnes is waiting outside by the west sign. You and Inji grab whatever you're carrying, and get going."

"We'll get the door first," Wince said, looking around. "Inji?"

And then, abruptly, the cracks in the hangar roof blazed with light.

"Cover!" Blair snapped at Wince as she sprinted toward her plane. *Damn* the HKs, anyway. "And get clear of the door!"

The words were barely out of her mouth when the silence of the night was shattered by the thunder of automatic weapons fire.

But not the drawn-out stutter of an HK's miniguns. It was the slower, higher-pitched sound of a Galil assault rifle.

Like the one Barnes had been carrying over his shoulder.

Blair swore under her breath. Leave it to him to pick a one-man fight with a flying weapons platform.

"Forget the winch!" she shouted to Yoshi as she bounded up the ladder and dropped into her cockpit. "Blast and burn."

"Right," Yoshi called over the gunfire as he headed for his own plane. "You or me?"

"Me," Blair shouted, punching for engine ignition. "Go as soon as it's clear." There was no time for her to do a proper flight checklist. She would just have to hope Wince and Inji had done the prep right.

They had. Even as she pulled the canopy closed she could feel the vibration of the twin GE turbofans behind her coming to life. Flipping up the safety bar on her stick, she raised the muzzle of her GAU-8 to point at the center of the hangar door and squeezed the trigger.

A normal door would have simply disintegrated at the center of fire, leaving the bulk of it still sitting there, blocking the way. But this particular door had been carefully warped most of the way out of its guide rails and fasteners, and its center had been heavily reinforced with large pieces of superhard alloy, scavenged from wrecked HKs and T-4 tanks. The result was exactly as planned:

even as the door's center began to shred in the face of Blair's onslaught, the sheer impact of two-pound shells striking it at a thousand meters per second blew the whole door out of its housing and hurled it in a twisting arc across the open area outside. Blair caught a glimpse of an HK swooping down toward the spot where she'd left Barnes—

And with a teeth-tingling screech of metal against metal, the flying door slammed into the HK's tail.

The HK nearly lost it right there and then, as the impact threw it violently to the side. Its left tail fin hit the ground and dug in, spinning the whole aircraft a quarter turn around the pivot point.

But the computer controlling the craft was faster than any human pilot. Before the HK's nose could slam into the tarmac, it managed to pull up and out of its spin, its engines revving madly as it tried to regain its equilibrium.

It was still trying when Barnes sent a final burst of fire squarely into its nose, igniting its fuel and munitions and blowing the whole thing to scrap metal.

The fireball was still billowing skyward as Blair snagged her helmet and jammed it on over her head.

"Jinkrat: go!" she barked into the mike.

"Roger," Yoshi's voice came back. The hum of his engines became a sudden roar, and Blair's plane bucked beneath her as the backwash blasted against the rear wall of the hangar and bounced off again in all directions. Yoshi's A-10 lurched forward, rolled up the ramp, and turned sharply right as he made for the pockmarked runway and the relative safety of the open air.

Blair grabbed for her safety straps and started pulling them on as she peered through the dust and fire and the pieces of raining metal. Wince and Inji were on the move, weaving their way through the buffeting turbulence of Yoshi's backwash as fast as the weight of their backpacks and shoulder bags would allow. Another few seconds and they should be out of the way of her own exit.

Until then, here she sat in an open hangar, as vulnerable a sitting duck as could be imagined.

Apparently, Yoshi had the same kind of imagination.

"Hickabick, what's the trouble?" his voice called through her headset. "Get your butt out of there."

"Can't—penguins are still on the move," Blair told him.

"The penguins may just have to hump it," Yoshi warned. "You've got three bandits on the way; repeat, three on the way."

"Check," Blair said, resetting her grip on the throttle as she watched Wince and Inji running across the open space.

Another three seconds...

Two...

One...

"*Clear*," she called, and threw power to the engines.

The A-10 surged forward, again swaying and shaking as the big turbofans bounced their streams of superheated air off the back wall. Blair maneuvered the plane up the ramp, easing back slightly on the engines as she negotiated the tight left-hand turn that would take her onto the other section of runway. She left the throttle where it was for another three seconds, rolling relatively slowly down the runway, giving Barnes and the ground crew as much margin of safety as she dared. Then, bracing herself, she kicked it into full power.

The runway here had been short to begin with, and the meteor storm of falling debris on Judgment Day had left it riddled with pits and ridges. But the A-10 was a close-air support fighter, specifically designed to work on the less-than-ideal airstrips typically found near the front lines of battle. The jet bounced badly as Blair did her best to steer around the worst of the damage, but it kept going, its speed increasing.

The three incoming HKs had just reached the edge of the grounds when she pulled back on the stick, sending the A-10 rocketing up into the sky.

"Three on your tail, Hickabick," Yoshi's voice snapped in her ear. "Jink right—I'll see if I can shake them off you."

"Check," Blair said, twisting the A-10 hard to the right. She caught a flicker of movement as Yoshi crash-dived from somewhere above them, his GAU-8 spitting armor-piercing shells at the deadly machines behind her.

Spitting it accurately, too. Blair was halfway through her turn when the ground lit up behind her as one of the three HKs blew to splinters. She straightened out momentarily, then jinked right again. Her turn brought her into sight of the two remaining HKs, and she armed one of her Sidewinders, locked it onto the nearest bandit, and fired.

There was another blast, this one even more spectacular than the last, and the enemy count was down to one.

But Blair's combat instincts were screaming like an Irish banshee. This was too easy. It was *way* too easy. She twisted the A-10 around as the final HK opened up with its own Gatling guns, reflexively dodging the enemy fire as she searched the sky.

The two backup HKs were coming in dark and low, weaving smoothly between the ruined buildings, hugging the ground where a careless pilot might easily miss them.

"Eight o'clock low," she snapped a warning to Yoshi,

twisting her stick hard around in an attempt to bring her plane into firing position before Skynet tumbled to the fact that its little sneak play had failed.

The race ended in a tie. She squeezed off her last Sidewinder just as both HKs opened fire, one targeting her, the other targeting the missile. A second later the Sidewinder blew up, well short of its intended targets, as Blair shoved her joystick forward, trying to duck under the lethal stream of lead coming in her direction.

She shoved the stick forward perhaps a bit too hard. The sudden change in direction, coupled with her lack of sleep, sparked a wave of lightheadedness that sent the universe tilting violently around her. Dimly, she was aware of her pulse throbbing in her throat, of Yoshi shouting in her ears, of the ground rushing up toward her—

She snapped out of it just in time, yanking back on the stick and pulling up out of the dive close enough to the ground to feel the buffeting as her shockwave bounced off it and up against the A-10's underside.

"You all right?" Yoshi called.

"I'm fine," Blair managed, twisting the A-10 sideways and clawing for some altitude. "Are you—?"

She broke off as another explosion ripped through the air.

"Jinkrat!" she snapped, looking frantically around.

"S'okay," Yoshi assured her. "Just reminding Skynet that we usually come in pairs."

And as the glare of the explosion faded, Blair saw that one of the two sneak-attack HKs had been turned into a heap of blazing rubble. The remaining newcomer, still running dark, had escaped and was angling across the airfield, clearly heading for a link-up with the last of the original three attackers.

"Looks like they're pairing up, too," she said. "What's your status?"

"I'm at Geth Pete," he said.

Blair grimaced. Geth Pete—Gethsemane Peter. *The spirit is willing, but the flesh is weak.* In other words, Yoshi was completely out of ammo.

But Skynet was unlikely to have picked up on such an oblique reference, in which case it might still think its HKs were facing two armed fighters.

"You cut around and hit their flank," she told Yoshi. "I'll take it down their throats."

"Check," Yoshi said, and Blair mentally threw him a salute. Charging into battle unarmed this way might help Blair, but it could easily cost Yoshi his own life.

Though not if Blair could help it.

She curved her A-10 around toward the two HKs, mapping out her strategy. Whichever one turned toward Yoshi, she would concentrate all her fire on the other, hopefully blowing it out of the sky quickly enough that she could get to the remaining bandit before it could engage with him.

Unfortunately, the HKs weren't playing to the script. Both of them were heading straight toward Blair, completely ignoring Yoshi's one-man Light Brigade charge at their flank.

Which meant the oblique reference hadn't been oblique enough. Skynet had figured it out, and wasn't going to waste its resources on an enemy who couldn't fight back. At least, not until it had dealt with the one who could.

"Better idea," Blair told Yoshi. "Break off and get back to the coop. I can handle them."

Yoshi muttered something Blair didn't quite get. But he

was smart enough to realize that, with the jig up, it was the only reasonable course. The Resistance didn't have nearly enough planes and pilots to let any of them get wasted without a good reason.

"Check, Hickabick," he said with a sigh. "I'm gone."

"Just watch for unfriendly eyes," Blair warned. "And don't forget to go in from the north."

"Check," Yoshi said again. "Good luck."

"You, too."

The two HKs, which had worked so hard to get into a single formation, now split apart again at Blair's approach, one swinging right as the other went left. Blair flipped a mental coin and turned to follow the one to the left. Her turn caught up with it before it could sidle out of range, and a single long burst from her GAU-8 took it out.

Unfortunately, that left the other machine sitting squarely on her tail. Even as she started to turn back to face it, the HK opened fire, sending a burst of lead across the A-10's belly.

There was only one thing Blair could do.

Throwing full power to her engines, she hauled back on the stick, turning the A-10's nose toward the sky in a power loop. She kept going, ignoring the enemy fire that was tracking up toward her, curving ever more skyward until the A-10 was nearly to stall configuration.

Then, twisting the plane around into half a barrel roll, she turned it right-side up again as she finished her half loop.

And with that single smooth maneuver, she was heading along an opposite vector, and had gained herself a good stretch of altitude along with it.

She cut back a little on her throttle, breathing out a

sigh of relief as she scanned the sky around her. The Immelmann turn was a standard fighter maneuver, one that had probably been taught to every military pilot since World War One. But that didn't mean anyone especially liked *doing* them.

Still, when the trick worked, it worked well, particularly against aircraft like HKs that had been designed more for hunting ground targets than for real aerial combat. And indeed, the sky around her seemed to finally be clear of enemies.

Though just because the current generation of HKs weren't particularly good at this kind of warfare, it didn't mean Skynet didn't have something more maneuverable already in the works. There were also rumors of some kind of plasma gun that would replace the HKs' Gatlings. Given time, she suspected, every advantage the Resistance had been able to find or carve out would be blocked.

It was her job, and the job of people like John Connor, to make sure Skynet was taken down before that happened.

She checked her mirrors. The HK she'd thought she'd left far behind was still in pursuit, moving as fast as its little midships turbofans could take it.

Skynet wasn't yet ready to call it a day.

Fine. If the massive computer system wanted to lose another HK, Blair would be happy to oblige.

In fact, there was a little maneuver she'd been saving for just such an occasion, and with three of Skynet's four radar towers currently down, it was the perfect time to try it. Watching the blip behind her, adjusting her speed just enough to let the HK start closing the gap, she headed due west, toward the edge of the city and the dark ocean beyond.

The HK had closed about half the gap between them by the time Blair came in sight of her objective: a pair of twenty-story buildings about fifteen meters apart, probably once the towers of a hotel, with a fair amount of wall and ceiling still clinging to their skeletons.

She didn't know why so much of their structure had survived, especially that high off the ground, unless there had been something even bigger and taller to the south that had shielded them from the worst of the nuclear blast. However it had happened, though, the buildings presented her with a golden opportunity.

Smiling tightly to herself, she reached over and shut down her starboard engine.

It was like throwing fresh meat into a shark tank. The HK behind her abruptly leaped forward, drawing on a reserve of extra speed that Blair had never realized the damn things had. As it closed the gap, it began firing, sending quick bursts across her wingtips and tail, clearly targeting her remaining engine.

Blair swore under her breath as she checked the distance back to the HK, then ahead to the two buildings, then back again to the HK. It was going to be tight, and with the enemy firing at her the whole way. Briefly, she considered restarting the starboard engine and getting back her speed advantage.

But the minute she did that, Skynet would know she wasn't as vulnerable as she was pretending and realize it was a trap. At that point, it would either break off the attack entirely or else send the HK in with more caution than Blair really wanted from it.

On the up side, after all the shooting tonight the HK had to be running low on ammo. On the down side, so was Blair. Of the 1100 rounds she'd started with, less than 150 were left. At the A-10's cycle rate of 3900 rounds per minute, that was roughly two seconds' worth.

It was definitely going to be tight.

They were nearly to the buildings now, and despite Blair's evasive jinking the HK was starting to get the range. She could feel the thuds and hear the whining screeches as the enemy's Gatlings tore bits and pieces off the A-10's skin and dug furrows into her wings and tail. *Just fifteen meters between buildings,* she reminded herself as she turned north, putting herself on a vector that would pass her along the left sides of the buildings. A fifteen-meter gap didn't leave much clearance for an HK, and on paper, at least, it was pretty much impossible for the A-10's own seventeen-and-a-half-meter wingspan.

The HK made another surge forward, closing the gap even more as Skynet apparently decided that Blair was on her last legs.

She shot past the first building.

And with a hard yank on her joystick, she turned the plane into a tight right-hand turn. The maneuver banked the A-10 halfway up onto its right wingtip, the angle shortening its effective wingspan, and without scraping even once against the half-demolished structures, she curved neatly through the narrow gap.

Putting the first of the two buildings directly between her and the HK.

Three weeks ago, with all four of Skynet's radar towers providing intermeshed coverage of the L.A. basin, this trick would never have worked. But three of those towers were down now, with only the one at Capistrano way to the south still in operation.

Which meant that unless there was a stray T-1 or T-600 somewhere nearby on the ground, being out of the HK's sight also meant Blair was out of Skynet's sight.

She had maybe five seconds before the HK maneuvered its own way through the gap. But she'd spent a lot of time mentally working this through, and she knew exactly what to do. With the A-10 still curving to the right, she fired up her supposedly dead starboard engine and simultaneously hauled back on the stick.

And with that, her tight right-hand circle turned into a tight right-hand upward spiral. She rode skyward, gripping the stick with two hands as she fought against the g-forces that were trying to pull the blood away from her brain. The spiral took her over the top of the first building, and she shoved the stick forward again, dropping her nose toward the ground, curving over the broken steel girders and into a power dive headed toward the narrow strip of ground between the two structures.

Which, exactly as she'd anticipated, put her directly above and behind the pursuing HK.

Skynet must have known instantly that it had lost this round. But it still wasn't willing to concede defeat without a fight. The HK tried to roll itself over far enough to bring its Gatlings to bear, just as Blair's last 143 armor-piercing rounds blew it to hell.

She puffed a little sigh as she pulled out of her dive and eased back on her engines. The sky around her finally showed clear, and it was time to head back to the new hangar Connor had set up near Fallback One. Blowing a drop of sweat off the tip of her nose, she sent the A-10 in a leisurely circle that would take her back eastward toward the team's territory. She glanced at the ground, scanning for the distinctive shapes and glowing red sensors of Skynet's Terminators.

And abruptly felt her heart seize up.

Six blocks to the south, squatting motionlessly on the ground like silent gray moths, were four more HKs.

And Blair was out of ammo.

Automatically, she kept the A-10 turning on the curve she'd set for it, her pulse pounding in her neck as she gazed at the enemy aircraft. They were sitting at the four corners of a narrow parking lot around a half-crushed warehouse surrounded by a lot of rubble, their lights dark, their turbofans either completely off or else turning slowly enough that they weren't throwing up any dust. Their noses were pointed outward from the warehouse, the kind of arrangement soldiers used when they had to bunk down for the night in enemy territory.

But HKs didn't sleep. *Skynet* didn't sleep.

Could Skynet somehow have missed the fact that Blair was still alive? Ridiculous, not with the Capistrano tower still functioning. Could it have decided it had spent enough of its precious resources for one night? That was at least possible. The honchos at Command were pretty sure that Skynet was still in the ramping-up stage, still building its fleet of HKs and its armies of tanks and Terminators.

But whatever the reason, all that mattered to Blair right now was that she seemed to be off the hook for the rest of the night.

The A-10 finished its turn, and Blair straightened the plane out again. Keeping one eye on the city in front of her and another on the view in her mirrors, she headed home.

CHAPTER THREE

Orozco was at his usual night-guard post, sleeping with his back to a broken pillar beside the archway that led into the half-crumpled building known to its residents as Moldering Lost Ashes, when he was startled awake by the sound of an approaching aircraft.

He pried his eyes open, wincing at the grit that had worked its way beneath the lids. His hands, which had been cradling his M16A2 rifle in his lap, shifted automatically into a proper firing grip on the weapon.

The plane was coming closer. Muttering a prayer under his breath, Orozco rolled half over and got to his feet. He hefted the M16, made sure his holstered Beretta was secure at his side, and stepped cautiously through the archway and out into the street.

It was a plane, all right, a dark shadow cutting across the patches of stars as it headed westward maybe half a klick south of him. It was too dark for a recognizable silhouette, but from the sound of the engine he guessed it was one of the A-10 Warthogs that the Resistance forces in the area liked to use for air support.

Orozco felt his lips press together as a second silhouette shot across the stars close behind the first. Unfortunately, the Resistance probably wouldn't be using this particular

A-10 much longer. The second shadow was one he *did* recognize: one of Skynet's cursed Hunter-Killers, moving in for the kill.

The A-10's engine pitch changed. Orozco frowned, trying to find it again against the dark sky.

And then, suddenly, there it was, bearing practically straight toward him.

Reflexively, he ducked as the A-10 shot past overhead, heading due north now with the Hunter-Killer right behind it. Probably making for the San Gabriel Mountains, Orozco decided. Maybe hoping to lose the HK among the slopes and valleys there.

But at this point, and from this distance, that was a pretty forlorn hope. Sure enough, a few seconds later there was a flash of reflected light and a rolling boom.

Closing his eyes, Orozco sent a prayer skyward for the dead pilot.

He opened his eyes again, frowning. The echoes of the explosion had faded, leaving the sound of a single aircraft drifting through the cold night air...and to his amazed disbelief, it was the sound of the A-10.

Shaking his head in admiration, Orozco let go of his M16 with his right hand and threw a salute in the fighter's direction. He wasn't very familiar with the A-10—it was an Air Force jet, and the Marines had always used Harriers and Cobras for their close-air support. But he *was* familiar with HKs, and any pilot who could take one down in single combat was worthy of admiration.

Turning away from the sound of the distant plane, he took a deep breath of the cold night air and let his eyes drift around the ruined street he'd called home for the past two years.

Los Angeles had been lucky, he mused, if such a word

could be applied to any spot on the globe these days. The nuke that had hit the city had been a smaller one, or else had misfired enough to lower its yield a little.

More importantly, its actual target had apparently been the Camp Pendleton Marine Base south of the city. Together, those two factors had worked to leave more of the city standing than had been the case with some of the world's other major metropolitan areas.

Paris, for one, was gone completely, at least as near as he'd been able to glean from the scattered Resistance reports he'd pulled in before his radio had finally died. New York and Chicago were in worse shape than L.A., and it sounded like everything for a hundred kilometers around D.C. had been turned to slag.

An empty can somewhere across the street rattled. Orozco swung the muzzle of his M16 in that direction, probing the darkness for movement. Most of the local gangs had learned to leave Moldering Lost Ashes alone—several of them learning the hard way. But you never knew when some loner would drift into the neighborhood and think he'd found easy pickings.

You also never knew when Skynet would decide it was this area's turn to be cleansed of the humans that infested its shiny, brave new world.

But the time for that final battle apparently wasn't tonight. The can across the street rattled again, and this time Orozco caught a glimpse of a large rat scurrying past and disappearing into the shadows. The rats, at least, had done all right for themselves in the post-Judgment Day world. So had the cockroaches.

Orozco knew eight recipes for rat and three for roaches. Some of the residents here knew even more. Some of those recipes were even pretty good.

Judgment Day. Sighing tiredly, Orozco continued his visual sweep of the street, the bitter irony digging under his skin like the ever-present dust dug beneath his eyelids.

A stupid name, "Judgment Day." Someone in the Resistance had apparently coined it, and it had spread by radio and word of mouth until it was the universally accepted name for the destruction that Skynet had unleashed upon the world.

But there had been no true judgment to it. None at all. Good and evil, rich and poor, sinner and saint—everyone had suffered equally in the attack.

Unless perhaps the judgment aspect was in the way death and life had been handed out. That the chosen had been the ones granted the quick death of nuclear holocaust, while the evil had been those consigned to this living hell of hunger and cold and darkness.

The good die young. The old saying echoed through his mind. He'd never believed that before.

Maybe it was time he did.

But tonight, at least, the darkness out there concealed no fresh horrors. Taking one last look around, Orozco went back inside.

He was heading to his sleeping mat when a pebble clattered softly across the ground at his feet.

His first impulse was to look upward, through the broken sections of flooring toward the building's top floor, where the group's lookouts were stationed. But a second later his brain caught up with him and he realized it couldn't have come from one of them. The lookouts always dropped their pebbles onto metal plates, where the clatter would alert Orozco or one of the other watchmen. The nearest such plate was a good twenty meters away, and impossible for the lookout to miss.

Which made the source of the pebble at his feet obvious.

He peered a few meters down the broken tiles and cracked walls of what had once been a luxurious apartment building lobby to the pair of sleeping mats tucked into a small alcove. Nine-year-old Star was half sitting up on her mat, her wide-open eyes gazing unblinkingly at Orozco, a taut questioning look on her face.

He gave the girl a reassuring smile and a thumb's up. Her questioning look lingered another few seconds, as if she was wondering if there really *was* something wrong and Orozco was merely humoring her. But then she nodded, lay back down, and closed her eyes.

He watched her a moment, then shifted his gaze to the sixteen-year-old boy sleeping soundly on the mat beside her.

People at the Ashes wondered about the two kids. They didn't wonder a lot, of course—with basic survival the top item on everyone's list, no one had much time left to spend pondering anyone else's oddities. Certainly everyone here had a long list of peculiarities of their own.

But even against that backdrop, Kyle Reese and Star stood out. They weren't brother and sister—that much Kyle would readily tell anyone who asked. But how and where and why the two of them had linked up, that no one knew. Not even Orozco, and he was closer to them than probably anyone else in the building. It was something Kyle simply wouldn't talk about. Not even when asked point blank, which a couple of the less tactful residents had done on occasion.

Star didn't talk about it either.

But then, Star didn't talk about anything. Whether she was physically unable to speak, or whether the trauma of Judgment Day or its aftermath had sent that part of her personality into a hole too deep for anyone to reach, was just another of the mysteries surrounding them. The system of hand signals she and Kyle used to communicate bore no resemblance to any formal sign language that Orozco had ever seen. Presumably it was something the two of them had created themselves over the years.

But for Orozco, at least, the most striking thing about the two of them was their almost symbiotic relationship. They did everything together, from their work to their sentry duties to the general struggle of life, often with only a hand signal or two between them for coordination.

Right now was a perfect case in point. Over the two years Orozco had been here, and apparently for at least a year before that, Kyle had politely but flatly refused all offers of a real room for him and Star to sleep in at night, preferring instead to stay down here as the night guard's backup. *Right* down here, in fact—Orozco had offered the two kids a comfy spot up on the mezzanine balcony, where Kyle could overlook the archway and act as a sniper backup. Alternatively, there were several anterooms off the lobby where he and Star would be at least partially out of harm's way.

But Kyle had politely refused both offers. He'd said that it didn't count as a victory to kill an attacker if the sentry himself died in the process. Far better, he argued, for a potential attacker to see *two* armed guards and thus abandon the attack entirely.

It was a duty the boy took very seriously. Normally, any time Orozco got up to check on a noise or movement Kyle would be instantly awake right along with him, one hand on his gun, while Star continued to sleep.

But on those rare occasions, like tonight, when Kyle was so tired that he slept through one of Orozco's spot-checks, Star invariably woke up instead, watching and waiting until Orozco gave her the all clear. It was as if on some subconscious level their two minds had agreed in advance which one would be on duty that night, and adjusted their sleep accordingly.

Orozco had seen that sort of near-telepathy before, but normally only between members of highly trained and highly experienced military units. He'd only rarely seen it in civilians, and never between kids this young who weren't related.

The A-10's engines had faded into the background now. Orozco wondered briefly whether it would find some hiding place before Skynet scrambled more of the HKs, then put the thought out of his mind. That was the pilot's problem, and Orozco had more than enough problems of his own.

His eyes drifted back to the two sleeping figures in the alcove. *No,* he decided, Judgment Day hadn't been about taking the good and leaving the evil. Not when people like Kyle and Star were still here.

Once again settling his back against the pillar, Orozco laid his M16 in his lap and drifted off to sleep.

CHAPTER FOUR

The half-underground complex of half-broken buildings that made up Fallback One was smaller than the group's previous bunker had been. It was also a bit more spread out and was thus, at least in Kate's estimation, more vulnerable to a pincer attack if and when Skynet finally tracked them down.

But it did have a few advantages over their last base. For one thing, it was partially underground, and had a direct connection into the city's old system of storm drain tunnels, which meant a somewhat safer escape route. For another, it had a large open space in the middle of the complex where the entire group could gather together for planning or conferences or just plain simple emotional support.

At the moment, though, having everyone here together was looking more like a liability than an asset.

"—glad you got your people out alive." The audio speaker crackled with the static-laden voice of one of the generals at Command. "Considering the scope of the attack, that's no small feat."

"Thank you," John said into the mike. "What we need right now is some assistance in replacing the gear we had to abandon. We could meet your people wherever it's convenient—"

"Unfortunately, we're not in a position to help you resupply at the moment," the general interrupted. "We can offer some organizational support, but that's all."

"Perhaps a partial resupply—" John began.

"I'm sorry, Connor," the other cut him off again. "There's another call coming in that I have to take. Good luck."

The radio went dead. For a couple of seconds John stared at the mike, his face giving away nothing of what Kate knew was going on behind it. Then he stirred, reaching over and shutting off his transmitter. He glanced once at his wife, then turned to the group huddled silently around him.

"Well," he said calmly. "Looks like we're on our own."

No one said anything. Kate looked around the room, her eyes touching in turn each of the faces she knew so well.

Fifty-four. There were fifty-four of them, now that Piccerno was gone: forty-two adults, plus six teens and four children under ten who the realities of life had put on the fast track to adulthood. There were also, at last count, two babies.

Most of the adults were seasoned, hardened fighters who had been with her and John for years, and on their faces Kate could see only small flickers of concern or annoyance. Hard experience had taught them that disconnecting from their emotions as much as possible was the easiest way to make it through the life they'd been given.

The half-dozen civilians hadn't yet learned that lesson. Their eyes were wide with disbelief, fear, and the beginnings of quiet panic, particularly the babies' mothers. They weren't fighters, and probably never would be.

They were with the group for the simple reason that there had been nowhere else for them to go.

Predictably, it was Barnes who finally broke the silence.

"That sucks," he declared.

As if that was the signal everyone else had been waiting for, a rustling of murmurs erupted across the room. Kate caught snatches of some of the conversations, curses or pithy complaints lifting themselves briefly out of the general buzz. John let it run for a few seconds, then cleared his throat.

The room went instantly silent.

"You can't blame Command for their decision," he said calmly. "They have limited resources, and they have to do triage, like anyone else does."

"With all due respect, sir," Barnes said, "I think that's a load of—" He glanced sideways at two of the children standing near him "—I think that's ridiculous. Some of us have been fighting this damn war longer than Command's even been in operation."

"They're career brass," someone from the back of the room put in sourly. "History doesn't matter, potential doesn't matter. All they care about is what you've done for them lately."

"I had a boyfriend like that once," Blair Williams murmured.

"Not for long, I'll bet," Tunney said.

Blair sniffed loudly.

"Shelf life of an egg."

A general chuckle ran through the assembly, and Kate sensed some of the tension fade away.

As usual, John was right on top of it, ready to take advantage of the altered mood.

"Simmons is right," he said. "What counts is not

whether we've delivered in the past, but whether we can *continue* to deliver. This is the ultimate in natural selection, where the weak not only die, but die very quickly. Command can't waste supplies, or risk being compromised, by a group that isn't going to make it anyway."

Barnes muttered something under his breath.

"Well, if they think we're gonna just roll over and die, they're full of—" He glanced at the children again. "You know?"

"Absolutely," John agreed. "They want us to deliver? Fine. We'll deliver." He straightened up in his chair, his eyes flashing with sudden fire. "And we're going to deliver so spectacularly that they will never, *ever* write us off again. Whether they like it or not."

Kate looked around, watching with a never-waning fascination as John's words, character, and unshakable strength of purpose quieted a room full of fear and despair and uncertainty. They would succeed, because John knew they would.

"What's the plan, sir?" David asked, putting the group's new sense of determination into words.

"Right now, the plan is for everyone to get some sleep," John said. "Almost everyone, anyway. David and Tunney will organize sentry duty, and then the seniors and I will sit down for a strategy meeting." His eyes swept the room one final time. "You behaved superbly tonight, and I want you to know how proud I am of every one of you. Go get some sleep, and by the time you wake up we should have a plan that'll make the other local Resistance groups, Command, *and* Skynet sit up and take notice."

David did a half turn to face the group and gave a brisk nod.

"Dismissed," he said.

Another low murmur of conversation started as the group began a general movement through the three doorways that led to the bunker's various sleeping and living areas. As they did so, David and Tunney slipped into the departing crowd, each picking two soldiers and sending them off to the appointed sentry posts.

Two minutes later, the only ones left in the room were John, Kate, Barnes, David, Tunney, and Blair.

"Good pep talk, Connor," David commented as they rearranged the handful of chairs into a circle. "Though may I suggest that the plan not make Skynet sit up and take *too* much notice?"

John's lip twitched in a half smile, and Kate felt her stomach tighten. If the others only knew how long Skynet *had* been taking notice of him.

"We'll see what we can do," John said, turning to Blair. "Yoshi *did* make it through, didn't he?"

"Yes, he's fine," Blair said. "He's at the hangar helping Wince check out the Hogs." Her nose wrinkled. "Afraid I took a little more damage than I'd hoped to."

"The important thing is that you got back alive," John reminded her. "Bringing your planes back—in *any* shape—is an extra bonus."

"So what exactly did you have in mind?" Tunney asked.

"There are a couple of possibilities," John said. "One obvious target would be the Capistrano radar tower."

"Won't be easy," David warned. "There's a reason Skynet built the damn thing so close to NukeZero—there isn't a single scrap of cover for at least a klick around it. Not even bushes."

"Not to mention that the whole area's still a little

hot," Tunney added.

"Both excellent reasons why the tower hasn't yet been taken down, and why Skynet might not expect us to go for it," John said. "Kate, do we have any actual readings on the radiation levels down there?"

"I haven't had an update since last summer," she said. "By now, though, I would think that the worst danger would be long-term cancer risks."

Barnes snorted. "Like any of us is going to live long enough to worry about *that*."

"You never know," John said. "Though that still leaves the lack of approach cover. Blair, you've flown around that general area. Anything of interest you noticed that someone on the ground might have missed?"

"Not down there," Blair said. "But I did notice something tonight that struck me as strange."

She described her final aerial battle, and the four darkened HKs that had allowed her to escape rather than join in the battle.

"Interesting," John said when she'd finished. "What did the ground around the warehouse look like? Would anyone at street level have been able to see the HKs?"

Blair's eyes unfocused a bit as she considered.

"Not from street level, no," she said. "Probably not even from the second or maybe even the third floor of anything nearby. There were heaps of rubble—*big* heaps—surrounding the place. More rubble than there *should* have been, now that I think about it."

"As if Skynet deliberately blew up all the nearby buildings so as to block the view?" John suggested.

Barnes snorted again.

"Or else they were just sitting there waiting for her to head back so they could follow her."

"No one followed me," Blair insisted, sending a dark look in his direction. "Trust me. I did a weave-and-duck the whole way back."

"I don't think Skynet's plan was to follow her," John said. "I think the plan was for her *not* to notice the warehouse."

"Then why position HKs there at all?" David asked. "If Skynet didn't want to draw attention to the place, it should have scrambled them when it launched the attack on our bunker."

"Except that Skynet couldn't have known I'd be going that far west," Blair pointed out. "*Or* that I'd live long enough to tell anyone about it."

"Exactly," John agreed. "I submit that by the time Skynet realized the danger, it was too late to move the HKs without revealing that they'd been sitting that far away from a known staging area. All it could do was go silent and dark and hope she didn't see them."

"You think the warehouse is a new staging area, then?" Kate asked quietly.

She saw John's throat tighten.

"I think it's the most likely possibility," he said.

For a moment the room was silent, and Kate watched a fresh layer of grimness settle onto their faces like drifting dust. They knew as well as she did what it meant when Skynet set up a staging area in the middle of a city.

Somewhere deep inside itself, the pitiless artificial intelligence that was Skynet had calculated that it could spare some of the resources it was throwing against the Resistance, and divert them to the job of killing a few blocks' worth of civilians.

Reaching to a tray behind him, John pulled out a map and spread it out on the narrow table beside the radio.

"Show us where it is," he said.

Blair stepped over and studied the faded paper as the others got up and gathered around her and John.

"The buildings where I dropped the HK are here," she said slowly, pointing at a spot on the map. "So the warehouse is...here."

"Mm," John murmured. "What do we know about that area?"

"Not much," David said. "I don't think there are any organized Resistance cells anywhere nearby."

"Except us," Kate said in a low voice.

"And we're not all that close," Tunney noted, leaning over the map. "There *could* be quite a group of civilians there, though. Looks like there were at least two major strip malls with grocery stores in the area, plus I think this thing here on the edge of the neighborhood was a warehouse outlet store."

"Lots of packaged food and other supplies, in other words," David added.

"In theory, anyway," Tunney agreed. "If enough of it survived Judgment Day, there could be, oh, anywhere from 400 to maybe even a thousand people living in the sixteen blocks around Skynet's new staging area."

Kate winced. Up to a thousand people, all of them struggling day in and day out, fighting hard just to survive.

And Skynet was going to send in its HKs and T-600 Terminators and simply wipe them all out.

She looked at John. He was still gazing down at the map, but she knew he could feel her eyes on him. They couldn't just abandon those people to sudden, violent death. Not if there was any way they could stop it.

Blair was obviously thinking along the same lines.

"If we could get hold of a Maverick, I'm pretty sure I

could get in there and deliver it before they could stop me," she offered. "No staging area, no slaughter."

"At least until Skynet rebuilds it," John said, his voice thoughtful.

"It would at least buy the people some breathing space," Blair pointed out.

"Yeah, but Skynet won't try playing possum twice in a row," Tunney warned. "Next time it'll be ready for you."

"Doesn't matter," Blair said calmly. "I don't know what kind of anti-aircraft setup the place has, but if I get in close enough it won't have time to lock up either me *or* the missile."

"Be an interesting race, anyway," Tunney said. "Unfortunately, we're a little short of Mavericks at the moment. Unless we can pry one loose from Command, I'd say you're probably out of luck."

"There might be a simpler way," David said, running a finger diagonally across the map. "It looks to me like one of the old drainage tunnels cuts under the parking area around the warehouse. We'll have to check, but if it actually goes under the building itself, maybe we can blow the place without Williams having to risk herself or her A-10."

"Skynet's bound to have plugged it already," Barnes said sourly.

David shrugged.

"Maybe. No way to know until we've checked it out."

"We can't destroy the staging area," John said. "Not if we want Command to take us seriously."

Kate frowned, replaying his words in her mind, convinced she must have heard him wrong.

"They won't take us seriously if we *do* destroy it?" she asked.

"Of course not." John gave her a tight yet oddly mischievous smile. "What we really need to do is capture it. Intact."

Blair's mouth dropped open half an inch.

David and Tunney exchanged startled glances.

Barnes just stayed Barnes.

"Excuse me?" David asked carefully.

"Skynet has a pattern in these operations," John said. "First thing it does is put out a ring of T-600s to seal off the kill zone. Then, once it's dark, it sends more T-600s through the neighborhood, usually with some HKs providing air support, and starts the slaughter. As the Terminators run out of ammunition they return to the staging area to reload, then head out again for a second wave, and so on."

"And you're suggesting Skynet might carelessly leave the lunch wagon unlocked while all the T-600s are out enjoying the picnic?" Tunney suggested.

"Why not?" John asked. "The first clue most people have that an attack is even coming is when the HKs lift and the miniguns start firing, and by then there's no time for anything but trying to escape or survive. As far as I know, this is the first time anyone's ever known in advance where Skynet's setting up shop."

"Of course, we don't know *when* the attack will happen," Tunney pointed out.

"Which is why we need to get started right away," John said. "Barnes, what's the status on Fallback Two?"

"It's mostly ready," Barnes said. He looked at Blair. "We don't have a good hangar setup yet, though."

"You want me to go hunting for something tomorrow?" Blair asked.

"Either you or Yoshi—you can sort it out between

yourselves," John said. "Make sure that whichever of you goes takes along an escort, just in case. We'll work out the details after everyone's had some sleep, but I'm thinking now that we keep the infiltration team to about twenty."

"That few?" David questioned, frowning.

"Any more than that and we'll leave the bunker and the rest of our people unprotected," John pointed out. "Besides, this whole thing hinges on surprise. If twenty of us can't pull it off, doubling the number isn't likely to make much of a difference."

"I suppose," David said. Kate could tell he wasn't convinced, but his voice and expression nevertheless showed his willingness to follow John's lead. "May I suggest that we go in as Resistance recruiters?"

"Good idea," John said. "Who knows? We might even find a few people who are ready to stop being victims and help us take the fight to Skynet. I'm thinking we'll go in two groups of ten, with me taking one group and Barnes taking the other. Once we've scouted the territory a bit, we'll regroup, compare notes, and set up a temp base as our launch point."

"Can I choose my own ten men?" Barnes asked.

Tunney cleared his throat.

"You know, Barnes, it really isn't our job to clear the streets of every brain-scrambled gang of punks that's out there."

"It is if they get in our way," Barnes said, his voice going flat and dangerous. Barnes had grown up in one of L.A.'s worst gang areas, Kate knew, and his hatred of them had never faded. "Besides, sometimes they've got spare ammo and other stuff." He looked back at John. "I get to choose my men?"

"Knock yourself out," John told him as he started folding up the map again. "Only you can't have your brother," he added. "I'll be leaving him in command of the group here."

"Will you want Yoshi and me as part of the attack?" Blair asked.

"I definitely *want* you," John said wryly. "Whether I get to have you or not will depend on how fast Wince can get your planes put back together."

"Oh, they'll be ready," Blair promised, her tone the exact same level of flat and dangerous that Barnes had just used.

Kate suppressed a smile. Blair and Barnes didn't always get along, not because they were opposites, but because they had far too many of the same hard-ass traits in common.

"Then we're adjourned," John told them as he stood up. "Get some sleep, and I'll see you back here in six hours. And don't forget to make sure the sentries get rotated."

John was silent as he and Kate walked down the long corridor to their new quarters. Kate, for her part, was content to allow him his moment of quiet. Particularly since she knew that it wasn't going to last.

They reached their room, a slightly bigger space than they'd had at the previous bunker, but with oddly angled walls and a rather lumpy floor. There was no door, either, just a curtain that could be pulled across the opening for minimal privacy. Together, she and John took off their weapons belts and pouches and outer jackets, keeping on enough clothing to push back the cold night air. Kate finished first and climbed beneath the sleeping mat's covers, trying to figure out how exactly she was going to broach the subject she and John needed to discuss.

Wasted effort, as it turned out. John knew her as well as she knew him. He climbed onto the mat and pressed himself against her side, one arm draped lovingly and protectively over her, his breath warm against her cheek.

"Let me guess," he whispered. "You want to go with my infiltration team."

Here we go, Kate thought.

"It's not that I want to go," she whispered back. "It's that I *have* to go."

"Because we need a medic?" He shook his head. "We can't risk you, Kate."

"It's not just that," Kate said. "It's that…John, I've seen how they look at me. Seen how they treat me. They respect me, yes, but as a surgeon and medic."

"Nothing wrong with that."

"Yes, but I'm also supposed to be one of their leaders," Kate said. "You and the others call me that, and I sit in on your meetings. But I never actually lead."

"Neither does Williams," John pointed out. "No one's thrown her out of a meeting yet."

"It's not the same," Kate said, hearing a hint of desperation creeping into her voice and ruthlessly forcing it back. She needed to convince him, not manipulate him. "I don't ever share the same risks they do. They respect me, John, but they wouldn't follow me. Not the way they follow you."

"And someday they'll have to?" he asked.

Kate felt her chest tighten. *Don't say things like that!* she thought fiercely.

But stifling the words wouldn't change the reality that

had already been foretold by that last Terminator they'd met before the horror of Judgment Day. Just as John would one day rise to lead all of Earth to victory over Skynet, one day he would also die at Skynet's hand.

"That's still a long way down the road," she said instead. "All I'm saying is that I need to do this. I *need* to do this."

John reached his hand up and stroked her cheek.

"I hate this," he said quietly. "You know that, don't you?"

Kate pulled her right arm from beneath the blankets and took his hand.

"More than I hate watching you go off without me?"

"Touché," he admitted. "Does anybody say 'touché' anymore?"

"You can say it in private," Kate assured him, feeling some of her tension fade away as she sensed his change from solid refusal to reluctant consent. "And I don't have to actually *lead* anyone, not this time. That part can wait until later. I just need them to see me fighting alongside them."

John didn't answer. Kate waited silently, her mental fingers crossed, letting him work it through.

"Compromise," he said at last. "You can come with the infiltration teams and help with the recruitment part of the trip. Actually, you can probably take point on that—you're much better at talking to people than Barnes or even Tunney."

"I'm better than Barnes, anyway," Kate said. "I think Tunney ought to handle the actual recruitment speech, though. I'd rather watch him this first time, and maybe just answer a few questions."

"Well, you can sort out the duties however you want,"

John said. "But once the actual attack starts, you'll stay put in whatever temp base we've set up in the neighborhood."

"At least until you need a medic?"

"Until we need work that our junior medics can't handle," John corrected firmly. "Is it a deal?"

For a moment Kate considered pointing out that sitting alone in the middle of a fire zone wouldn't be a lot safer than being out in the middle of the action. But bringing that up would probably get her summarily left here at the bunker instead. "Okay," she said. "So I can recruit, hide, and maybe bandage."

"You just can't shoot," John said, nodding.

"Well, I *can* shoot," Kate said in the prim voice a couple of her mother's upper-crust friends had always used. "I'm a woman of many talents, you know."

John squeezed her shoulder, pulling her closer.

"Definitely," he said. "Come on, let's get some sleep."

CHAPTER FIVE

Breakfast at Moldering Lost Ashes that morning consisted of a handful of dried seed pods from one of the wild plants that had popped up around the city over the past few years, plus a slice of three-day-old coyote.

Kyle and Star ate quickly, which was usually the best way to get three-day-old coyote down, and then made their way up the untrustworthy stairways to the highest inhabitable part of the rickety building.

Kyle didn't really like sentry duty. Not so much because it was boring, but because if Skynet ever launched an attack he and Star would be stuck up here, instead of downstairs where they could help.

Chief Grimaldi, the man running the building, didn't think that would happen as long as the people here minded their own business. But Orozco said it would, and that was good enough for Kyle.

The southeast sentry post had once been the outside corner of a fancy apartment's living room. It wasn't so fancy now, though. The firestorm that had swept the city on Judgment Day had blown off one of the living room's outer walls, along with half of the other wall and most of the ceiling. The result was a roughly three-meter-square section of floor that gave a clear view of that part of the city, but which was largely open to the elements.

Today, those elements consisted of a sporadic southwest wind that grabbed at the collar of Kyle's thin coat as he and Star stepped off the stairway onto the platform. He pulled the collar back into place as he went to the equipment alcove set into the sentry post's inner wall. There was supposed to be a spare blanket up here, but a quick check of the alcove showed no sign of it. Apparently, whoever had been on duty during the night had taken it with him when he left.

That, or else someone had sneaked up between shifts and stolen it. Chief Grimaldi said things like that didn't happen here, but Kyle knew they sometimes did.

Orozco didn't much like Grimaldi. He'd never actually said anything, but Kyle could tell. Grimaldi had run some sort of group before Judgment Day, something called a corporation, which had made him think he could run anything. Some of the other people on the Board that made all the decisions had worked in the same corporation he had, which was probably how Grimaldi had been chosen chief.

Orozco hadn't been there when the Board was set up. He'd arrived only two years ago, a year after Kyle and Star had stumbled across the building and had been allowed to move in. What Kyle couldn't figure out was once Orozco *had* shown up, why he hadn't been put in charge instead of Grimaldi. Orozco had been a soldier once, and in Kyle's book that had to count more than anything anyone else had been doing before Judgment Day.

But Kyle was only sixteen, so of course he wasn't on the Board. He didn't get a voice in any of their discussions, either, the way some of the adults did. The way it worked was that Grimaldi or one of his men told Kyle where to go scrounging for food or supplies, or Orozco told him which post he'd been assigned for sentry duty, and Kyle would do it.

It irritated him sometimes, especially when Grimaldi tried to use words like *tactics* or *strategy* or *logistics* when Kyle could tell from Orozco's expression that Grimaldi didn't have the slightest idea what he was talking about. Sometimes, usually late at night, Kyle thought about saying good-bye to Orozco, packing up his and Star's few belongings, and getting out of here.

But bad moods like that never lasted very long. The Ashes could be annoying, but he and Star were eating at least one meal every day here, and had a safe place to sleep. Considering some of the places they'd been, that all by itself made it worth putting up with a little irritation.

Beside him, Star shivered. "Cold?" he asked.

I'm okay, she signed back even as she shivered again.

"You could go sit over there by the alcove," Kyle suggested. "You'd be out of the wind there."

But then I won't be able to see anything, she pointed out.

"That's okay," Kyle assured her. "I can watch alone for awhile."

Star shook her head. *I'm okay.*

Kyle sighed. Star considered his sentry duty to be *her* sentry duty, too, and she took the job every bit as seriously as he did. Aside from physically carrying her over to the alcove, there was no way he was going to get her there, and aside from physically sitting on her, there would be no way he could make her stay.

"Fine," he said. Standing up, he walked around her and sat down again so that he was at least between her and the wind.

She gave him one of those half patient, half exasperated looks that she did so well, and for a moment Kyle thought she was going to get up and go sit in the wind again just to show him she didn't need babying. But Kyle was as stubborn as she was, and they both knew it, and so rather than playing a pointless game of leapfrog with him and the wind, she just rolled her eyes, drew her knees up to her chest, and wrapped her thin arms around them.

Smiling to himself, Kyle turned his eyes back to the ruined city.

The wind apparently wasn't nearly so potent down at street level, and he could see a soft mist rolling in from the direction of the ocean, the drifting tendrils masking some of the jaggedness of the streets and rubble-filled lots below.

Unfortunately, the mist did an equally good job of masking the movements of people and animals, which was going to make Kyle's job that much harder. Keeping his eyes moving, paying particular attention to the spots where he knew some of the neighborhood's troublemakers liked to gather, he settled down to the long hours ahead.

There wasn't much activity today. A few of the other residents were out and about, mostly scrounging for canned food that might have been missed by earlier searchers. Some of the Ashes' residents were out, too, though mostly they were digging through the rubble for building materials to prop up a section of the building's southern wall that Grimaldi's people said was in danger of collapsing. There was very little gang movement, with only a few members of one of the packs roaming the streets several blocks to the south. That would change when darkness came, though.

As for Skynet, all Kyle could see of its presence was a single HK moving back and forth across the eastern sky. If any of the T-600 Terminators were out and about, they were someplace he couldn't see them.

Noon came and went. He and Star each had a few sips from the post's water bottle, and about an hour after noon they shared a small piece of coyote that Kyle had saved from breakfast. By mid-afternoon most of the locals had finished their foraging, either finding what they were looking for or else giving up, and had headed back to secure their homes against the nighttime gang activity.

It was late afternoon when Star tapped Kyle urgently on the arm and pointed to the east. Hunching over a little, Kyle sighted along her arm, searching for whatever it was that she'd seen.

There it was: a group of people approaching down one of the area's better east-west streets. There were six men in the main party, escorting two heavily-laden burros each, and there were at least two outriders Kyle could see traveling along a block ahead of the others. The main group was keeping to the middle of the street, where it would be harder for someone to ambush them.

"Did Orozco say anything about traders coming here today?" he asked Star.

Not to me, she signed.

Kyle pursed his lips. This could be exactly what it looked like: a visit by the traders who came in sometimes from the hardscrabble farmlands to the east and north. Just because Star or even Orozco hadn't heard they were coming didn't necessarily mean anything. Traders didn't exactly operate on a regular schedule.

But it could also be a gang of robbers masquerading as traders in hopes of getting the people in the area to let their guard down. The burros might not be carrying trade goods, but merely the robbers' collection of loot. It was a ploy that Orozco had often warned his sentries to watch out for.

"Binoculars, please," he said.

She nodded and retrieved the scuffed leather binocular case from the equipment alcove. She handed the case to Kyle, then returned to the alcove, standing ready beside the tray of signaling stones.

Carefully, Kyle removed the binoculars from the case. Technically, he remembered Orozco saying once, this was actually a *mon*ocular, since the left set of lenses was broken. Lifting the instrument to his eyes, he focused on the approaching men and animals.

They were definitely not the same men who'd been with the traders who'd come through the neighborhood six months ago.

Kyle grimaced. The fact that he hadn't seen them before also didn't necessarily mean anything. People out in the farming regions came and went as often as people here in the city did. Still, Orozco's number one rule was that it was better to be safe than sorry. Lowering the binoculars, he gave Star a nod.

"Three and two."

She nodded back and selected five of the fingertip-sized stones from the tray. Crossing to the ragged-edged opening between the alcove and the stairway, she got down on her knees and carefully dropped the first three stones, one at a time, down the hole. She paused, and Kyle watched her lips move as she counted out five seconds, then dropped the other two, again one at a time.

And with that, there was nothing for them to do but wait and continue watching. Lifting the binoculars again, Kyle first gave his whole sector a careful sweep, then turned his attention back to the approaching men.

The party had made it about half the distance to the Ashes when Kyle heard the sound of footsteps on the stairway. He lowered the binoculars just as Beth, one of the building's fourteen-year-olds, stepped into view.

"I'm supposed to take over," she announced, panting with the exertion of her climb. "Orozco wants you down at the main entrance."

"Got it," Kyle said, standing up and handing her the binoculars. The girl winced like he was offering her a live snake, but gamely took them. A few months ago Beth had been unfortunate enough to be present when her older brother Mick had been goofing around and had dropped one of Orozco's other sets of binoculars. She'd also been present when Orozco chewed the boy out over the incident, and had been terrified of binoculars ever since.

Going down the stairs was just as hazardous as going up, but at least it was faster and didn't take as much effort. Kyle and Star reached the main entrance to find Orozco and three of Grimaldi's men in quiet but earnest conversation beneath the archway. All four were armed, Orozco with his usual M16 and Beretta, the others with some of the building's collection of hunting rifles and shotguns.

Orozco looked up as Kyle and Star approached and beckoned them over.

"Report," he said.

"At least eight men and twelve burros approaching from the east," Kyle told him. "Could be traders, but I didn't recognize any of them."

One of the others, a short balding man named Wadleigh, gave a snort.

"You scrambled us for *traders?*" he demanded.

"I didn't recognize any of them," Kyle repeated, standing his ground. "Who knows who they are?"

"They're traders, kiddo," Wadleigh explained with exaggerated patience. "The animals alone prove that. Unless you think someone's opened a Hertz Rent-A-Burro for the L.A. gangs to use?" He looked at Orozco. "I thought this stone system was supposed to have enough nuances to keep us from having to drop everything every time one of your sentries got nervous."

"Is that what you think?" Orozco asked calmly. "That Reese just got nervous? That's your *professional* military opinion?"

"Don't pull that *professional military* crap on me," Wadleigh said scornfully. "I may not have been a *sergeant* in the army, but I *do* know something about tactics and strategy, thank you."

"I'm sure you do," Orozco agreed. "And your suggested course of action?"

Wadleigh rolled his eyes.

"Fine," he growled. "As long as we've been interrupted anyway, we might as well play it through."

"Thank you," Orozco said. "Get your fire teams together, and get to your posts."

"Sure." Wadleigh threw another look at Kyle, then gestured to the other two men and strode off across the lobby toward the hallway that led to the rear of the building.

Orozco let them get to the far side of the cracked fountain basin in the center of the lobby before clearing his throat.

"By the way, Wadleigh," he called after them, his

voice loud enough to be heard all the way at the back of the balcony, "*scramble* refers to aircraft. The proper term for activating ground forces is either *turn to* or *lock and load*."

Wadleigh threw a glare over his shoulder. But it seemed to Kyle that the glare was tinged with embarrassment, and the man turned and kept going without saying anything. A few seconds later, he and the others disappeared down the hallway.

"Idiot," Kyle said quietly.

"That the way a soldier talks about his superiors?" Orozco asked.

Kyle grimaced. "No, sir. Sorry."

"Better," Orozco said, nodding. "Doesn't change the fact that Wadleigh *is* an idiot, of course. But he's an idiot who's willing to pick up a gun and help defend our home and our lives, and for that he deserves your respect. Now, what's your reading on our visitors?"

"They probably really are just traders," Kyle admitted. He'd stood up to Wadleigh's scorn just fine, but under Orozco's steady gaze he could feel his confidence melting into a vague feeling of foolishness.

"But the back of your neck's still prickling?" Orozco persisted.

Kyle thought about it.

"I guess so," he said. "Yes, it is."

"Then you made the right call," Orozco said. "Always listen to your neck and your gut. What's their ETA?"

"Probably about ten minutes," he said. "Maybe less. They were moving pretty fast."

"Were they, now," Orozco said. "Interesting."

"Why?" Kyle asked.

"Because quick movement attracts the eye, which is

something to be avoided these days," Orozco said. "Besides that, peddlers and traders working a neighborhood don't generally want to rush through it. Not without a really good reason."

He shifted his M16 to his left hand and drew his Beretta.

"Here," he said, reversing the pistol and handing it to Kyle. "You and Star take backup position around the right side of the fountain. I'll hold my rifle either across my chest or else pointed at the visitors. If everything's okay, I'll lift the muzzle to point at the ceiling."

"And we should come out then?"

"Or you can stay hidden," Orozco said. "Your choice. *If* I instead lower the muzzle to point at the floor, start shooting. Remember to take out the ones with weapons first."

"Right." Kyle took the gun, checking the safety, the clip, and the chamber the way Orozco had taught him. Then, heart pounding, he gestured to Star and headed across the lobby to the fountain.

Orozco counted out seven minutes before he heard the sound of shuffling feet and clattering hooves coming along the street from the south.

That alone was unusual. A short block and a half south of the building's archway, lying on its side across the street, was an old city bus that had probably been sitting there rusting since Judgment Day. The bus's body was in remarkably solid condition, though, which made it an ideal spot from which to launch an ambush. Orozco had occasionally toyed with the idea of using it as an observation post, but had concluded that the lines of communication back to the building were too iffy for it to be safe for any of his young sentries.

But strangers had no way of knowing the bus was harmless, which was why those approaching Moldering Lost Ashes usually avoided the whole questionable situation by coming in from the north. Either this new group was strong enough not to care about possible traps, or else there was someone—or something—to the north that they were even more anxious to avoid.

Whichever it was, this could end up being a very unpleasant morning. Lifting the M16 to ready position across his chest, Orozco mentally prepared himself for combat.

If it *was* a raid, though, the bandits were playing it cool. The first man to come into view was wearing a holstered sidearm, but both hands were busy with the leads of two of the burros Kyle had mentioned. His face was turned upward as he walked, his oriental eyes clearly searching for something on the wall above the archway.

Orozco let him get three more steps, then cleared his throat.

"Afternoon," he called.

The man jerked and came to an instant halt, his eyes snapping from his survey of the building to Orozco and his rifle.

"Afternoon," he said cautiously. His voice carried a slight accent, just enough to show that English probably wasn't his first language. "Excuse the intrusion. I'm looking for the Moldavia Los Angeles."

"I've heard of the place," Orozco said, nodding. "Luxury condos in the heart of greater Los Angeles, starting in the low 800s."

The other man drew back a little, probably wondering if the man with the military-issue rifle also had a radiation-scrambled brain.

"Uh…" he began.

"Long gone, of course," Orozco continued, watching the man's face closely. "However, if you're interested in Moldering Lost Ashes, where the rooms are a lot cheaper, that's a different story."

The other's forehead wrinkled even harder. Then, suddenly, it cleared.

"Oh, I see," he said, visibly relaxing. "You've changed the name." He frowned again. "Moldering Lost *Ashes*?"

Orozco shrugged. A second and third man had now entered the field of fire, both also armed, both with their hands also visible and safely occupied with burro leads.

"It fits the place better than Moldavia Los Angeles," he said. "Who are you?"

"My name's Nguyen," the man said, nodding back over his shoulder at the first of the two men who'd come up behind him. "This is Vuong, my second. We're from Chuck Randall at Keeper's Point."

"Are you, now," Orozco said, feeling his tension ease a bit. But only a bit. Nguyen had the names right, but there were a hundred ways he could have come by them. "How come Randall didn't come himself?"

"He's not traveling much these days," Nguyen said grimly. "Lost his right leg below the knee two months ago. Something new Skynet's started putting in the rivers."

"A new model Terminator?"

Nguyen shrugged. "All we know is that it's metal, travels in water, and has lots of big teeth. No one's gotten a pedigree for it yet."

"Not to be rude, but could we possibly take this inside?" Vuong put in, throwing a look northward past Nguyen's shoulder.

"What's your hurry?" Orozco asked.

"A mile or so back we spotted a group of nasties paralleling us a few blocks to the north," Nguyen said. "Eight to ten of them, all heavily armed. I don't know if they spotted us, or if they're even planning on turning in this direction, but we'd just as soon be out of sight before either of those things can happen."

Orozco grimaced. More swaggering young men with guns who would need to be taught to stay away from his building. Just what he needed.

"We're almost done," he assured Vuong. "So if Randall really sent you, he must have told you who you'd be dealing with"

"Yes, after a fashion." Nguyen's lips tightened. "But then, he also told us to look for the Moldavia Los Angeles. Obviously, losing his leg hasn't affected his sense of humor."

"Apparently not," Orozco said, a little more of the tension easing. Only someone who knew Randall would also know what sorts of things the man found funny. "So who did he send you here to see?"

"He just told us to ask for Auntie Em," Nguyen said. He frowned. "I don't suppose...that's not *you*, is it?"

"Hardly," Orozco said as the last remnant of tension faded quietly away. That had been his and Randall's private joke, one the grizzled farmer had come up with the last time he was here. "Go ahead and bring your people and animals inside—we've got a room over to your right past the fountain where you can put them."

"Thank you," Nguyen said, making no effort to take Orozco up on his invitation. "But even a private joke has two sides."

"In other words, how do you know I'm the one Randall said you could trust?" Orozco asked.

"Correct." Nguyen inclined his head slightly. "No offense."

"None taken," Orozco assured him, his estimation of the man going up a notch. That kind of caution, that refusal to ever take anything for granted, was how you stayed alive these days. "Here's Auntie Em."

He hoisted his rifle to point at the ceiling, giving Nguyen a full profile view of the weapon. "Nguyen, say hello to Auntie Em. Auntie M16, say hello to Mr. Nguyen."

Nguyen gave a slightly twisted smile.

"Pleased to meet you, Ms. Em," he said. "I take it, then, that you must be Ms. Em's keeper and guardian, Mad Sergeant Justo Orozco?"

"Call me Huss," Orozco said, beckoning to Kyle and Star. "This is Kyle and Star," he added as the two kids rose from their concealment and started across the lobby. "They'll help you get your burros inside and unloaded."

"Ah...you may have slightly misunderstood our intentions," Nguyen said carefully. "We're not necessarily planning to sell *all* of our goods to you."

"I understand that," Orozco said. "But given the late hour, and given that the Ashes is the safest place around, I'd hoped you would accept our hospitality for the night."

For a moment Nguyen studied Orozco's face. Then, he again inclined his head.

"Thank you. We would be honored."

"Good."

Orozco turned to Kyle as he and Star came up beside him.

"Mr. Nguyen and his party will be our guests for the night," he told the boy. "They and their animals will be in the Lower Conference Room. Take them there, and on your way tell Pierre I want him to stay at his post, but that the rest of his team can stand down and give you a hand getting our guests settled in."

"Got it." Kyle gestured to Nguyen. "This way."

They boy headed off toward the conference room, walking sideways so that he could watch the traders' progress as they picked their way across the lobby. He hadn't stuck the Beretta into his belt, Orozco noticed, but still had it ready in his hand. Like Nguyen, like Orozco himself, the boy knew better than to take anything for granted.

Orozco waited until the last of Nguyen's group was inside. Then, stepping beneath the archway, he signaled the man in the sniper's nest across the street to come in. Once he was back in the building, Orozco would have him take over the post here at the entrance.

And then Orozco would have the unpleasant task of admitting to Wadleigh and the others that, yes, the party Kyle had spotted *were* just traders. The information would probably lead to more snide comments about Kyle's paranoia, which thanks to the politics of life here, Orozco would have to endure in silence.

As Kyle had already noted, Wadleigh was an idiot. What was worse, he took things for granted, and this incident would simply reinforce the man's mental laziness.

If there were any justice in the world, Orozco mused, *Kyle would survive for a long time, while Wadleigh would suffer a quick and unpleasant death.*

Baker appeared from the sniper's nest and headed briskly across the street. Orozco gestured to him, then pointed to the floor beside the archway to indicate his new post. Then, cradling his M16 under his arm, he headed across the lobby to close down all the rest of the fire teams.

Including Wadleigh's.

No, there was no justice left in the world. Not anymore. Justice had died on Judgment Day.

CHAPTER SIX

The storm drainage tunnel was dank, fungus-infested, shin-high in fetid water, and tight enough that Connor and David couldn't walk without stooping over.

But it was underground and out of sight of HKs and T-600s. That alone elevated the experience to the level of a walk in the park.

They were nearly to their target when Connor spotted a narrow slit of pale light angling in from the tunnel's roof. David, in the lead, noticed it about the same time and signaled for a halt.

"Does that look suspicious to you, too?" he whispered to Connor.

Connor studied the dim light. They'd passed beneath similar openings at various points along their journey, most of them a result of warped or broken manhole covers that had once protected access points into the tunnels.

But none of those other covers had been inside a Skynet staging area. This one was, and it demanded a higher degree of caution.

"We've come this far," Connor whispered back. "Let's take a look."

David nodded, taking a moment to fold up the strip map he'd made of the tunnel and tucking it away inside his jacket. Then, getting a grip on his shoulder-slung MP5 submachine gun, he started forward.

They reached the ray of light without anything jumping out of the darkness or, worse, opening fire. The manhole cover was at the top of a five-meter concrete cylinder, accessible via a set of rusty rungs set into the cylinder's side.

Connor peered up at it. This particular cover wasn't cracked, but had merely been angled slightly up out of its proper position, either by movement of the ground around it or by a small warping of the cover's seating. The gap itself was very small, no more than half a centimeter across at its widest.

More significant than the gap's origin was the fact that it had clearly been there a long time. A single tenacious vine had taken root in the tunnel wall where the light shone, its roots poking through cracks in the concrete, its leaves positioned to drink in the meager bit of sunlight.

Of even greater significance was the thick layer of rust and grime visible on the cover itself, which meant it had lain undisturbed since long before Skynet had set up its staging area in the warehouse above. Possibly since Judgment Day itself.

David had apparently come to the same set of conclusions.

"Looks clean," he whispered. "Be careful not to move it."

Connor nodded, rotated his own MP5 downward on its shoulder sling, and started up the rungs. Caution was definitely the order of the day—if there was a similar layer of rust on the upper side of the cover, moving the plate would probably disturb it. Skynet's Terminators were experts at ferreting out such subtle clues of Resistance presence.

The rungs, fortunately, were sturdier than their coating of rust suggested, and Connor reached the top without incident. Hooking his right arm through the top rung, he pulled out the snoop kit with his left and unrolled its length of bendable but slightly stiff fiber optic cable. He slipped the elastic band around his head, adjusted the eyepiece over his right eye, then bent the tip of the cable into a right angle and eased it up through the opening.

The good news was that David's map and navigation had been right on the mark. They had indeed reached the warehouse Blair had spotted the previous night. Turning the optic cable in a slow circle, Connor could see two of the HKs she'd described, still maintaining their silent guard at the parking lot's corners.

The bad news was that the tunnel wasn't going to take them beneath the warehouse itself, as David had suggested might be the case. It was close, certainly—the tunnel ran nearly parallel to the building, angling slightly away at the far end. Unfortunately, the entire passageway was very definitely *outside* the wall.

He looked down at David, still waiting at the bottom of the shaft, and shook his head. The other grimaced and nodded acknowledgment.

Connor raised his head and once again focused on the view through the eyepiece. The wall the tunnel was paralleling didn't look all that healthy, he noted. In fact, it looked way too fragile to still be holding up that much roof. Some trick of the warehouse's internal structure, perhaps, that made the wall look weaker than it actually was?

Or had Skynet actually taken the time and trouble to reinforce the building?

There was no way to tell without actually getting inside. But whatever the situation, it probably wasn't anything they couldn't fix with a few chunks of C4 along the bottom edge of the wall.

He was figuring out the best places to set the charges when a T-600 appeared around the far corner, striding alongside the south warehouse wall like a sentry on patrol.

Coming directly toward the manhole cover.

Connor's first impulse was to yank the optical fiber down out of sight. But movement attracted the eye, especially a Terminator's eye, and the machine was already close enough to notice even a movement that small.

But if Connor could mask that movement with something else...

Shifting control of the optic cable to his right hand, he reached over to the vine and pinched off the largest leaf and its stem with his fingernails. He held it up against the opening, making sure to keep it below ground level. Then, watching the Terminator closely, he eased the leaf a couple of centimeters up through the opening as he simultaneously pulled the end of the cable back down. Holding the leaf in place, feeling the breeze tugging at it, he held his breath.

Even through the ground and the concrete of the shaft, he could feel the vibration of the T-600's steps as the machine approached and then came to a halt. For a moment nothing happened. Connor forced himself to hold the leaf steady, wishing he could see what the Terminator was doing, wondering if it and Skynet were merely contemplating this green intruder into their lifeless domain or whether they'd seen through the deception and had spotted the soft, vulnerable humans below.

And then, abruptly, the cover was slammed back into position, sealing the gap, cutting off the faint light and crushing the leaf.

And as a soft rain of rust particles drifted down onto Connor's face and shoulders, he felt the fading thuds as the Terminator continued on its way.

Carefully, in full darkness now, he made his way down the shaft to where David was waiting.

"Terminator?" David whispered.

Connor nodded. "Regular sentry patrol, I assume."

"What were you doing with that leaf?"

"I didn't want the T-600 to spot the cable vanishing," Connor explained, "and I sure as hell couldn't risk leaving it out there. So I gave the Terminator something more innocuous to notice."

David grunted. "Good thing their motion sensors require a visual follow-up," he said. "Who knew they hated plants, too?"

Connor grimaced. "Of course they hate plants. Plants exhale oxygen, which oxidizes metals. If and when they wipe out humans, you can bet animals and plants will be next."

"Well, as long as they start with lima beans, I'm good with it," David said philosophically. "So what's the story with the warehouse?"

"I think there'll be something we can do from the tunnel," Connor told him. "It wasn't a wasted trip, if that's what you mean."

"Good," David said. "So now we get the hell out of here?"

"In a bit," Connor said as he carefully coiled up the snoop kit and returned it to its case. "As long as we're down here anyway, let's take some time and see where else these tunnels go."

There was a short pause.

"Any particular reason you want to know?" David asked at last.

"Not really," Connor said. "Any particular reason you don't?"

"Not really," David said. "After you."

One of Orozco's fondest childhood memories was the farmer's market that came to his neighborhood every Saturday. He could still remember the sights and sounds of the people and vendors, the spicy aromas from the food carts mixed in with the subtler scents of melon and strawberry and fresh corn. He could feel his mother's grip on his hand, lest they be separated in the crowds, and the precious weight of the grocery bag he'd been entrusted with clutched tightly to his chest.

Nguyen's display of goods wasn't nearly up to those memories. But in the world beyond Judgment Day, it was as close as anyone was likely to get.

"These are apple seeds," Nguyen said, pointing to a small collection of black seeds. "Not for everyone—they take a lot of space and soil. But if you've got all that, I guarantee you'll love them."

"Afraid we don't have that kind of space here," Grimaldi said, gazing over the collection of seeds, seedlings, ripe vegetables, and grains Nguyen's people had laid out on a long plastic display sheet. "We could use some of that lettuce, though."

"Good choice," Nguyen said. "But you really need some zucchini to go with it."

"Yes, that does sound good," Grimaldi agreed, stroking his lip carefully.

Standing back against the conference room wall, Orozco gave a quiet sigh. They had some pretty extensive gardens in Moldering Lost Ashes, and they could certainly use more vegetables to supplement the canned and packaged goods they continued to scrounge from the wreckage of the city.

The problem was that they really didn't have any room available for expansion. The only practical areas for gardens were on the third and fourth floors, and every square centimeter up there that received even limited sunshine was already packed with either traditional dirt-grown plants or the hydroponic setups Morris and Clementi had put together. There was literally nowhere else in the building where they could set up more gardens.

Just as importantly, they didn't have any more of the wire mesh they used to shield the plants from casual observation by either Skynet or potential raiders who might be lurking in nearby buildings.

But Grimaldi didn't care about that. He was still locked into the corporate grow-or-fold mindset that he'd ridden to the top of the stack before Judgment Day, and he was hell-bent on applying that philosophy to this struggling colony he'd built amid the ruins of his former dukedom. In his eyes, Moldavia Los Angeles—as he still insisted on calling it—was destined to become a thriving community, a self-contained city-within-a-city that would someday pull the rest of L.A. out of the ashes along with it.

It wouldn't happen, of course. What Moldering Lost Ashes was really destined to become was a shattered graveyard. Sooner or later, Skynet would see to that.

Orozco looked over at Kyle and Star, standing at the edge of one of the clumps of residents who were drooling over Nguyen's display. Kyle, like a good bargainer, was pretending he wasn't nearly as interested as he really was. Star, without Kyle's sophistication or craftiness, was gazing at the wares in open, wide-eyed fascination.

"...for ten gallons of gasoline," Grimaldi finished.

Orozco snapped out of his reverie. What the *hell* had the chief just promised?

"Wait a minute," he spoke up, leaving his wall and working his way through the crowd to the chief's side. "Ten *gallons*?"

"Is there a problem, Sergeant?" Grimaldi asked coolly, his eyes daring Orozco to argue with him in front of everyone.

"I just wanted to point out to Mr. Nguyen that we have many other items available for trade," Orozco said. "We've got mechanical systems, tools, plumbing equipment, electrical parts—"

"I appreciate the reminder of our current inventory," Grimaldi interrupted. "I'm sure Mr. Nguyen does, too. But he seems mostly interested in our gasoline supply."

Orozco looked at Nguyen, noting the cautious fervor in the man's eyes. He wanted their gasoline, all right. Wanted it very badly.

"I trust you to remember that our supply is *not* unlimited."

"Of course," Grimaldi said evenly. "But gasoline is a promise for the future. Food is a promise for the present."

Orozco grimaced. So much for any further argument. Once Grimaldi started in with the slogans and aphorisms, it meant his mind was completely made up. From that point on, not even the Board could sway him.

"Fine," he said. "We'll get it first thing tomorrow."

"I'd prefer to have it now, if you don't mind," Nguyen

spoke up. "Chief Grimaldi indicated that he wanted to start transplanting the seedlings as soon as possible, and I'm sure you understand that once our plants are mixed in with yours, it will be very difficult to tell which ones are which."

"I hope you're not suggesting that we might renege on our promise," Grimaldi said, raising his eyebrows slightly.

"Of course not," Nguyen assured him. "But things happen. You understand."

"All the same—" Grimaldi began.

"It's not a problem," Orozco said, cutting off what could only be a useless argument. It was still plenty light out, and most of the gangs in the area didn't come out until it was full dark. "Give me one of your burros, and Kyle and I will go get it. You brought your own containers, I trust?"

"Yes, we have some collapsible plastic ones," Nguyen said. "If you'd like, I or some of my men can come with you and give you a hand."

"That won't be necessary, thank you," Orozco assured him, gesturing to Kyle. Like he was naïve enough to show a group of perfect strangers where their stash of gasoline was hidden. "Kyle, go check out the Colt from the weapons locker and put it on. Mr. Nguyen, just bring the burro to the front entrance, if you would."

Five minutes later, Orozco and Kyle left the archway, crossed the street, and headed down the somewhat narrower cross street that ran along the north side of their sniper nest building. A container-laden burro led by a frayed rope walked beside Orozco. Star, as always, walked beside Kyle.

"Keep your eyes open," Orozco warned quietly as

they reached the first corner and turned south. He glanced back, checking to make sure none of Nguyen's men were following. "We should be okay, but one of the gangs could be out trying for an early-bird special."

"What's an early-bird special?" Kyle asked.

Orozco grimaced. "Something restaurants and stores used to use to draw in customers. People who got there early could snatch up the easiest pickings. We don't want those easy pickings to be us."

"Oh," Kyle said. "Speaking of stores, the blanket that's supposed to be stored at the southeast sentry post is missing."

"I know," Orozco said. "Don't worry about it."

"Did Ellis take it?" Kyle persisted. "I checked, and he was the one on shift before Star and me."

Orozco sighed.

"Yes, he took it," he said. "He also took some food and one of the .22s."

Kyle stared at him.

"He *left*?"

"So it would seem," Orozco said. "Keep that to yourself, please. I haven't told the chief yet, and there's going to be hell to pay when he finds out. Might as well wait until our visitors leave and we can hash it out in private."

"Okay," Kyle said, still sounding confused. "Why would he just leave like that?"

"Probably just got tired of the place," Orozco told him. "Or got tired of the people, or the food, or the work. Or he's just one of those kids who can't stand to stay in one place very long. I've known some like that."

Their gasoline stash, the underground fiberglass storage tank from a long-demolished service station, was located three blocks from the main Moldering Lost

Ashes building. There had been hundreds of such stations in the L.A. area, and Orozco suspected that a large percentage of that supply was still down there, just waiting to be found.

The trick, as always, was to make sure that once you found something valuable, it stayed yours. The passageway Grimaldi and his people had created leading to the tank went a long way toward accomplishing that, with the main entrance disguised as just another section of demolished building and a couple of decoy tunnels leading off the main route to guide any casual visitors harmlessly back to the surface.

But Grimaldi's real genius was the hidden door he'd constructed that led into the storage tank chamber. He'd rigged a sliding door that would only open far enough for a child of ten or younger to squeeze through. Once inside, it was a simple matter of shifting a couple of two-by-fours to allow the door to open the rest of the way. Until that was done, though, adults and teens were out of luck.

The door was strong enough to stand up against all but the most determined physical attacks, and even if someone managed to force it open all he would get for his trouble would be a booby-trapped ceiling collapsing on top of him.

Orozco's personal contribution to that genius was in tapping Kyle for this particular duty whenever possible. Very few people in the Ashes even knew where the gasoline was located, and of those only Orozco, Grimaldi, and a couple of others knew about the special door and how it operated. Star was so much a part of Kyle's every movement that no one gave her a second thought anymore as she wandered around in the boy's shadow.

Certainly no one would ever dream that her presence on a gasoline run had anything to do with the operation itself, let alone provided a vital key to it.

Which was exactly the way Orozco and Grimaldi wanted it. The gasoline was used almost exclusively as a trade good, and then only sparingly, with virtually none of it going to the building's own activities. As a result, after five years of gradually drawing down the supply the tank was probably still half full.

Orozco had every intention of making sure that it was Moldering Lost Ashes—and *only* Moldering Lost Ashes—that finally drew down the last drop.

Unlike some of the beasts of burden Orozco had dealt with over the years, this particular burro had no problem letting itself be led into the cramped tunnel beyond the disguised entryway. Orozco kept a firm hand on the animal's lead, alert to any sign that it might suddenly bolt. They reached the door, Star slipped inside, and two minutes later Orozco was carefully filling Nguyen's canisters from the tap they'd drilled into the gasoline tank.

The tap had been specifically designed for low flow in order to minimize the chance of spillage, and drawing the promised ten gallons took over fifteen minutes. Orozco made sure the tap was securely closed, reset the backup safety system that would hopefully prevent a catastrophic spill if the tap's seals somehow failed, then led the way out of the chamber back to the tunnel.

Star closed the door back down to its usual crack, reset the two-by-fours, and rejoined them. Turning the burro around would have been difficult, so Orozco opted instead to leave via one of the decoy tunnels. It brought them back to street level a block from where they'd entered; getting his bearings, Orozco turned them back toward home.

They still had two blocks to go when a pair of gaunt and filthy teenaged boys suddenly appeared from broken doorways on opposite sides of the street five meters ahead.

"Freeze or bleed," one of them ordered, hefting a long-barreled revolver in both hands and pointing it at Orozco's chest.

Orozco felt his stomach tighten. Neither of the kids was a local, or at least not a local he recognized. Was this the vanguard of the gang Nguyen and his people had spotted on their way in?

"Take it easy," he said soothingly. "I'm sure we can make a deal."

"Well, would ya look at that?" another voice came from the right. Orozco turned, to see six more youths file out of a long ganghouse shack that seemed to be built mostly from cracked pieces of drywall. The boy in front was gripping an even bigger revolver than the sentry, the others sporting knives or clubs made from pieces of broken rebar. "We've hit the jackpot tonight, kiddies," the teen with the revolver went on. He pointed the gun at the burro. "We got dinner—" he shifted his aim to Orozco's holstered Beretta—"we got more guns—"

He leveled the gun at Star.

"And we even got ourselves some entertainment."

CHAPTER SEVEN

Never panic.

Orozco's frequently repeated warning echoed through Kyle's mind as the six teens spread out into a loose semicircle and started toward the three of them. Never, ever *panic.*

But it was very hard not to. He and Orozco had guns of their own, but they were still holstered at their sides. The teens' two guns were already out and aimed.

"Take it easy," Orozco called again. "There's no need for trouble."

"Maybe we *like* trouble," the leader retorted. He had pulled a couple of paces ahead of the rest of his pack, his revolver pointed at Orozco's stomach as he strode toward his victims.

"Maybe so, but I'll bet your buddies would rather have goodies than broken bones," Orozco countered, reaching behind him to give Kyle a gentle but imperative push backward and a little to the right.

Star plucked at Kyle's sleeve.

"Not now," Kyle muttered, trying desperately to come up with a plan. If he took a long step to his right, the direction Orozco had just nudged him, he would end up with the burro between him and the main group of teens.

That might at least give him a chance to draw his Colt and even the odds a little.

But no, that wouldn't work. Even though the burro might block shots coming from that direction, Kyle would still be exposed to the kid with the revolver standing down the street.

Unless Orozco was planning to block that line of fire with his own body. Was that what the little push had meant? Was Kyle supposed to duck into shelter, and try to take down as many of the attackers as he could before one of them got Orozco? Or him? Or Star?

There was another tug at Kyle's arm, even more insistent than the first.

"What?" Kyle bit out, glaring at her.

Her eyes met his evenly, her hands tracing out a single word. *Empty.*

Kyle frowned. Empty? What was that supposed to—?

And then he got it, and his eyes lifted from Star to the gun pointed at them from down the street. To the gun, and the faint hints of light he could see peeking coyly through the revolver's cylinder.

The gun was empty.

Kyle looked back at the gang leader, still bearing down on Orozco. Was his gun empty, too? The kid was holding it low, pointed at Orozco's waist instead of his chest or head, too low for Kyle to see if its cylinder was also empty.

But it almost didn't matter. The minute the boy reached them and got his hands on either Orozco's Beretta or Kyle's Colt, he *would* have a loaded gun. If Kyle was going to do something, he had to do it right now.

The kid was nearly there, his free hand reaching toward Orozco's holster. Setting his teeth, Kyle took a quick step to his right, ducked down behind the burro's side, and yanked out his Colt.

"Freeze!" he ordered.

The gang leader's head snapped toward Kyle, his eyes burning with surprise and rage, his gun swiveling toward this sudden new threat. As he did so, Orozco took half a step forward.

And in a haze of motion that Kyle never did completely figure out, the gang leader was spun 180 degrees around, his gun hand yanked up behind his back with the revolver pointed harmlessly down the street, and Orozco's left arm snaking its way around the kid's neck to press tightly against his throat.

"Like my friend says," Orozco said. "Freeze."

"Let him go!" the gunman down the street snarled, jabbing his empty revolver threateningly toward Orozco as he and his friend unglued themselves from their positions and charged toward the would-be victims.

There was a sudden muffled crack from the direction of the gang leader's twisted arm. The kid cried out in pain, and his revolver thudded onto the broken pavement. An instant later, Orozco had released the kid's wrist, drawn his Beretta, and had his arm crooked around the front of the leader's face with the gun pointed toward the two incoming teens.

"We only say *freeze* twice," he warned quietly.

The boys came to a sudden halt.

"Join the group," Orozco invited them, twitching the Beretta's muzzle toward the five who were still spread out in front of him. "Put the gun on the ground first."

Silently, the two teens complied. Orozco's Beretta followed them the whole way over to the rest of the pack, and now there were seven sets of hate-filled glares washing at Kyle over the muzzle of his Colt.

"Here's how it's going to work," Orozco said into the brittle silence. "You're going to put down your weapons—*all* of them—and you're going to walk away. And you're not going to come back. Ever."

The leader began cursing. Orozco tightened his grip slightly around the other's neck, and the swearing abruptly stopped.

"That's the easy way," Orozco continued. "The hard way is that we make sure you don't bother us again by killing all of you." He cocked back the hammer on the Beretta. "Right now."

Kyle felt sweat gathering on the back of his neck. He'd seen Orozco use this same threat on other gangs, and so far all of them had backed down.

What if this one didn't? Would Kyle be able to cold-bloodedly open fire on other human beings if they decided to make a fight of it? Even to save his own life?

Beside him, he felt Star brush his arm…and with that, all the questions and indecision faded into a cold determination. Because he wouldn't just be protecting himself. He would be protecting Star.

And whatever it took, he would do that. *Whatever* it took.

Maybe the other teens saw the subtle change in his face. Maybe they didn't, but had just finished running the odds. Whichever it was, one of them took a deep breath and dropped his knife onto the pavement. A moment later a second followed suit, and then a third, until all of them were standing unarmed, looking forlorn and a little ridiculous, as they continued to glare with impotent rage.

"Good," Orozco said. Removing his arm from the

leader's throat, he gave the kid a shove toward the rest of the group. The kid stopped a couple of feet in front of the pack and turned around, adding his glare to the others' as he clutched his wrist.

"I suggest you head south," Orozco went on. "The population density goes down as you get closer to NukeZero, so there should still be places where you can carve out a home for yourselves. And the radiation should be well below danger levels by now."

"Like we care about that when we're starving to death," one of them muttered.

"There's still plenty of food to be had for the scrounging," Orozco assured him. "Or you can starve, if you'd rather. Makes no difference to me."

Abruptly, Kyle heard the sound of running feet coming from his left. He turned, to see Wadleigh and three more Moldering Lost Ashes men appear around the corner, rifles and shotguns at the ready.

The teens saw them, too, and with that the last thoughts of resistance or treachery crumbled away. They might be vicious and depraved, but the fact they'd survived this long proved they weren't stupid.

"But wherever you go," Orozco went on, "please believe me when I say that you have no future in this neighborhood."

The leader's eyes came reluctantly back to Orozco.

"Yeah, we got it," he bit out.

"Good," Orozco said. "Now go collect whatever you've got in your flophouse and hit the road. I'll give you half an hour. After that, if we see any of you around here again, you'll be shot on sight."

"Go to hell," the leader muttered. But the words had no fire behind them, only dull resignation.

"I'm already there," Orozco said grimly. "So is every-one else. Save your strength for fighting Skynet and the Terminators, not your fellow humans."

The kid snorted. "Right."

"I'm serious," Orozco insisted. "You like leading? Fine. We need leaders. But lead a Resistance cell, not a gang."

The kid just grunted and turned his back. Pushing his way through the rest of the group, he stomped back into their flimsy ganghouse. One by one the others followed, some of them glancing at Orozco as they went, others ignoring him completely.

They had all disappeared inside by the time Wadleigh and the others arrived.

"You okay?" Wadleigh asked, panting as he trotted to a halt. "The sentry signaled that you were in trouble."

"We were, but we're not anymore," Orozco assured him. "Thanks for the timely arrival. Made it much easier to convince them to vacate the premises."

"Let's hope so," Wadleigh growled. "What about that stuff?" He gestured at the knives and revolvers scattered around the street.

"We'll take it with us," Orozco said. "Kyle, you and Star go gather everything up. You can put it in that extra bag on the burro's harness."

"Sure," Kyle said. Gesturing to Star, he holstered his Colt and grabbed the bag. Walking around the burro, he went to the abandoned weapons and started collecting them. One of the knives in particular caught his eye, and he took a moment to heft it in his hand, feeling the weight nestle comfortably in his grip.

A couple of the teens, he had noticed, had held their knives like they really knew what they were doing. Carefully setting the weapon in the bag with the others,

Kyle made a mental note to ask Orozco about that later.

Orozco had already taught him how to shoot and make explosives. Maybe later Kyle could learn how to fight with a knife, too.

The sun was setting behind a line of drab, pink-edged clouds when Blair finally arrived at the new hangar where she and Yoshi had stashed their A-10s.

Considering the shape her plane had been in when she delivered it to Wince last night, she'd expected to find the place buzzing with activity. But the big open space was quiet and dark, with no hum of grinding wheels or flicker of welder fire.

"Hello?" she called softly into the darkness, stepping back to put her shoulder blades against the wall beside the door, her hand dropping to the grip of her Desert Eagle. "Anyone home?"

There was another moment of silence. Then, a shadow behind her A-10 shifted subtly and Wince's familiar shock of white hair appeared around the tail.

"Oh," he said. "It's you."

"You were expecting someone else?" Blair growled, looking around the otherwise deserted hangar. This was *not* the level of security they were supposed to have around here.

"Yoshi, actually," Wince said. "He's been here all day, and I finally sent him back to the bunker to get some sleep. But you know how well he obeys that kind of order."

"About as well as I do?"

"About that, yes," Wince agreed. "But since you're here and he isn't, could you give me a hand?"

"What do you need?" Blair asked, keeping her grip on

the Desert Eagle as she headed toward him. If there was someone back there holding a gun on the old man...

But she rounded the tail to find that Wince was indeed alone.

"I'm trying to get this attached without attracting attention," he told her, pointing to a replacement armor plate lying beneath an open section of her A-10's tail, a section completely surrounded by bullet holes. Those HKs last night had really done a job on her plane. "HKs have been buzzing the neighborhood all afternoon," Wince continued, "and I've been afraid to fire up the welders."

"So what are you going to use, duct tape?" Blair asked, eyeing the hole. It looked way too small for the plate Wince was planning to jam into it.

"Close," Wince said with a grin as he pried the top off an unlabeled one-quart can. "I'm going to glue it in."

Blair cocked her head.

"You're kidding."

"Well, temporarily, anyway," he said. "Tomorrow when I don't have to worry so much about stray light leaking out I'll do a proper welding. But the glue should hold it together until then."

"Okay," Blair said, looking at all the other bullet holes on the tail as the scent of the adhesive curled her nose hairs. Wince's inventory included some of the worst-smelling concoctions in all of creation. "Don't you think you should take off all those other plates before you glue this one down?"

"By that I assume you mean I should take them off so that I can replace them?" Wince suggested as he select-ed a paintbrush and started to layer the glue onto the exposed section of fuselage. "I'd love to do just that.

Problem is, we haven't got anything to replace them with."

Blair looked at the other damaged plates.

"Oh."

"It's worse than just 'oh,'" Wince said grimly. "Another round like last night and you and Connor can say goodbye to any hope of continuing air support. My inventory of spare parts and armor is going fast, and as for jet fuel, we're down to a single fill-up each." He glanced over at her. "Just between us, I'm starting to get a bit concerned."

"Join the club," Blair said. "I just hope we'll find some useful stuff in that depot."

"The Skynet staging area," Wince said, nodding. "Yes, Yoshi told me about that. Sounds perfectly insane, if you ask me."

"No argument there," Blair agreed. "But it's better than going out with a whimper. Besides, in theory all the Terminators will be out making trouble when Connor hits it."

Wince snorted. "In theory. Right. Famous last words if I've ever heard 'em."

"Maybe, maybe not," Blair said. "You ever hear that bumblebees can't fly?"

"Unscientific urban legend," Wince scoffed, studying his new layer of glue and reaching the brush in to touch up a few spots. "There's not enough wing surface if the bumblebee functioned like a fixed-wing aircraft, but its wings actually work more like reverse-pitch semi-rotary helicopter blades. You get a lot more lift that way, obviously more than enough for a bumblebee to tootle along just fine."

"That's my point," Blair said. "Skynet's got its rules

and logic, and if we play by them it'll eventually grind us down. So we have to find new ways and new logic."

"Such as hitting a staging area?"

"Exactly."

Wince shook his head.

"I'm just a simple country mechanic. Okay, I think we're ready. You get that end of the plate, and I'll take this end."

Lying on the floor, the plate had looked much bigger than its intended hole. Once held up to the gap, though, it turned out to be precisely the correct size.

"Now what?" Blair asked as she and Wince pressed it into place.

"We need to hold it here for a minimum of fifteen minutes," Wince said. "I hope you didn't have anything else you wanted to do just now."

"I think I can spare a bit from my busy schedule," Blair said. "Especially given that it's *my* plane you're putting back together."

The minutes dragged slowly by. Blair pressed against her end of the plate, feeling the warmth of Wince's shoulder nearby. The silence of the hangar and the city beyond it settled in around her, the smell of oil and metal and adhesive tingling at her nostrils. Her stomach grumbled once, reminding her that she hadn't eaten since breakfast, and the plate began to feel increasingly heavy as her arm and shoulder muscles started to fatigue.

On the theory that the glue must surely be ready to take some of the strain, she shifted to pressing against the plate with only one hand at a time. It seemed to help.

"Why 'Hickabick?'" Wince asked suddenly.

Blair frowned sideways at him.

"What?"

"Your call sign," Wince said. "I've wondered about it for months, only I never think about it when you're actually around to ask."

"It's an acronym," Blair told him. "HKBK—Hunter-Killer Butt Kicker. Throw in some vowels so you can actually pronounce it and it comes out Hickabick."

"Cute," Wince said. "A little mild, though, isn't it? I mean, why not go with 'Hunter-Killer Ass Kicker?' Let's see—HKAK—Hikak. Works even better."

Blair turned her eyes back to the plate, a hard lump forming in her throat.

"It's already taken," she said, trying to keep the old pain out of her voice. "A friend of mine had it. Pete Teague. He was killed by the HKs a month before I joined Connor's group."

"Oh," Wince said quietly. "I'm sorry."

"It's okay," Blair said. "But like I said, that was his call sign. It's—I can't use it."

"Because it's his memorial?"

"Something like that," Blair said. "Probably sounds silly."

"No, not at all," Wince assured her. "Thank you for sharing that."

The room fell silent again. Blair found herself staring at Wince's hands as they pressed against the plate beside hers, images of Pete flashing with bittersweet clarity across her mind. She'd watched his plane go down in flames even as what was left of their group fled yet another Terminator attack.

Blair hadn't had a chance to say goodbye to him, or to give him a final kiss. She hadn't even been able to give him a proper burial.

But she could make sure his call sign remained *his*.

That much she could do.

That, and do her absolute damnedest to make sure his death ultimately counted for something.

"Okay, that should be enough," Wince said, breaking into her thoughts. "Let's let 'er go and see if she stays put. Keep your toes out of the way, though, just in case."

Carefully, they eased their hands off the plate. Blair watched it closely, but it showed no sign that it was even thinking about coming off.

"Perfect," Wince said after a minute. "It should survive the night just fine. Thanks."

"No problem," Blair said, peering at her plane's underside. The missile pylons, she noted, were still empty. "You'll be rearming me once you get all the holes fixed?"

"You mean the holes, the hydraulics, *and* the left aileron?" Wince asked.

Blair grimaced. "I *thought* the aileron was acting a little funny."

"It's not just funny, it's hilarious," Wince said dryly. "But I think I'll be able to sober it up a little."

"I know you will," Blair said. "You can do anything."

"But...?" Wince asked.

Blair frowned. "But what?"

"Come on, Blair," Wince said with a knowing look. "Flattery is always followed by an insane request. Go ahead, but do bear in mind that I've only got three Sidewinders left, and even I can't make new ones out of cheese and ten-year-old Army MREs."

"I wasn't going to ask for more Sidewinders," Blair protested, mentally scratching them off her list. "I was just going to ask if you could give me a few extra rounds for my GAU-8 this time."

"And how would you suggest I do that?" Wince asked. "Those ammo drums only come in one size."

"I know," Blair said. "But we just agreed that you can do anything."

"*You* agreed I could do anything," Wince said. "I'm not sure my vote was even asked for, let alone counted. Wouldn't it be simpler to just lighten up on the trigger a little?"

"It's not that I'm spending them too fast," Blair said. "It's that Skynet always seems to know when I'm dry. I swear the damn computer's counting every round as it comes out."

"Actually, it probably is," Wince conceded. "No, really, it's a fine idea. I just don't know if I can—"

"*Shh!*" Blair cut him off, snapping up her hand for silence. A familiar hum had appeared at the edge of her consciousness, the low-pitched vibration of an HK's turbofans working its way through the hangar's walls.

Wince had heard it, too. He nodded understanding, his face drawn and tense. The hum was getting louder...

And suddenly, the hangar's boarded-up west wall exploded into a hundred fiery spots and slashes of light as the HK's searchlights found their way through the cracks and gaps.

Wince twitched, but remained silent. Blair found her hand again gripping her holstered gun. Pure reflex—it would be a lucky shot indeed that would let even the Eagle's .44 caliber rounds do anything against one of Skynet's flying horrors.

The angle of the lights shifted as the HK passed overhead, and for a few seconds it was the ceiling, not the wall, that was leaking intense beams of light.

Abruptly, the lights went out. Blair held her breath, peering into the darkness, trying to figure out if the HK's rumble was moving away or circling back for a second look.

And then, the light reappeared, coming through the series of cracks and gaps in the east wall. But this time it wasn't the eye-burning, full-power glare of the HK's searchlights. It was the softer glow of that same blaze as it was reflected from the ground and rubble and distant buildings.

Blair and Wince looked at each other, and Wince puffed out his cheeks in a pantomimed puffy sigh. Blair nodded, then lifted a finger to her lips to remind him not to make any actual noise until the HK had left the area. Wince nodded in turn, and together they waited as the growl turned again to a distant hum, then faded out completely.

"That's the sort of nonsense we've had to put up with all day," Wince murmured, making a face as he stretched muscles and joints that had been frozen too long in the same position. "God, but we're vulnerable here. The sooner Connor gets us out of L.A., the better."

Blair ran her fingers gently over the jagged rims of the bullet holes in her plane. He was right, of course. Skynet had way too good a bead on them here, and the noose was only going to get tighter each time they were forced to run from one rat hole to the next.

But where could they go? L.A. surrounded them for dozens of kilometers in every direction, a hell of a long walk when you had to carry everything on your own back. The team itself had no vehicles, and even if they could find a truck that still worked there was no gasoline to put into it.

But that was Connor's problem, not hers. He would figure something out.

He always did.

"At least until then we've got this nice building to keep the rain off," she said.

"Actually, a little rain would be nice," Wince said, almost wistfully. "Might clear the air a little." He shook his head. "Anyway, you'd probably better get back to the bunker. Get some food, and then get to bed."

"Don't worry about me—I had almost six hours last night," Blair said. "I was just thinking you probably need sleep more than I do." She cocked her head. "And food, too."

"I've got some lunch over there I never got around to eating," Wince said, nodding toward the back of the hangar. "We could split it if you'd like."

"No, that's okay," Blair said. Wince was famous for trying to foist food off on people he suspected were hungrier than he was. Blair had fallen for that trick five times in a row before she'd finally caught on. "I'm not hungry."

"That *was* your stomach sending out audible distress signals, wasn't it?" he reminded her dryly. "Come on, there's plenty for both of us."

"In which case we can deduce that you missed at least *two* meals, not just one," Blair countered. "So go eat, then get some sleep. That's an order."

Wince shook his head sadly.

"You young people," he said, mock-mournfully. "Always ordering around your elders."

"Call it enlightened self-interest," Blair told him. She had a few tricks of her own, after all. "I don't want someone tired and hungry working on my plane."

"Ah," Wince said. "Well, when you put it *that* way…"

"I do," Blair said. "Now go. I'll stay here until Yoshi gets back."

"Okay," Wince said. "Thanks, Blair." He touched her shoulder, almost shyly. "Don't worry, I'll find a way to get you those extra rounds."

"Thanks," Blair said. "You pull it off, and I guarantee they won't go to waste."

"I know they won't," Wince said. "See you later."

He headed off toward the back, where the hangar's compact housekeeping corner had been set up. Blair waited until he was digging ravenously into his neglected food pack, then took a few minutes to wander around the hangar, checking on the security of walls and boarded-up windows and doors. By the time she'd finished her tour, Wince was stretched out on one of the hangar's two sleeping mats, sound asleep.

Blair shook her head. A meal that disappeared that quickly had definitely not been enough to share. Just as well she hadn't let him talk her into it.

Her stomach rumbled again. Ignoring the emptiness down there, she picked up the other sleeping mat and moved it to a spot where she could keep a simultaneous eye on the door, both of the planes, and Wince.

Drawing her gun, she sat down on the mat, laying the weapon beside her. Nearly out of fuel, nearly out of spare parts, nearly out of ammo, nearly out of food. Life, she reflected, was definitely not looking good for the good guys. All the more reason to be glad this mess was in Connor's hands, not hers.

She just hoped he could still find a trick or two up his sleeve.

CHAPTER EIGHT

For Orozco, the day began as so many of them did: with a fight over food.

"But it's *mine*," Candace Tomlinson insisted, her plaintive five-year-old's whine especially jarring coming from a seventeen-year-old's mouth. "I found it. It's *mine*."

"But it was *my* stuff she found it in," Sumae Chin, the twenty-two-year-old complainant snapped back.

"And where exactly was this private cache of yours?" Grimaldi asked, his eyes steady on Sumae as he stared at the two girls across his scarred office desk. "In your room?"

"She can't just steal my stuff," Sumae insisted, glaring at Candace.

"Where was the cache?" Grimaldi asked again, his voice going a few degrees sterner. "Sumae?"

Sumae sent Orozco a hooded look.

"In the lower storage room," she said reluctantly. "Under some cracked drywall."

Orozco sighed to himself. All the residents had their own rooms, as well as lockers Grimaldi's men had lugged all the way from the remains of a high school, almost a mile away. In theory, everyone had all the room they needed for their personal items.

But too many of them had gone the squirrel route, hiding stuff around the building. Some did it because they didn't want anyone else even knowing how much they'd managed to accumulate, while others were out-and-out paranoid about the Board swooping down someday and confiscating everybody's private treasures.

The problem, of course, was that one battered can of processed lunchmeat looked pretty much like any other. Once it was outside anyone's official storage, it was well-nigh impossible to establish ownership. Especially since—even after all this time—it *was* still possible to occasionally find food items everyone else had missed buried in the building's rubble.

Which left Grimaldi with really only one possible ruling.

"I'm sorry, Sumae," the chief said, his voice regretful but firm. "If you choose to hide items outside your designated areas—if the pickles Candace found were, in fact, yours to begin with—"

"But they *were*," Sumae protested. "I told you where I'd—"

Grimaldi stopped her with an upraised hand.

"Even if they *were* yours to begin with, you forfeited all claims when you left the jar unattended outside your area. You know that. I'm sorry, but Candace owns them now."

Sumae flashed the younger girl a look of pure hatred.

"Just wait," she said, her voice low and menacing. "Someday you'll drop something—"

"Sumae," Grimaldi warned.

"—and I'll be right there to pick it up," Sumae finished.

"And if and when that happens, I suspect I'll be seeing the two of you again," Grimaldi said wearily. "You may return to your rooms or your work now. And you,

Sumae, had best collect anything else you might have hidden around the building."

Sumae held her glare on Candace for another heartbeat, then tried to transfer it to Grimaldi. But Grimaldi wasn't sixteen, and he'd no doubt been glared at by experts. Sumae's expression faltered as her glower bounced harmlessly off the stone that his face had become.

"Yes, sir," she muttered, and slunk away out of the room. Candace triumphantly snatched up the dusty jar of pickles and followed.

"And so begins another glorious day in Moldavia Los Angeles," Grimaldi said with a sigh.

"So it does," Orozco agreed. He and Grimaldi had their differences, God knew, but Orozco had always respected Grimaldi's insistence on handling these disputes personally, instead of hiding behind his desk and title and foisting the unpleasant duty off onto someone else. "Let's hope things go uphill from here."

"I don't think they will," Grimaldi said. "I talked to Evans and Kemper last night. They're pretty sure they've seen your empty-revolver gang before."

"Over on the far southern edge of the neighborhood," Orozco said, nodding. "Yes, I got the same thing from Hamm."

"Which means those kids were not, in fact, the new gang Nguyen and his buddies spotted on their way in yesterday afternoon," Grimaldi said. "Which means that group is still out there, and we're eventually going to run into each other."

"I've already doubled the sentry shifts and put two of the fire teams on quick-response," Orozco told him. "Unless you want to go out hunting, there's not much more we can do."

"We definitely don't want to go looking for them," Grimaldi said firmly. "The lower the profile we can keep, the better."

"Agreed," Orozco said. "Unfortunately, we're about five years past the low profile stage. Everyone for ten or twelve blocks around at least knows we're here somewhere, even if they don't know exactly which building we're in. We have to assume our newcomers will try to pick up as much intel as they can on the territory they're trying to move into."

"Fortunately, everyone who knows we're here also knows that everyone who's tried taking us on has lost," Grimaldi said. "Maybe they'll be smart enough to learn from the mistakes of others."

"We can hope," Orozco agreed. "But in case they don't—"

He broke off as the door was suddenly thrown open, and Mick the Binocular-Breaker ran into the room.

"Sentry signal," he said, panting. "Four and one."

"Damn," Orozco snarled as he rose quickly from his chair. Four and one was a positive threat coming from the north. Ten to one it was Nguyen's gang. "Chief—"

"I got it," Grimaldi interrupted. He was on his feet, checking the chambers of the shotgun he kept under his desk. "Get to the entrance—I'll roust the fire teams."

Ninety seconds later Orozco was back at the archway. Kyle and Star were already there, Kyle with Orozco's M16 gripped in his hands.

"They're coming," he reported tightly.

"I know," Orozco said, stepping to the arms locker and pulling out their one true sniper rifle, a Remington 700 with a Leupold VX-1 scope "Are they visible?"

Kyle stepped beneath the archway, leaning cautiously

out from behind the building's broken façade.

"Not yet," he said. "They may be on the other side of that broken truck three blocks up."

"Take this," Orozco said, taking the M16 from Kyle and handing him the Remington in exchange. "Go to the sniper nest."

Kyle's forehead creased uncertainly as he fingered the Remington.

"Evan's a better shot than I am," he said.

"Evan's not here," Orozco said. "You are. Get going."

With a grimace, Kyle nodded and headed across the street, Star right on his heels.

Orozco waited until the two kids had disappeared into the sniper's nest. Then, checking the M16's clip and chamber, he settled in to wait for their visitors.

He had received one follow-up report from the sentry, and was waiting for a second, when they arrived.

In impressively sophisticated military fashion, too. The sentry had said there were ten of them, but only four came striding into Orozco's view along the street, spaced far enough apart that they couldn't be taken down in a quick four-shot. The other six weren't visible, but Orozco suspected they could see *him*, or at least they could see the building's archway. Backup forces, ready to provide covering fire or a second attack wave, whichever was needed.

Not that the first group wasn't a wave and a half all by itself. Orozco counted ten heavy weapons among the four men, plus holstered sidearms and whatever hidden grenades or knives they might be carrying.

They were well-armed, well-trained, and at least slightly better-fed than the average L.A. citizen. If they had been a new gang trying to move into the area,

Orozco would have been worried.

But they weren't a gang. The red sashes tied around their sleeves showed that. They were, in fact, Resistance.

Which made it even worse.

"Morning," Orozco called courteously, keeping the muzzle of his M16 moving gently back and forth between them. "Just passing through?"

"Mostly," one of them said. He was a big black man with a fringe of a beard and a totally bald head. Along with his guns he was also carrying a couple of ammo packs, but he didn't even seem to notice all the weight. His eyes flicked once to the M16, then came back to Orozco's face. "You must be the Orozco everyone talks about."

"*Sergeant* Orozco, actually," Orozco said. "Formerly of the U.S. Marine Corps."

The other gave a snort that seemed to double as a laugh.

"That supposed to impress me?"

"Just want to make it clear I know how to use this," Orozco said, hefting the M16 a bit. "You have a name?"

"Barnes," the man said. He nodded toward the red armband. "This is *my* unit."

"Yeah, I see it," Orozco said. "Is that supposed to impress *me*?"

"It should," Barnes growled. "We're the ones keeping Skynet off your back."

"Or you're the ones drawing Skynet's fire onto everyone else," Orozco countered. "That's the way a lot of people around here see it."

Barnes gave him a long, measuring look.

"You can't be that stupid," he said at last. "Not if you were really a soldier."

"Marine," Orozco corrected automatically.

"Whatever." Barnes nodded past Orozco's shoulder.

"Mind if we come in? We've got some snacks to share out with your people in there."

Orozco suppressed a grimace. He'd called it, all right, straight from the top, the minute he'd seen those red armbands. These guys were here to recruit.

Grimaldi, if he were here instead of up on the balcony, would absolutely forbid them to pass the archway. He saw the people of Moldering Lost Ashes the same way he'd seen his inventory list back in the day, and he took it badly—and personally—when any of them chose to leave. The best thing Orozco could do right now would be to send Barnes and his team away.

And then, Orozco's eyes fell on all the weaponry the men were carrying.

A hard knot settled into his stomach. Recruiters didn't lug that much stuff around. Not if all they were doing was looking for fresh faces and able bodies.

Something was about to go down. Something bad.

And if Barnes's recruitment pitch meant even a couple of the people here got out before it was too late...

"If you're here to sign folks up, you're going to be disappointed," he warned. Some people, he knew, worked better and harder if you told them something couldn't be done. Barnes looked like that type. "But if you want to try, it's your time to waste."

"Thanks," Barnes said. He lifted his left hand above his head—

"But you'll have to leave your weapons here at the archway," Orozco added. Grimaldi, he knew, would insist on that.

Barnes froze, his arm still lifted.

"You thinking about trading up?" he asked, looking pointedly at Orozco's M16.

"Not at all," Orozco assured him. "You're welcome to leave a guard with the gear. Two or three of your six backstops should be enough."

Barnes grinned suddenly, bright white teeth against his dark skin.

"I guess maybe you *were* a Marine," he said. He flashed a couple of hand signals, then lowered his arm again to his weapon, swiveling the muzzle to point it at the ground. "That's okay—the rest of the crowd can stay out here," he added. "Don't want to make your people nervous."

"I appreciate your concern," Orozco said dryly. "What do you want me to do?"

"Just call 'em in and line 'em up," Barnes said as he and the other three men walked in under the archway. "Tell 'em we're springing for breakfast."

Orozco nodded. "I'll pass the word."

This whole "Breakfast with the Resistance" thing had been one hundred percent Connor's brainstorm, and Barnes had disliked it right from the start.

He'd argued vigorously against it, in fact, the minute he'd been able to get Connor alone. The group barely had enough food for its own, and the idea of handing out freebies to a bunch of civilian parasites had struck him as complete and utter insanity.

But he had to admit that the scheme had gotten them into a lot more places over the past two days than they probably could have managed without it.

Not that they'd actually gotten any new recruits out of all that time and effort. Most of the people they'd talked to were small, close-knit family groups that you couldn't break up if you lobbed in a brick of C4.

But for once, Barnes didn't mind the lack of results. When you were in the process of infiltrating a Skynet staging area, every hour spent off the street and out of sight was a good hour. Even if all the civilians did was eat your food, listen to your sales pitch, and then throw you out.

This place was the last one on Connor's list, and it was looking to be more of the same. Barnes couldn't tell about Orozco—the man had a poker face like a T-600. But the boss man who'd showed up as soon as the team had cached their weapons had been as easy to read as a Terminator's footprint.

Grimaldi didn't like Barnes, he didn't like the Resistance, and he especially didn't like these intruders breathing his nice, clean non-violent head-in-the-sand civilian air. He'd been picking restlessly at the strap of his shotgun ever since slinging it, and Barnes could tell the man would like nothing better than to swing that gun back up to firing position and order Barnes and the others back onto the street.

But the man also knew better than to buck the crowd, and the swarm of children, teens, and adults that had come out of the woodwork at the mention of free food was definitely a crowd and a half.

"So what exactly are you offering my people?" Grimaldi asked as he stood beside Barnes, watching as the team passed out snack bars to the eager residents.

"Mostly, the chance to fight back," Barnes told him.

"And to die while they're doing it?" Grimaldi countered, raising his volume a little. A few nearby heads turned toward them in response. "Very heroic, I suppose, if you buy into all that glorious epic hero nonsense. But what I meant was what can you offer in the way of safety or community compared to what we have here already?"

Barnes snorted a laugh.

"Safety?" he bit out. "You think you're safe here? From T-600s and HKs? *Here?*"

"Gentlemen, please," a soft voice came from behind Barnes. "There's no need to frighten the children."

Barnes turned to see a slender, almost gaunt man standing a respectful two paces behind him. The man's skin was darker even than Barnes's, his face pock-marked with tiny scars, probably from some childhood disease. First or maybe second generation African, Barnes guessed.

"You have a problem with fear?" he challenged the newcomer.

"Not at all," the man said calmly. "Fear is an excellent motivator, though not as strong as duty, honor, or love." He inclined his head toward three young children digging eagerly and blissfully into their snack bars. "But hopelessness isn't." He held out his hand. "Reverend Jiri Sibanda."

"Barnes," Barnes said, taking the proffered hand carefully. He had already seen the telltale bulges of arthritis in Sibanda's knuckles. "You the chaplain?"

"The pastor," Sibanda corrected. "I was just thinking that there are several children and young adults who haven't been able to avail themselves of your generosity. If you're willing, I'd like to take you to them."

Barnes scowled. First Connor wanted him to waste food on civilians, and now Sibanda wanted him to waste it on the sick and dying.

"If they can't take the time to get here on their own—"

"Oh, no, it's not like that," Sibanda said. "I'm talking

about the sentries on duty on the upper levels." He looked past Barnes at Grimaldi. "With your permission, of course."

Barnes looked at Grimaldi as well. The man didn't look happy at the idea of a stranger touring his building, but he didn't seem ready to get in Barnes's way, either.

"Go ahead," he growled.

"Thank you." Sibanda took a step back and gestured toward a wide stone staircase. "This way, please."

The trip to the top of the building was more of an adventure than Barnes had expected. The stone staircase, which led up to a mezzanine balcony and a whole group of what had probably once been a selection of retail stores, was as sturdy as anything Barnes had run into over the years since Judgment Day. The next three floors were all right, too, though the stairways that led between them were now the more standard types tucked alongside the empty elevator shafts.

But starting with the fifth floor, things got trickier. Some of the stairs were missing, while others were solid only in certain places along their width. Between the sixth and seventh floors half the steps had vanished completely, forcing a quarter-building detour through a set of hallways even more treacherous than the stairs.

Fortunately, Sibanda knew all the danger spots and was agile enough to make the jumps and long steps necessary to avoid them. Still, Barnes could see why Orozco had delegated most of the high sentry duty to the more nimble kids and teens.

Finally, to his quiet relief, they emerged once again into the open air.

"Here we are," Sibanda said cheerfully. "This is our southeast sentry post."

Barnes looked at the two kids sitting by a partial wall at the side of the building. One of them, a boy, looked to be thirteen or fourteen, while the other was a six- or seven-year-old girl. Both of them were staring wide-eyed at the big newcomer.

"This is Zac Steiner and this is Olivia Womak," Sibanda said, gesturing to the kids. "Olivia's just learning how to be a sentry."

"You like it?" Barnes asked the girl.

Her lip twitched.

"Kinda cold up here."

"It's kind of cold everywhere," Barnes pointed out.

"And at least here you have this wonderful view," Sibanda said.

Barnes turned to look. The city stretched out in front of him, broken but still surviving, its streets and empty areas green with the vines and grasses and weeds that had slowly been coming back across the whole nuke-blasted region. To the far east and south, a haze had set in, softening the edges of the vista.

"It's okay," he said with a shrug.

"But you didn't come up here for the view," Sibanda continued. "Zac, Olivia, Mr. Barnes is with the Resistance, and he'd like a word with you."

Barnes turned back to the kids.

"That's right," he said. "In the Resistance our job is to fight against Skynet and the Terminators."

"Are you one of the people Kyle saw yesterday?" the boy asked.

"I don't know," Barnes said. "Who's Kyle?"

"One of the other sentries," Sibanda explained. "No, Zac, that was a different group. From what I understand, Mr. Barnes's group was coming in too far north to be visible from this particular station."

"Oh," the boy said. "What's Skynet?"

"It's a big computer that's taken over most of the world," Barnes told him. "You know those HKs—Hunter-Killers, those big metal flying things—and the Terminators, those metal robot sorts of things that walk around with big guns?"

"I've seen them," the boy said, shivering. "Not very close."

"You want to try very hard to keep it that way," Barnes told him grimly. "People who see Terminators up close usually die. That's what the machines do. That's all they do."

"That's…kind of scary," the boy said.

Barnes looked at Sibanda. But this time there were no speeches or warnings about fear or hopelessness coming from the man. Maybe the preacher really did understand the reality of the world these kids were living in.

"It's very scary," Barnes agreed, looking back at the young sentries. "That's why we fight."

"Mr. Barnes is offering you—and all the rest of us—the chance to join them and be part of that fight," Sibanda explained. "It's something you both need to think about, very hard."

The boy looked at Barnes, then back at Sibanda.

"Do we have to go right now?"

"Not right this second, no," Sibanda said. "But soon. We'll be visiting the other sentry posts, and then Mr. Barnes and his people will want to talk to the people downstairs, so you both have a little time to make up your minds." Looking at Barnes, he raised his eyebrows. "In the meantime, I believe Mr. Barnes has something for each of you."

"Oh—right," Barnes said, digging into one of his jacket pockets and pulling out two of the snack bars. "This is to thank you for listening to me."

"Though I'm sure that even in the Resistance they don't get these things all the time," Sibanda cautioned as the kids' faces lit up and they started eagerly unwrapping the bars.

"No, we don't," Barnes admitted, remembering Connor's number one rule of not sugar-glazing what the prospective recruit was getting into. "Mostly, what we get is that when the Terminators start shooting, we get to shoot back."

"And with that, we'll leave you to your duty," Sibanda said, touching each of the children lightly on the shoulder before heading back into the building.

They were a quarter of the way around the floor, heading for the southwest sentry post, before Sibanda spoke again.

"You'll take care of him, won't you?" he asked Barnes quietly.

"Who?" Barnes asked.

"Zac," Sibanda said. "He's going with you."

Barnes frowned. Last he'd heard, the kid was still undecided.

"When did he say that?"

"He didn't have to," Sibanda said, a deep sadness in his voice. "I know these people, Mr. Barnes. Olivia is interested, but she's not yet ready to leave her family and friends. But Zac is older, and he's been listening to Sergeant Orozco. He understands the danger lurking out there."

Barnes grunted. "He's ahead of Grimaldi on that one, anyway."

"The chief's heart's in the right place," Sibanda murmured. "You must give him that. He also understands organization and resource management. Under other conditions, he would be the ideal man to run a place like Moldering Lost Ashes."

"You mean conditions like no Skynet?"

Sibanda sighed. "He's not blind, you know. We see your planes battling the Hunter-Killers, and we get word from other parts of the city. He knows what Skynet is doing. But he truly believes that you Resistance people are baiting it, that it's just reacting to your attacks. He believes that if we stay quiet and leave Skynet alone, it will leave us alone, too."

Barnes barked a laugh.

"Yeah. Right."

"I know," Sibanda said with another sigh. "But what else can we do? We can't fight, not all of us—we have women and children here. We can't run, either—where could we go where Skynet couldn't find us?"

"There isn't any place," Barnes agreed grimly. "But don't sell your women short. We've got women in our group, too. Most of them are damn near as good at fighting as the men."

"Perhaps," Sibanda said. "But there are still the children. I doubt you have any of *them* in your group."

Barnes grimaced. "We've got a few. Civilians. Mostly because they didn't have anywhere else to go."

"Then you see our problem," Sibanda said. "Even if Chief Grimaldi was willing, there's little he *can* do."

The southwest post had a lone sentry, a teenaged boy who clearly wasn't interested in anything but Barnes's snack bar bribe. The lookouts in the northwest and northeast posts were pretty much the same, though the girl in the northwest post was at least willing to listen to Barnes as she ate.

"Is that it?" Barnes asked as they headed back down toward the lobby.

"There's a sniper's nest in the building across the street," Sibanda said, "and I daresay Sergeant Orozco probably has a few other places around the neighborhood where people can watch or shoot from. But I would guess he's already called all of them in to hear your recruitment talk."

Barnes nodded. "I can check with him on that before we go."

By the time they returned to the mezzanine balcony, the snack bars had been distributed and Tunney had formed the residents into the circle he liked to use on these occasions. In this case, there were enough folks to form a circle three people deep, centered around the broken fountain in the middle of the lobby.

Tunney himself was standing on the inner part of the circle facing the balcony. A dozen steps behind him, a few meters inside the distinctive entrance archway, the other two men of their foursome were standing in a loose guard circle around their cached weapons, their arms folded or clasped parade-rest style behind their backs, eyeing the two men who'd taken up guard duty at the entry. From the voices drifting up to the balcony, Barnes gathered that Tunney had finished running through his standard sales pitch and was in the process of answering questions.

There were a *lot* of questions, too, Barnes noted as he and Sibanda walked down the stone staircase and settled in unobtrusively at the rear of the circle. Maybe the preacher was right, that the people here didn't have anywhere else to go. But that didn't mean they'd all bought into Grimaldi's ostrich plan, either.

And it was pretty clear that Grimaldi didn't like that. He was standing a quarter of the way around the circle to Tunney's right, flanked by three other men. All four of them had rifles or shotguns slung over their shoulders, and all four of them were glowering.

But for the moment, at least, they seemed willing to let Tunney talk.

Finally, the people ran out of questions. Tunney let the silence hang in the air for a few seconds, just to make sure, then cleared his throat.

"If there are no more questions," he said, "it's time for you to make your decisions. What we offer isn't much, but it's better than sitting here waiting for the inevitable. Are there any who would like to come with us?"

For another handful of seconds no one moved. Then, from the front row directly across from him, a young man took a step forward.

"I will."

A quiet stir rippled through the crowd.

"Your name?" Tunney asked, gesturing him forward.

"Callahan, sir," the young man said, circling the fountain and going up to Tunney. "I'm not very good at fighting. But I can learn."

"Indeed you will," Tunney promised, motioning the man over to stand beside him. "Anyone else?"

A young couple stepped out from the middle row, the woman clutching at the man's arm like she was afraid to let it go.

"Leon and Carol Iliaki," the man said. "I'm not much of a fighter, either, but I can also learn. And Carol has some skills you might find useful."

Barnes looked at Grimaldi. The boss man hadn't looked happy when Callahan had deserted him, but that was nothing compared to the stiffness of his expression now as he watched the Iliakis cross the circle.

"She's a master seamstress," Sibanda told Barnes quietly. "Amazing woman. She can take nearly random bits of cloth or leather and fashion them into clothing that's both warm and durable."

Barnes nodded. No wonder Grimaldi didn't want to lose her.

"Anyone else?" Tunney called.

"Can I come, too?" a familiar voice called from behind Barnes, and he turned to see the kid Zac Steiner hurrying down the stone staircase.

Apparently, that was the final straw.

"Hold it, Steiner," Grimaldi called, stepping into the circle. "What are you doing down here?"

The boy faltered to a confused-looking halt.

"Mr. Barnes said I could—"

"You're on sentry duty, boy," Grimaldi cut him off. "You think these people want someone who deserts his post?"

Zac sent Barnes a look that was full of sudden guilt and fear.

"But I sent Amy Phao up—"

"*You* sent Phao up?" Grimaldi echoed. "Since when are *you* authorized to make changes in the duty roster?"

"It's all right," another voice put in, and Barnes turned in mild surprise to see Orozco step into the circle across from Grimaldi. Either the Marine had just arrived, or else he'd managed to blend into the crowd so well that Barnes hadn't spotted him a minute ago from up on the balcony. "The sentries have permission to leave their posts under extraordinary circumstances."

"This is *not* an extraordinary circumstance," Grimaldi countered. He shot a glare at Tunney. "This is a circus."

Barnes's mind flashed back to the gangs he'd locked horns with so many times when he was growing up. They'd all had the same kind of single-man rule he could see happening here...and with most of them, this kind of ridicule had been the next-to-the-last resort when they didn't have any other way to counter someone's argument or demand.

If ridicule didn't work, it was always followed by violence.

Carefully, Barnes shifted his weight, picking the path he would take through the people in front of him on his way to telling Grimaldi up close and personal exactly what he thought of him—

A hand touched his arm.

"No," Sibanda murmured. "Let him talk."

"I'd hardly call matters of life and death a circus," Tunney said mildly.

"I wasn't referring to matters of life and death," Grimaldi said. "I was referring to *you*. You and your little band of amateurs."

"Amateurs?" Tunney asked, his voice still calm.

"Listen to me," Grimaldi said, raising his voice as he looked around the circle. "We've been here, some of us, for over ten years now. We've kept ourselves and each other alive, and fed, and clothed." He leveled a finger at Tunney. "And yet now these men come along promising the moon; and you're actually *listening* to them? These men who were so eager to talk you out of here that they were foolish enough to give up their guns?"

And without warning, the three men alongside

Grimaldi swung their weapons up, leveling the barrels at Tunney.

"*This* is the tactical brilliance these men have?" Grimaldi went on sarcastically. "And yet they promise to keep you alive while they pick and poke and prod at Skynet and the Terminators?" He snorted. "I don't think so."

Sibanda's hand was still on Barnes's arm. Gently but firmly, Barnes pushed the hand away.

"Please," Sibanda pleaded. "They have guns. You don't."

"The man needs a lesson," Barnes told him grimly. "It's time he got one."

CHAPTER NINE

Orozco felt his heart seize up inside his chest. Suddenly, in a single instant, the whole thing had gone straight to hell.

"Put those down," he said sharply, walking swiftly around the fountain toward Grimaldi. "Have you lost your *minds*?"

"Stay out of it, Sergeant," Grimaldi ordered, raising his own shotgun now to point not quite at Orozco's feet. "Our people need to see the hollow shell these men really are."

Orozco looked through the stunned crowd toward the archway where Tunney's other two men were guarding the group's weapons. But they, too, were standing motionless, with Barney and Copeland now holding their rifles on them.

"This isn't an object lesson," Orozco ground out, shifting his glare back to Grimaldi, his body tingling with the adrenaline of impending combat. The man had drawn down on a *Resistance group*, for God's sake. "This is mass suicide."

"Is it?" Grimaldi countered. "Do you see anything to indicate that they aren't helpless?"

"Chief, you're playing with fire," Orozco warned.

"Do you see *anything* to indicate that they aren't help-less?" Grimaldi repeated.

Orozco clenched his hands into fists.

"Not at the moment," he had to admit. "But—"

"But nothing," Grimaldi said firmly. "As I said: these men—this John Connor they go on and on about—have the tactical skill of hamsters. They'll be lucky to keep *themselves* alive, let alone anyone they con into going with them."

And then, at Orozco's left, the crowd abruptly parted and Barnes stepped into the circle.

"Maybe you need to run the odds again," he said, his voice dark and menacing.

"No!" Orozco snapped as Grimaldi's shotgun shifted to point at Barnes. "Grimaldi—"

"Relax, Sergeant," he said, his voice dripping with contempt. "I'm not going to kill him. Not unless he insists on it."

"You know, Grimaldi, you have a really big mouth," Barnes said. He looked around the circle, his dark eyes touching each of the residents in turn as if he was mem-orizing their faces for future reference. "Is this the kind of leader you people want?" he went on. "A leader who uses guns to keep you here, instead of letting you make your own decisions?"

"I'm not keeping anyone here," Grimaldi insisted.

"You're the ones holding the guns," Barnes countered. "You're like a gang leader, Grimaldi. I hate gang leaders."

"Hate me all you want," Grimaldi said. "But the fact of the matter is that you and your group haven't sur-vived by any kind of skill. If you've really been togeth-er as long as you claim, it can only be because of sheer dumb luck. If my people want to go with you, that's their business. But they have a right to know exactly what they're getting themselves into."

"Fair enough," Barnes said. "But like I said, maybe you ought to recalculate. For starters—" He reached down to the hem of his jacket.

And suddenly there was a shining Bowie knife gripped in his hand.

"—maybe we didn't leave *all* our weapons in that pile over there."

"Stop it, both of you," Orozco snapped. He absolutely, positively had to stop this before it got any more out of hand than it already was.

But down deep, he knew it was too late. Grimaldi would never back down, not when he had a gun against the other man's knife. Pride alone would keep him from doing that.

And Barnes wasn't going anywhere, either. His men were in harm's way, and he would free them or die in the attempt. He had the glint of death in his eye, a look Orozco had seen all too many times before in the midst of combat.

Maybe Grimaldi recognized that look, too. He muttered something to the men beside him, and suddenly two of the three guns that had been pointed at Tunney were pointed at Barnes instead.

"I said stop it," Orozco tried again. "Barnes—put the knife away. Skynet's the enemy, remember?"

"Your chief needs a lesson, Orozco," Barnes said loudly, his voice echoing across the lobby as if he was trying to intimidate Grimaldi by sheer lungpower.

Maybe it was working. Barnes still hadn't moved from the spot where he'd pulled the knife, but Orozco could see that Grimaldi was starting to have some belated second thoughts. With Barnes's challenge—even one so patently futile—the chief had suddenly gone from a position of absolute authority and strength to one of dangerous uncertainty.

Orozco had never seen Grimaldi backed into a corner this tight before. But he'd seen the man in lesser corners, and he knew that the road ahead could only lead to disaster. At Barnes's first threatening move, or whatever Grimaldi considered a threatening move, the chief would order his men to open fire. Barnes would die, right there in front of everyone. After that, Tunney and the others would also have to die. Grimaldi could hardly leave witnesses to take back the news to the rest of their team.

And Moldering Lost Ashes would have the blood of four murders on its hands, and would have lost its soul.

There was only one chance, one move that might at least buy Orozco enough time to make them all see reason. Stepping directly in front of Barnes, he turned to face Grimaldi. "No," he said firmly.

"Out of the way," Grimaldi ordered.

"No," Orozco said again. He could feel Barnes's breath on the nape of his neck, and the skin of his back prickled with the awareness of the knife poised only inches away from it.

If Barnes had already crossed the line from calculating strategist to mindless berserker, Orozco had only seconds before he died with that blade buried in his back. If Barnes *hadn't* crossed that line, giving him a human shield this way could still get Orozco shot, and by the very people he had been protecting for the past two years.

Not that most of those people were probably thinking

very highly of him right now. He could feel the eyes of the whole crowd on him, but didn't dare look away from Grimaldi long enough to see if they were looking on him as a peacemaker or as a traitor. Very likely the latter, he suspected. It had been Orozco, after all, who had let these strangers in and had thus sparked this confrontation in the first place.

What was worse was the fact that Grimaldi had a point. From a strictly tactical point of view, for Barnes and the others to have voluntarily disarmed themselves *was* foolish, even if that had been the price of entry.

Orozco had considered their gesture to have been one of trust and goodwill. Perhaps he'd been wrong. Perhaps trust was a luxury people could no longer afford.

Certainly their trust in Orozco's implied promise of safety had betrayed them. Barnes probably considered Orozco a traitor, too.

And then, from somewhere behind him, cutting through the thick silence like a knife through freshly churned butter, Orozco heard the distinctive *chink-chink* of a pump shotgun action. Grimaldi's eyes flicked upward.

Abruptly, the man froze.

Carefully, Orozco turned his head. Standing in a nicely spaced line on the mezzanine balcony were six men and women. All of them had heavy rifles or shotguns pointed downward at Grimaldi and his men.

All of them except one of the women in the middle. Her hands hung empty at her sides as she gazed coolly down on the scene below her.

And the look in those eyes...

Behind Orozco, Tunney cleared his throat. "Chief Grimaldi," he murmured, "meet Kate Connor."

"There are two ways this can go, Chief Grimaldi," Kate Connor called, her voice glacially calm. "Your choice."

Orozco looked back at Grimaldi. The other's breath was starting to come in quick, shallow gusts, his gun still pointed at Orozco and Barnes.

His back to the corner...

"Be smart," Orozco said quietly. "Put the guns down."

Grimaldi's gun didn't waver. But if the chief was frozen in pride and fear and indecision, his cohorts weren't. All three of them quickly squatted down and set their weapons on the floor. Steeling himself, Orozco stepped forward into the bore of Grimaldi's shotgun and gently but firmly took the weapon away from him. Turning around, lowering the muzzle to the ground, he offered it to Barnes.

To his surprise, Barnes waved it away.

"Keep it," he said calmly. He flicked his hand again, and the knife vanished once more beneath his jacket.

So, too, did his death's-head scowl.

"A lesson, you said," Orozco said as he suddenly understood. "Only you weren't the lesson. You were the distraction."

"We all were," Tunney put in as he came over and retrieved the weapons Grimaldi's men had set on the floor. "First lesson of warfare: if you can get your opponent looking in the wrong direction, you're halfway there."

"And if you can talk your opponent into treason, that gets you the rest of the way?" Grimaldi bit out. He still looked a little shaken, but he was rapidly getting back on stride. "So, Sergeant. What did they pay you?"

Orozco stared at the man in disbelief.

"What are you talking about?"

"Don't play innocent with *me*," Grimaldi said, raising

his voice so that the entire confused crowd could hear. "You're the one who handles the building's security. Either you deliberately let them in, or else you screwed up in your duties. Which is it?"

Orozco was still trying to unfreeze his tongue when the crowd parted like the Red Sea and Kate Connor walked into the circle.

"You need to enlarge your thinking, Chief Grimaldi," she said, her voice mildly reproving. "You also need to forget about finding someone to dump the blame on. Not everything is someone else's fault."

"Then how *did* you get in?" Grimaldi demanded.

Kate smiled. "So that you can plug up the hole?" She shrugged. "Fair enough. There's an old underground drainage tunnel that runs past the northern edge of your building. My husband John found it. It's outside where your outer wall used to be, but the debris blow-out covered one of the manhole covers so it's not visible from the street or any of your windows. We got it unblocked and then came in through one of the broken windows that you didn't bother to seal up, since the whole side was already blocked by a heavy wall of junk."

Grimaldi's lips compressed.

"Very clever," he growled. "So now what? You kill me and take over?"

Kate sighed.

"This isn't about you, Grimaldi," she said. "We came in here for one reason: to recruit willing people into the war against Skynet. Some of your neighbors suggested that you might take exception to our efforts, so we decided extra caution might be in order. It appears we were right."

"Yes, you're very clever," Grimaldi said. "So again: now what?"

"We take those who've decided to go with us and we leave." Kate looked around the group. "Anyone else?" she called.

The lobby remained silent.

"Looks like you've already got all the rash fools we had," Grimaldi said bitterly. "So get out." He raised his voice. "And all the rest of you can get back to your jobs. The circus is over."

A few of the residents glanced uncertainly at each other.

"You heard me," Grimaldi snapped. "Back to your jobs. We work together, or we die together."

Still silently, the crowd began to disperse. A minute later only Orozco, Grimaldi and his men, and the Resistance team and their four new recruits remained in the lobby.

Grimaldi's eyes had never left Kate Connor since the residents began their exit, Orozco noted, and he could tell there was considerably more that the chief wanted to say. But as the last of his people disappeared down the hallways and up the staircase, he merely gave Kate a curt nod and strode off across the lobby toward his office. His men followed, trailing after him like sullen sheep.

"Keep an eye on the doors and staircases," Barnes ordered as Tunney set aside the confiscated weapons and he and the others started collecting their own from the cache by the door.

"What about you, Sergeant?" Kate added.

Orozco frowned at her.

"What about me?"

"Are you coming with us?"

Orozco felt his lip twist.

"Is this standard Resistance procedure, Ms. Connor?" he asked. "You come into an area a few days ahead of the Terminators, and glean out all the best and the brightest?"

The lines in Kate's face seemed to deepen.

"Would you rather we stayed away and let *everyone* die?" she countered.

"That depends," Orozco said.

"On...?"

"On whether or not Chief Grimaldi's right," Orozco said bluntly. "On whether or not you're the flame that draws the damn Terminator moths in the first place."

Kate shook her head.

"You know better than that," she said. "Skynet's purpose is to destroy humanity. *All* of humanity. Yes, it keeps track of our activities, but hardly to the point of sending Terminators trailing along behind us to punish the locals for talking with us."

Orozco felt his stomach tighten.

"I suppose not," he conceded.

"I understand how you feel, though," Kate added. "It would be easier to be able to blame someone for what was happening. If you could see some kind of direct cause-and-effect at work. But that's not how things are. Skynet's not so much an opponent as it is a force of nature."

"Like a hurricane," Orozco said. "You don't try to reason with a hurricane. You try to figure out where it's going, and get out of its way."

"Exactly," Kate said, a sudden fierce edge to her voice. "Except that unlike a hurricane, Skynet *can* be defeated. And it will be, if enough people are willing to take a stand against it."

"Which gets back to her question," Barnes said. "You coming with us?"

For a long moment Orozco was tempted. Very tempted.

Grimaldi and his friends didn't really appreciate all the work he had put into making the Ashes as safe as it was.

Nor did they have any understanding of the true situation they were in. In fact, they seemed to almost pride themselves on their ignorance of the danger Skynet posed. There would definitely be poetic justice in letting them find out the hard way.

But Grimaldi didn't speak for everyone in the Ashes. And the rest of the people didn't deserve to die just because the chief had a double helping of boneheadedness.

"You know I can't do that," he said.

"I suppose not," Kate agreed, her voice heavy with regret. "But we needed to ask."

She nodded at him, then gestured the others toward the archway.

"How soon?" Orozco asked.

Kate paused mid-turn. "We think you've got until tomorrow night," she said.

Less than two days. "Any suggestions?" Orozco asked, forcing his voice to stay calm.

"Explosives are always a good place to start," Tunney said. "T-600s have electromagnetic cores built into strategic joints so that they can reassemble themselves if you blow off their arms or legs. Blow them far enough off, though, and that trick won't work anymore."

"Do you have access to explosives?" Kate asked. "We might be able to spare you some."

"I have some," Orozco assured her. "And the makings for quite a few more."

"Good," Tunney said, glancing around the lobby. "You could also consider rigging a few booby-traps. There's a lot of heavy stonework in here, especially this archway and the stone facing above it. Collapse a wall on a Terminator, and even if you don't destroy it you'll put it out of action for awhile."

"Of course, blowing up walls could also bring the whole building down on top of us," Orozco pointed out.

"There is that," Tunney conceded. "I notice you also have a fair number of guns, which is good. How many of them are large caliber—9mm, .45, or bigger?"

"A fair number," Orozco said. "Unfortunately, a lot of our armament is smaller than that."

"Those won't do much against Terminators," Kate said grimly.

"But if you can get in enough head shots with the larger rounds, the T-600s will usually go down," Tunney said. "You can also go for the joints—if you can cripple them, they aren't as much trouble." He pursed his lips. "Of course, if Skynet throws in more than a couple of HKs, life will get trickier."

"Your other choice is to run," Kate said. "Collect everyone you can, collect everything you can, and get out."

"And go where?" Orozco countered. "Is there any place that's safe from Skynet?"

Kate's lip twitched.

"No," she admitted.

"Then there's not much point in running, is there?" Orozco said.

Barnes snorted contemptuously.

"Or you could just roll over and die," he growled. "Guess that's up to you."

"I wish it *was* up to me," Orozco said ruefully. "Unfortunately, it isn't."

From behind him came the sound of an opening door, and he turned to see Grimaldi's men filing out of the chief's office. Apparently the skull session—or chewing out—was over. A couple of the men glowered at Orozco and Kate as they all headed together across the lobby and into the hallway that ran along the north side of the building.

"Excuse me a moment," Orozco said, and he headed after them.

Halfway across the lobby, as he circled the old fountain, he glanced back over his shoulder to discover that Kate and her people had quietly disappeared.

He caught up with the nearest of the men, Wadleigh, halfway down the hallway.

"What are you doing?" Orozco asked him.

"What do you think?" Wadleigh retorted. "We're going to find Connor's back door and plug it."

"Go ahead and find it," Orozco said. "But don't plug it. Not yet."

Wadleigh snorted. "Sorry, Orozco, but the chief gave orders." He turned away.

Orozco caught his arm and turned him back around.

"Find the door," he repeated, enunciating each word carefully and distinctly, "but don't plug it. Put a bar across it if you want, or pile a few bricks on it that can be quickly removed. But *don't plug it.*"

Wadleigh started to speak, took another look at Orozco's face, and nodded silently. Orozco held his arm another moment, then released it. Wadleigh turned and continued down the hallway, hurrying but trying not to look like it.

Orozco watched for another moment, then returned to the lobby.

Four people. Only four people had been willing to leave the Ashes' false sense of security in order to take on the more immediate risks of standing up against humanity's common enemy. Only four people. And *one* of them had been just a teenager—

Orozco felt his breath catch in his throat.

Damn.

Damn.

CHAPTER TEN

His measured tread switched to a reckless sprint as he tore across the lobby toward the entrance. He reached the archway, automatically getting a grip on his holstered Beretta as he dashed outside.

But Connor and his people were already gone.

Orozco took a couple of deep breaths, swearing viciously and uselessly to himself as he looked up and down the street. His plan had been to wait until Tunney's recruitment talk was over, then quietly call them in from the sniper's nest so they could meet the Resistance team.

But in all the excitement and tension it had completely slipped his mind. Now, it was too late. Swearing one last time under his breath, he gave the hand signal to call Kyle and Star back in.

A minute later the two kids emerged through the battered doorway, Kyle with the Remington cradled ready in his arms, a taut look on his face.

"Where did all those other people come from?" he called as they started across the street. "They went south—I couldn't see how far. Zac and Callahan and the Iliakis were with them. They weren't being—I mean—?"

"No, they weren't being kidnapped," Orozco assured

the teen as he took back the Remington. "They left entirely of their own free will."

"Should I have tried to stop them?" Kyle persisted, clearly still concerned that he'd failed in his assigned duty. Maybe he was assuming Orozco's frustration was directed at him. "Maybe pinned them down until you could get there? I didn't hear any shots, but there were all those others with them—"

"Kyle, you did fine," Orozco said firmly, resting a reassuring hand on the boy's shoulder. "Just relax, okay? I'm just sorry you didn't get a chance to meet them."

"Okay," Kyle said, still sounding a little uncertain, as Orozco led the way back under the archway into their building. "Who were they, anyway?"

"Resistance recruiters," Orozco told him. "They—"

"They were *Resistance*?" Kyle interrupted sharply, an unreadable expression on his face.

"That's what they said," Orozco answered, taken aback by the unexpected intensity of the boy's reaction. "Why? Did you recognize any of them?"

Kyle looked away.

"No," he said, his voice back under control again. "I just…wondered."

"Ah," Orozco said, letting the subject drop and looking around the lobby. Barney and Copeland, who had ostensibly been guarding the entrance, and who had really been put there to draw down on Barnes's men, had of course disappeared with the rest of Grimaldi's crowd.

"I guess you and I are on guard duty," he commented to Kyle. "Unless you need to get some sleep."

"I'm okay," Kyle said, looking at Star. "So's Star." He peered closely at Orozco. "*You're* the one who needs sleep."

"I'll be fine until Johnson and Baker show up for their shift." Orozco handed the Remington back to Kyle. "Go put this away, if you would, and get me the M16."

Kyle nodded and headed for the arms locker, Star trailing as always behind him.

Orozco watched them go, a dark heaviness settling in around his heart. Of all the people in their sorry little community, Kyle and Star were the ones who should have gone with Barnes's group. They were the ones who could have been of the most value to the Resistance's war against Skynet.

But Barnes was gone, and Orozco didn't have the faintest idea where to go looking for him. Even if he had, he didn't think he would appreciate having someone trying to chase him down, what with Skynet and the whole world right there watching.

Still, the universe was a crazy place. Maybe Kyle and Star would have another chance someday.

Kyle was swapping out the Remington for the M16 when Orozco spotted movement across the lobby. It was Nguyen, heading toward him, his expression ominously rigid.

Orozco winced. Nguyen and his fellow traders had been conspicuous by their absence during Tunney's big sales pitch and Grimaldi's botched attempt to show him up, but Orozco had no doubt they'd been listening closely to the proceedings. From the look on his face, it was a safe bet that the man had some piquant things to say about the whole fiasco.

Things Kyle and Star probably didn't need to hear.

"Thanks," Orozco said as Kyle handed him the M16. "You and Star never got breakfast this morning, did you?"

"Not really," Kyle said.

"Neither did I," Orozco said. "Why don't you go see what Bessie's got going in the kitchen. And bring me some back, too."

Kyle glanced over his shoulder at Nguyen.

"Okay," the teen said. Nodding to Star, he headed across the lobby toward the kitchen.

Nguyen watched them go, and it seemed to Orozco that he perhaps slowed down his pace a bit. Maybe he didn't want the kids hearing this, either.

"Morning," Orozco said, nodding politely at Nguyen as he came into conversational range.

"And to you," Nguyen replied. "Interesting morning it's been, too. May I ask what in the name of hell and all its little demons you and Chief Grimaldi thought you were *doing*?"

"Actually, that was all Chief Grimaldi's idea," Orozco said, eyeing Nguyen closely as an odd thought suddenly struck him. If Kyle and Star couldn't go with Barnes and Kate Connor...

"In that case, it would appear that Chief Grimaldi has lost his mind," Nguyen said. "You'll excuse us if we don't bother to make our formal farewells before we go." He lifted a hand, and across the lobby the rest of the traders appeared, Nguyen's second-in-command Vuong in the lead, with the group's harnessed burros trailing closely behind them.

"I understand completely," Orozco said. "But before you go, I have one last deal to offer."

"We don't deal with madmen, Orozco," Nguyen said bluntly. "Anyone who pulls weapons on a Resistance group—"

"You won't be dealing with madmen," Orozco cut

him off. "This is my deal, not Grimaldi's. All I want is for you to take a couple of our kids back to the farm with you."

Nguyen shook his head.

"Impossible. We can barely grow enough for ourselves and for necessary trade."

"They could work," Orozco offered. "Both of them."

"We already have as many people as we have work for them to do," Nguyen said. "There's no more farmable land in our area."

"But there will be someday," Orozco persisted. "The soil is detoxifying as the short-life radioactives disintegrate. It's happening here—it must be happening out there, too."

"The radioactivity may be fading, but the soil is still contaminated with dangerous levels of heavy metals," Nguyen said. "We have some techniques for clearing them out, but they're slow. We're still years away from more arable soil."

"What if I paid their room and board until you had work for them to do?"

Nguyen snorted. "With what?"

Orozco braced himself. "Gasoline."

Nguyen seemed to draw back, his expression changing subtly.

"I thought Chief Grimaldi made all gasoline deals personally."

"I'm making this one," Orozco said. "You interested? Yes or no?"

Nguyen glanced around the lobby.

"How much are we talking about?"

"All of it," Orozco said, feeling his pulse thudding in his neck, the words *treason* and *betrayal* whispering in his ears. "I'll take you to our cache and show you the secret of how to get in without killing yourselves. In return, you'll take Kyle and Star out of the city and keep them safe."

"No one can promise safety," Nguyen said. "Not these days."

"Then you promise to keep them as safe as you can," Orozco said. "And you pledge Randall to do the same."

Nguyen hissed thoughtfully between his teeth.

"You know I can't make a pledge for another," he reminded Orozco. "But for gasoline, I think he'll be willing." He paused. "*And* for Mad Sergeant Orozco. Very well, it's a deal. How soon can our new charges be ready?"

"They can be ready very quickly," Orozco said. "Unfortunately, I still have some preparations to make for them, and I'll need a couple of hours for that."

"Which I presume you can't do while you're on guard duty."

"Correct," Orozco said. "Still, everything should be ready by mid-afternoon."

Nguyen pursed his lips, studying Orozco's face. Doubtless wondering whether the promise of free gasoline was worth the price of staying within Grimaldi's reach for all those extra hours.

"I doubt the early afternoon will be nearly as interesting as the morning has been," he said at last. "Very well, we'll stay."

"Thank you," Orozco said. "I'll get it done as quickly as I can."

"Yes," Nguyen said. "In the meantime, I trust you won't mind if we do a little trading elsewhere in the neighborhood?"

Mentally, Orozco threw the man a salute. How to stay out of Grimaldi's reach while still making the deal with Orozco, in one easy lesson.

"Not at all," he assured the trader. "Just be back by mid-afternoon."

The traders were gone by the time Kyle and Star returned with a small bowl of something.

"Breakfast was all gone," Kyle said as he handed over the bowl. "But she said we could have some of the soup she was working on for dinner."

"Thanks," Orozco said, sniffing at the bowl. The soup looked thin, but it smelled pretty good. "And now you two need to get some sleep. I'm going to have a special assignment for you later this afternoon."

"What kind of assignment?" Kyle asked.

"The kind that you'll need to be rested for," Orozco said evasively. Eventually, of course, he would have to give them the whole truth. But not yet. Not yet. "So get going."

"Okay." Touching Star's arm, Kyle turned and headed toward their sleeping mats.

Orozco lowered himself to the floor against his favorite pillar, settling himself into guard position, already feeling the fresh hole in his life. Kyle and Star were the best and the brightest Moldering Lost Ashes had to offer. They were also the closest thing to friends he still had. A few hundred gallons of gasoline was a small price to pay to buy their safety.

And it wasn't like the gasoline was going to do anyone in Moldering Lost Ashes any good. Not once the Terminators came through.

Cradling his M16 across his arms, Orozco settled down to watch. And to think.

* * *

The building David had found was decrepit, drafty, and made largely from discarded drywall, which meant the place would be pretty uncomfortable in a serious rainstorm.

It had also been recently occupied, Connor noted as the group began unloading and sorting their equipment. Briefly, he wondered what the chances were that the former inhabitants might return and try to reclaim the place. That could be awkward, not to mention noisy.

But aside from that, the place was ideal. It was unobtrusive, it had a back door they could use in an emergency, and it was only four blocks from the Skynet staging area.

"Is this your headquarters?" one of the new people, Leon Iliaki, asked as he gave the place a dubious look.

"No, it's just a temporary base," Connor assured him. "We'll be moving to better quarters in a couple of days."

"Once we're there, we'll start your combat training," Tunney added as he walked past with an ammo box under each arm.

One of the other newcomers, Callahan, stirred.

"Why wait?" he asked.

Connor eyed him. Usually new recruits needed a day or two to get their bearings. "You want to get started now?" he asked.

"What else are you going to do with us?" Callahan countered. "I mean, unless you've got some other work we can do." He hunched his shoulders uncomfortably. "I don't like the idea of eating someone else's food without working for it."

"Very commendable," Connor complimented him. "There's certainly enough work back at our main base.

Unfortunately, we've got a mission coming up soon, and I can't spare anyone to escort you back there just now."

"Is it a mission in this neighborhood?" Leon Iliaki asked.

"The general neighborhood, yes," Connor confirmed.

Callahan hunched his shoulders again. "Then all the more reason for us to learn as much about fighting as we can," he said, his voice quavering a little. "This is where our friends are. We need to do whatever we can to help them."

"Unless you can't spare anyone for that, either," Carol Iliaki offered hesitantly. "You seem awfully busy."

"We are, a bit," Connor confirmed. "But we're never too busy to teach people who are ready to learn."

Callahan glanced at Leon Iliaki, then at Zac, then back at Connor.

"In that case, I guess we're ready," he said.

"I am, too," Carol Iliaki said.

Her husband looked at her in surprise.

"You're not here to fight," he protested. "You're here to sew."

"I doubt the Terminators will care where I stand in the table of organization," she reminded him, her eyes on Connor. "Am I correct, Mr. Connor?"

"Your husband's right about your primary duty," Connor replied. "But you're also right in that everyone needs to know at least the basics of combat. Tunney? Over to you."

"Got it," Tunney said. "Let me stow these boxes, and I'll be right with you."

"He'll take you in hand," Connor told the recruits. "Learn well."

"We will," Callahan promised. "Thank you."

Connor nodded and moved off, long experience allowing him to cut through the apparent chaos swirling around him and assess each person and task with a single glance.

Some of the men and women had already completed their work, and while a few of them were taking a moment to rest or grab a quick bite, most were gathering around the table where Tunney had laid out the maps Connor and David had made of the Skynet staging area. Connor's eyes flicked across that group, then shifted over to the corner where Kate was organizing her medical supplies.

He frowned, studying her more closely. A dark and serious look had settled onto his wife's face, a look that couldn't be wholly explained by the magnitude of the task facing them.

Interestingly enough, as Connor again glanced around the room he noted that Barnes had an almost identical look on *his* face. And Barnes *never* worried about the jobs Connor took them on.

Which, of course, made it obvious.

Connor waited until Barnes happened to glance in his direction. Then, crooking his finger to the man, Connor headed toward Kate.

She looked up as the two men approached.

"Everything set?" she asked.

"Still working out a few details," Connor told her. "How about you?"

"I've just started, really." She waved a hand toward the bandages, antiseptics, and painkillers laid neatly out around her. "Since we're going for speed and maneuverability, I thought I'd try consolidating most of the supplies into one bag per squad, with only small personal packs for each individual soldier."

"Freeing up more carrying capacity for ammo and munitions," Connor said, nodding. "I assume you'll be giving the big bags to the people with the best medical training?"

Kate nodded. "I was thinking Vincennes, Sung, one of the Tantillo brothers—probably Tony—and Simmons. And of course, I'll be here as backup."

"Sounds good," Connor said. "Now, you want to tell me what has you and Barnes so bothered?"

Kate threw a slightly furtive look at Barnes.

"I'm not sure what you mean," she hedged.

Which was more or less the answer Connor had expected. Kate never liked questioning his orders or decisions, especially not in front of the others.

"How about you?" Connor asked, turning to Barnes.

Barnes, fortunately or unfortunately, had little of Kate's reticence and none of her diplomacy.

"I don't like using all these civilians as bait," he said flatly. "Especially the people in that last place—Orozco's group."

"Is that what you think I'm doing?" Connor asked.

"We're going to wait until all the T-600s leave and start shooting up the neighborhood before we move in, right?" Barnes countered.

"Would you rather we attack the warehouse with the T-600s still inside?" Connor asked.

Barnes scowled. "No," he muttered. "But I still don't like it."

"There are a lot of children in there," Kate added quietly.

Connor raised his eyebrows. "Did you offer everyone the chance to come with us?"

Kate sighed. "Yes," she said. "You saw how many accepted."

"So we made an offer, and were mostly refused," Connor said. "We also found them a potential escape route, the drainage tunnel you went in through, which they can use if they want to."

"Except that Grimaldi's probably already welded it shut," Barnes said with a sniff.

"Again, their choice," Connor said. "There's really not much else we can do for them."

"Yeah, but Grimaldi's the one making all the decisions," Barnes protested. "The people aren't."

"The people made the decision to accept him as their leader," Connor reminded him.

"I suppose," Kate said.

Connor looked at Barnes. He grimaced, but gave a reluctant nod.

"Yeah," he seconded.

"Then let's get back to work," Connor said, looking back and forth between them. "Barnes, Tunney's starting basic with our new recruits. As soon as you've finished stowing your gear, I'd like you to give him a hand."

"Sure," Barnes said. Nodding to Kate, he headed back across the room.

Connor looked at Kate. "You okay?"

"As okay as I am with anything these days," she said, her voice a mixture of tension and sadness. "I'm sorry, John—I don't mean to be questioning your decisions. It was just—all those children—"

"I know," Connor said quietly. "But you have to try to put them out of your mind, along with all the rest of the misery and injustice that's out there." He touched her shoulder. "Focus on the fact that our primary job is to survive long enough to destroy Skynet, so that people won't ever have to die this way again."

Kate gave him a faint smile. "I know. Thanks for reminding me."

Connor smiled back, and turned away. *Well, that's them convinced*, he thought as he headed over to join the group at the maps.

Now, the only one he still had to convince was himself.

CHAPTER ELEVEN

"Kyle?"

The teen started awake, chagrined by the sudden realization that he had, in fact, been asleep. That hadn't been his plan, certainly not with Orozco handling guard duty all alone. He must have been more tired than he'd realized.

Way more tired, in fact, he realized as he peered through half-open eyes out into the street. Nguyen and the other traders were standing outside the archway, and even in the limited sunlight making its way through the overcast sky he could see enough shadow to tell that it was at least a couple of hours past noon. He'd not only slept the morning away, but a good part of the afternoon, too.

He looked over at Star. To his surprise, he saw the same grogginess in her face that he himself was feeling. She must have slept as long and as deeply as he had.

"Come on, Kyle, get it together," Orozco said.

Kyle looked up at the man kneeling over him. There was a grimness on his face that made Kyle wince even harder. Had he and Star slept straight through the mission Orozco had talked about earlier?

"Sorry," Kyle apologized as he scrambled to his feet.

"Didn't mean to sleep so long."

"Don't worry about it," Orozco said, his voice as gruff as his face. "In fact, I'm glad you did. You've got a long day still ahead of you."

"We're ready," Kyle said, checking to make sure the Colt was still riding snugly in his holster. "What's the mission?"

"Come over here," Orozco said. He offered a hand to Star, who ignored it and climbed to her feet without assistance. "You're going to start by taking Mr. Nguyen and his people to our gasoline supply."

Kyle felt his eyes widen. The first rule hammered into the skulls of everyone who knew where the gasoline was located was to never, *ever* take strangers there.

"But—"

"And after that," Orozco said, "you and Star will be going back to their farm with them. And you won't come back."

For a handful of seconds Kyle just stared at him, the words spinning through his brain like moths around a candle.

"What do you mean?" he managed at last. "Are you? —We can't do that."

"You have to," Orozco said, his voice low and earnest and with a pain that Kyle had never heard there before.

"There's no future for you here. Out there, at least you have a chance."

And then, abruptly, the circling words fell into place in Kyle's mind. Into a horrible, terrifying place in a horrible, terrifying reality.

"They're coming, aren't they?" he breathed.

"I think so, yes," Orozco said quietly. "That's why you and Star need to get out of here."

"What about the others?" Kyle asked, throwing a look across the empty lobby. "We have to warn them."

"We will," Orozco promised. "And we'll do our best to get them all out. But you and Star are going first."

Kyle looked at Star. Her eyes were wide, her lower lip trembling. Moldering Lost Ashes was their home, the best and safest they'd ever had. To just throw all that away...

He looked back at Orozco.

"Are you coming with us?" he asked.

"No, but if I can I'll catch up with you later," Orozco said. "But whether I do or not, you have to promise me you won't ever come back here again. Not to look for me, or for anyone else, or to try to collect anything you might leave behind. Once you pass under that archway, you're gone forever. Understand?"

Kyle looked again at Star. She was gazing up at Orozco, her face solemn and troubled. Then, lowering her eyes, she silently took Kyle's hand.

"Yes," Kyle said for them both.

"Good," Orozco said. "Then go get anything you have that you want to take. And not a word to anyone else, okay?" He reached down and took Kyle's Colt from its holster. "Here, I'll load this for you."

It took Kyle and Star only about five minutes to collect their few belongings. They returned to the lobby to find Orozco standing beside Nguyen, talking to him in a low voice. Lying on the ground at his feet was a bulky canvas shoulder bag.

"Ready?" Orozco asked briskly as Kyle and Star came up. "Good. Here's your gun, Kyle, plus an extra clip."

"You sure you can spare them?" Kyle asked as he hesitantly took the weapon and clip. If the Terminators were coming, Orozco and the others would need all the guns and ammunition they could get their hands on.

"Don't argue with your sergeant," Orozco chided, though his tight smile showed he didn't really mean it. "Yes, we can spare them. We can spare this, too." He nudged the bag with his foot.

Kyle stooped over and picked it up. It was heavier than it looked.

"What is it?"

"Six pipe bombs," Orozco said. "I made them up this morning. And don't worry—I kept plenty for us, too."

Kyle swallowed hard. So that was what Orozco had been doing that had given him and Star time to sleep so much.

"Thanks," he said.

"It's just a precaution," Orozco added. "Even if we're in Skynet's crosshairs, its attacks nearly always come after nightfall. You should be well out of the area by then. There's a lighter in there with the bombs, too. But it's stoked with a gasoline mixture and burns really hot, so be careful with it."

"I will," Kyle said, looping the bag's strap over his shoulder. "I..."

He was still searching for a way to say good-bye when Orozco stepped close and wrapped him and Star in a single, massive bear hug. Kyle gripped the man tightly, his eyes squeezed shut, drinking in the warmth and the deepness of human contact.

For a long moment they held each other that way. Then, gently, Orozco disengaged.

"You'd better get going," he said, and Kyle could see the tears in his eyes. "Take care of yourselves and each other. May you both live long enough to see a world finally at peace."

Kyle tried to say something. But his throat and voice weren't working right, and he had to settle for giving his friend a quick nod instead.

A minute later, he and Star were walking down the street beside Nguyen, wrapped in a silence broken only by the crunching of their footsteps and the snuffling of the burros. Kyle had lost many friends and acquaintances over the years, either through death or simple desertion, to the point where he no longer cried over those losses.

But it was a near thing. It was a really near thing.

Nguyen and his men were very impressed by the gasoline stash, commenting several times on both its layered concealment and the booby-traps set up to protect it. Kyle had expected them to take as much of the gasoline as their burros could carry, and was therefore surprised when they quit after siphoning off only thirty gallons.

Still, pulling even that much of the precious liquid took nearly an hour, and by the time the group emerged again into the open air the faint glow in the clouds that marked the sun's position was already halfway to the horizon.

"What now?" Kyle asked as they headed east.

"We get out of this neighborhood," Nguyen said grimly, "and then cover as much distance as we can before we have to turn in for the night."

Star touched Kyle's arm. *Where will we stay?* she signed.

"You have some place in mind for that?" Kyle asked Nguyen.

"There are a couple of possibilities," the other said. "We have to see first how far we get."

"What are they like?" Kyle asked. They were passing the spot where he and Orozco had had the confrontation with the new gang yesterday, and he wondered whether they'd actually left like they'd said they would.

Apparently not.

Even as Kyle eyed their ramshackle headquarters the door opened a crack and a single eye peered out. The eye flicked back and forth, taking in the size and armament of the group, and then the door quietly closed again.

"One's just an empty building," Nguyen said. He'd noticed the door and the eye too, Kyle saw, and his gaze lingered there another moment before turning away. "The other's the home of some of our other customers. Much safer, but they'll charge a hefty fee for putting us up."

Kyle nodded, looking up over the broken buildings and piles of wreckage to Moldering Lost Ashes. Up there on the eighth floor, he knew, the sentries were watching, and he wondered if they'd spotted him and Star among the crowd of men and animals.

If they had, what were they thinking? Did they think he and Star had deserted them, the way Ellis had?

The group had made it three blocks east of Moldering Lost Ashes when Kyle spotted two figures standing motionlessly in the shadow of a broken wall, just two blocks farther ahead.

"Nguyen?" he murmured.

"I see them," Nguyen said grimly. "Vuong?"

"Terminators," Vuong said, squinting toward the figures. "T-600s, probably—haven't seen a T-400 in ages."

"Agreed," Nguyen said. "I wonder what they're doing. Terminators usually don't just stand around like that."

Vuong shrugged. "Maybe they're on break."

Someone in the rear of the group snorted.

"Well, whatever they're up to, we don't want to know about it," Nguyen said. "We'll turn north at the next street and try to get around them."

Kyle peered at the distant figures. He didn't know much about Terminators, only the little that Orozco had been able to tell him. He'd never even seen one close up, which Orozco had assured him was the way he wanted to keep it.

"Maybe we should split up," he said. "Some of us head north, the rest head south."

"Too risky," Nguyen said. "If they decide to come after us, we'll need all our firepower to stop them."

Kyle stole a look at the gun in Nguyen's holster. *Did* they in fact have enough firepower to stop a pair of Terminators? Orozco had always been a little vague on what it took to bring the machines down.

"Then let's all just go south," he suggested. "There's an alley about half a block south off the next street, that would get us across that block without being seen. If they stay where they are by that wall, we should come out on their blind side."

"Unless they take maybe two steps forward," Nguyen countered. "No, I think the northern route would be safer."

"But there's no way of crossing the street without them seeing us up there," Kyle persisted. "Not unless we go four or five blocks, and there are a couple of gangs up there we really don't want to get close to."

"There's a big gang to the south, too," Nguyen said. "There are gangs everywhere."

"Right, but if we go south and the Terminators *don't* take those two steps forward, we can get past without them ever seeing us," Kyle said. "Star and I are willing to try it."

"Forget it," Nguyen said flatly. "I promised Orozco

I'd keep you safe."

Vuong murmured something in another language. Nguyen answered back, and for a few steps the two men talked quietly back and forth.

"I suppose it's worth a try," Nguyen said at last reluctantly. "But Vuong will go with you."

Kyle nodded. "Where do we meet up again?"

"Vuong knows the rendezvous spot," Nguyen said. "Just watch yourselves, okay?"

The two Terminators still hadn't moved by the time the group reached the next street and split up. But Kyle could feel their eyes on him as he, Star, and Vuong headed south, and felt a sense of relief when they passed the nearest building and were out of the machines' sight.

At least the Terminators hadn't come charging straight for them. Maybe they really *were* on some kind of break.

Kyle hadn't been in this part of the neighborhood for several months, but the place hadn't changed very much.

"There's the alley," he told Vuong, pointing out the opening just past the midpoint of the block. "The footing's kind of tricky, but we should be able to get through."

"I don't know," Vuong said doubtfully. "We'll be coming out awfully close. If those Terminators spot us, we'll be sitting ducks. You sure we can't go a little farther south?"

Kyle shook his head. "Not unless we go all the way around the Death's-Head Gang's territory. They're the ones with all the cars up on their sides blocking the street."

"Yes, we saw those on our way in," Vuong said grimly. "We can't go around them—if we do, we won't be in position to back up Nguyen's group if they need us. I guess it's your alley, or nothing."

"It'll work," Kyle assured him. "Besides, if we have to backtrack, the alley's a good place to do it from. There's a gap in a brick wall at the far end you need to get through, and I don't think one of those Terminators could."

"You don't, huh?" Vuong said. "Ever seen a Terminator in action?"

"Not really," Kyle admitted.

Vuong grunted. "Let's hope we can keep it that way."

The alley was as treacherous as Kyle remembered it, filled with angled slabs of pavement, a pair of rusting pickup trucks, and a small forest of exposed rebar. The three of them picked their way through, squeezed through the gap in the final brick wall, and reached the far end. Crouching down beside a bush growing tenaciously through a wide crack in the sidewalk, feeling terribly exposed now that they were back on an open street, Kyle looked carefully around it.

Half a block north, he could see the partial wall where the two Terminators had been loitering. The Terminators themselves were nowhere to be seen.

"Anything?" Vuong murmured from behind him.

"I can't see them," Kyle murmured back. "They could be there, but they could have moved."

Carefully, Vuong lifted his head above the bush for a look of his own.

"Yeah," he said. "I guess for the moment we stay put."

"Stay put *here*?" Kyle asked, looking around. Except for the bush, they had no cover at all.

"We have to be able to see when the others get to their jump-off point," Vuong explained patiently. "Once they're there, we'll figure out our next move."

The minutes ticked slowly by. The cloud cover was starting to thicken, bringing a new chill to the air, and Kyle could feel Star shivering at his side. Slipping off his jacket from beneath his bag's shoulder strap, he wrapped the garment around her. She flashed him a quick smile of thanks, then went back to watching the street.

More minutes went by. Kyle was starting to wonder just how far north Nguyen had decided to go when Vuong touched his shoulder.

"There they are," he murmured.

Kyle leaned a little farther around the bush. Three blocks north, he could see Nguyen and the others creeping as furtively across the street as the uneven footing and the presence of a dozen burros allowed.

"I don't see anything," Vuong said. "Maybe the machines left while we were climbing over all that rebar."

"And went where?" Kyle asked, looking around.

"As long as they're not here, who cares?" Vuong said. "Looks like our alley continues on past the street, through that gap in the vines. That's where we're going."

"Okay." Taking a deep breath, Kyle gathered his feet beneath him for a quick sprint.

And found himself suddenly off-balance as Star grabbed his arm and yanked backward.

"Hey—*easy*," he protested, glancing at her.

What he saw made him take a second, longer look. The girl's face had gone rigid, her eyes wide and terrified. Something had spooked her, but good.

"What is it?" Kyle asked. A movement past the bush caught the corner of his eye, and he looked up.

To see the two Terminators emerge from a broken doorway half a block south of Nguyen's group and head straight toward them.

"Vuong!" he bit out.

"Stay here," Vuong ordered. Drawing his pistol, he dashed around the bush and headed toward the figures that were closing in on his friends.

Again, Kyle gathered his feet beneath him. If he could get Star across the street and into the relative safety of the alley while the Terminators were focusing on the traders....

But again, Star's grip brought him up short.

"Star, we have to go," Kyle insisted, trying to pry her fingers off his arm.

She shook her head violently, wrapping her other hand around his arm for emphasis, and nodded sharply in Vuong's direction. Wishing the girl could just *talk* to him, Kyle looked up again.

Vuong was still running, his arms pumping at his sides. The two Terminators were still marching stolidly toward Nguyen's group, apparently oblivious to this new threat coming up behind them. Vuong slowed a little, lifting his gun into a two-handed marksman's grip and leveling the weapon at the Terminators' backs.

And then, to Kyle's stunned horror, as Vuong passed the half-broken wall, the two Terminators they'd seen earlier stepped into view.

Vuong spotted them the same time Kyle did. Twisting half around, he opened fire.

The Terminators jerked with the multiple impacts as the rounds slammed into their metal bodies. But they didn't fall or even falter, but just kept moving.

Vuong must have known in that moment that he was a dead man. But that didn't mean he was just going to lay down and give up. He veered away from the approaching death machines, emptying his pistol into them.

Kyle held his breath. But aside from more jerking the Terminators seemed completely unaffected by the attack. Shaking the clip from his gun, Vuong slammed in a fresh one and emptied it as well. Again, the Terminators shrugged off the hail of lead.

Vuong was reloading with a third clip when a second, more distant crackle of gunfire erupted. Nguyen and his men had formed a line behind their burros and were making their own stand against the Terminators bearing down on them. But their attack was no more effective than Vuong's.

And then, suddenly, Kyle's brain unfroze and he remembered his bombs.

He reached into the bag, snatching out the lighter and one of the cold metal cylinders.

"Stay down," he muttered to Star as he popped the lighter's top and thumbed the flame to life. He ignited the bomb's fuse, gauged the distance, then rose to his feet and hurled the bomb as hard as he could toward the Terminators closing on Vuong.

But not hard enough. The pipe bounced off the pavement and skittered to a halt a good twenty feet back from the two Terminators. Even over the noise of the gunfire filling the air, the machines apparently heard the sound as the bomb hit the ground, and one of them turned to look.

And then the bomb exploded, and Kyle ducked back down as the shockwave blew through the bush's branches and leaves. The sound of the blast faded away into silence.

Complete silence.

Kyle looked at Star, his throat tightening. Then, steeling himself, he lifted his head again for another look.

To find that it was already over.

Kyle stared, unable to believe his eyes. Vuong was down, lying unmoving on the pavement, his shirt bright with blood. The two Terminators stood over him, gazing down at his body like hunters assessing their prey.

Away to the north, the other pair of Terminators were wading through Nguyen's group, metal arms slamming and punching and throwing the men around like rags. Kyle wondered why the traders hadn't at least tried to run, only then spotting the two additional Terminators striding toward the doomed men from further north, blocking any chance of escape in that direction.

Nguyen had tried to take his men away from a clear and present threat. Instead, he'd led them into the center of a trap.

And as far as Kyle could tell, none of the Terminators had even bothered to use the massive guns strapped to their right arms.

Then, as Kyle stared at the carnage, sickened yet somehow unable to turn away, one of the two machines standing over Vuong's body stirred and turned its head. Its glowing eyes seemed to lock onto Kyle.

And with a sudden surge of energy, it turned and headed toward him.

"Come on," Kyle muttered, grabbing Star's hand and pulling her back into the alley. He pushed her through the gap in the brick wall, then squeezed through himself, and again got a grip on her hand as he took the lead. If they could get back to the next street over and find some building they could disappear into before the Terminator caught up with them, they might still have a chance.

But the alley's footing was as treacherous going in this direction as it had been going in the other, and

Kyle was forced to slow down as he balanced their need for haste with their equally urgent need for safety. A broken leg or twisted ankle now would mean quick and certain death.

Kyle could feel the sweat gathering around his neck as he picked his way along the alley, not daring to turn around, wondering whether he would even hear the sound of the Terminator's gun as the killing rounds tore into his back.

But that line of thought led only to panic. Pushing it away, he concentrated on finding the best possible route for him and Star. They would make it, he told himself firmly. Luck favored the prepared, Orozco had always told him, and they were prepared. They would make it.

They were halfway through when their luck ran out.

The crash of breaking brick exploded from behind them. The Terminator had reached the wall and was battering its way through, sending bricks flying with each blow from its free left hand. Kyle spun round to see that the top of the wall was already gone, and even as he tried to get his own feet moving again the rest of the wall collapsed. Kicking its way through the rubble, the Terminator strode toward them.

And with that, it was all over.

Kyle froze, gripping Star's hand, staring helplessly as the killing machine bore down on them. Its glowing red eyes burned into them from its expressionless face, its rubbery skin and coverall-type clothing torn and scorched where Vuong's bullets had shredded them. Beneath the dangling tatters, Kyle could see the Terminator's gleaming metal skeleton. Gripped in its right hand, the multi-barreled gun looked as big as a cannon.

And then, abruptly, a completely unexpected question

popped into Kyle's mind. *Why didn't the Terminator open fire?*

They hadn't used their weapons against Nguyen and Vuong, either. Instead, they'd simply bludgeoned the traders to death with their bare metal hands.

And in a burst of desperation-induced inspiration, Kyle suddenly got it.

Orozco had said Skynet was planning an attack against the neighborhood. But he'd also said that the big computer probably wouldn't launch that attack until nightfall.

It didn't want anyone escaping before then, which was why it had set out all these Terminators as sentries. But it also didn't want to panic the inhabitants into a premature stampede, which might create enough confusion to allow some of the intended victims to escape.

Random gunfire, even at the levels Nguyen and his men had been putting out, was a common enough occurrence, and would probably be dismissed by anyone who heard it as simple gang activity. But a Terminator's multi-barreled gun would have a very distinctive and recognizable sound, and opening fire with one might well start the panic Skynet wanted to avoid.

Which meant that the Terminator striding toward them would probably hold off using its gun until and unless it calculated that its latest victims were on the verge of getting away. The trick would be to keep it thinking it was in control, right up to the moment when it suddenly wasn't.

All Kyle had to do now was find a way to do that.

He glanced around the alley, then turned back to the Terminator. Bracing himself, he reached into his bag and pulled out the lighter and another bomb. If the machine decided these bombs were a threat and that it needed to open fire...

But it didn't, not even when Kyle touched the lighter's flame to the fuse. Having already watched one of the bombs go off, the Terminator had apparently concluded that the weapon didn't have enough yield to stop it.

It was probably still thinking that as Kyle ran the fuse down to two seconds and then lobbed it beneath the rusting pickup truck the machine was passing. The bomb exploded, flipping the pickup up onto one side and straight on top of the Terminator, slamming it to the ground with a horrendous crash.

Slamming it squarely on top of the forest of rebar protruding through the concrete.

Kyle didn't know how much damage being shoved into all those metal spikes would do to the Terminator. But for the moment, all he cared about was that the killing machine was temporarily immobilized. Shoving Star out of the way behind one of the angled slabs of pavement, he pulled out two more bombs and lit their fuses. He ran over to the pickup, already starting to shake as the trapped Terminator tried to free itself, and shoved the two bombs between the twisted stalks of rebar directly beneath the Terminator's torso and hips.

The Terminator's arm snapped out, the metal hand trying to grab Kyle's wrist. Kyle managed to jerk back out of the way in time, then turned and sprinted for the pavement slab where he'd left Star. He ducked around behind it, wrapping his arms around the little girl, and squeezed his eyes shut.

The bombs went off together, the blasts much louder this time. Kyle waited until the sound had faded, then peeked cautiously around the slab.

The pickup had been blown up against the alley's side and was half leaning, half sagging against the wall. Still pressed into the rebar where the truck had been was the Terminator.

The machine was a mess. Nearly all of the rubber skin directly over the bombs had been disintegrated, exposing the scorched and blackened metal body beneath it. On the Terminator's face and legs, which had been farther from the blasts, some of the skin remained, smoldering with an acrid smoke.

But its lack of skin was the least of the machine's problems. The bomb that Kyle had wedged beneath its hips had shattered the joints there, severing the legs from the rest of the body. The arms were in nearly as bad a shape, with the left completely disconnected from the torso and the right just barely hanging on by a couple of cables. The Terminator's neck had managed to survive the blast, but the back of the head showed a deep dent, probably sustained during the pickup's initial impact.

There was a hesitant touch on Kyle's arm, and he turned to see Star staring wide-eyed at the wreckage.

Is it dead? she signed.

Kyle took a deep breath and looked back at the Terminator.

"I think—"

Without warning, the machine's metal skull turned toward Kyle, its red eyes glowing balefully up at him.

Kyle jerked backward. The Terminator's right arm twitched, and Kyle tore his gaze from the blazing eyes to look at it.

Slowly, moving in starts and stops, the arm was creeping back toward the shoulder.

Kyle felt his eyes widen. How in the world—?

There was a sudden gasp from beside him, and he jerked again as Star pounced forward to grab the Terminator's detached left arm. She lifted it up, staggering and grunting with the load.

"Careful," Kyle warned as he reached over and took it from her. The metal arm wasn't just heavy—it was somehow pulling itself toward the Terminator's shoulder.

The Terminator was trying to put itself back together.

Clutching the metal arm to his chest, Kyle leaned against the pull and managed to take a step backward. To his relief, the pressure eased, and the next step was even easier. Two steps more, and there was no pull at all.

He looked down at the arm that was pressed to his chest. So it wasn't some sort of evil Skynet magic. It was just a simple electromagnet, or set of electromagnets, embedded inside the gleaming metal to help the Terminator reassemble itself if someone managed to blow it apart.

But apparently only if its severed pieces were close enough together.

"Yeah, I think we can do something about that," Kyle muttered. Tucking the spare arm under his right arm, he reached into his bomb bag.

And twisted to the side as something shot past his face.

He ducked down, spinning around. Another Terminator had appeared in the far end of the alley, and was striding toward them with a piece of broken brick gripped in its left hand.

"Run!" Kyle snapped at Star, ducking again as the Terminator hurled the brick at him.

This time, the machine's aim was better. The sharp-edged missile slammed into Kyle's right shoulder, sending a stab of pain down his whole side. He threw the mechanical arm he was holding at the machine, then snatched out his Colt and fired a quick shot before turning and running for all he was worth. He caught up with Star at the alley mouth, grabbed her hand, and yanked her to the left. Another brick whistled past just as they made it around the corner.

The footing was better here on the street, allowing them to pick up their speed a little. Kyle glanced over his shoulder as they ran, wondering if the two Terminators who had attacked Nguyen's men had also joined in this new hunt. But to his relief, the street north of them was clear.

So far.

He turned back around, gripping Star's hand and trying to come up with a plan. The minute that second Terminator made it through the alley he and Star would be back in its line of fire. And this time, it might decide it would be easier all around to simply shoot the two of them down.

Which meant Kyle had to find them a hiding place.

Or else he had to find someone more worthy of getting shot at.

Despite his fatigue and fear, he felt a tight grin touch his lips. Maybe, if he was lucky, he could do both at the same time.

CHAPTER TWELVE

Connor was going over the approach plan with David's group when he heard the faint sound of gunfire.

"Quiet!" he snapped.

The room went instantly silent. Everyone froze, all ears tuned toward the distant noise. It was coming from a single weapon, Connor decided, probably a large-caliber handgun. There was a pause, just long enough for the shooter to change clips, then more shots, then another pause.

And then, abruptly, the first gun's reports were buried beneath a cacophony of new gunfire.

Connor listened intently, trying to sort out the types of weapons being fired. Most were handguns, but he could also hear the deeper roar of rifle fire in the mix, along with the distinctive boom of shotguns. Across the room, the sentry opened the door a few centimeters, bringing the sounds more sharply into focus.

And then, briefly overwhelming even the noise from the guns, came the thud of an explosion.

Connor looked at Kate, seeing his own tension mirrored in the tightness of her face. Gunfire—even this much gunfire—could be gang warfare or even ordinary residents defending their property and lives.

But very few people, gangs included, threw bombs at each other these days. The people who knew how to make such devices usually saved them to use against the Terminators.

"Could they have started already?" Kate murmured tautly.

"God, I hope not," David murmured back. "We're not ready yet."

The echoes of the explosion faded away, and as they did so the gunfire itself abruptly ceased. Connor strained his ears, even though he knew that the brief battle had been too far away for them to hear any moans or screams from the wounded. If there were, in fact, any wounded still left to scream. Into the silence came the sound of a second explosion, followed a few seconds later by a third, this one louder than the first two had been.

And then, silence again returned.

"Anyone get a direction on that?" Connor asked, looking over at the sentry. "Vincennes?"

The other shook his head.

"If I had to guess, I'd say it was somewhere to the east," he said. "But there's so much echo off the buildings I couldn't tell for sure."

Connor looked back at Kate, then turned to David.

"Opinions?" he invited.

"It wasn't Terminators," Barnes put in before David could speak. "They weren't the ones shooting, anyway."

"I agree," David said. "You can pick those miniguns of theirs out of a crowd any day of the week."

"True," Connor said. "But not shooting doesn't necessarily mean not there."

"It was a sentry line," Kate said quietly, a look of understanding appearing on her face. "Skynet has closed off the neighborhood."

Connor nodded heavily. Someone, maybe that group of men and burros who had passed them awhile back, had tried to get out of the neighborhood and had been stopped.

"Which means we don't have until tomorrow night, like we've been assuming," he said. "We have until tonight."

He looked around the room, watching as their expressions went from stunned to overwhelmed, and then to hard and cold and determined. They were a good team, and a tough team. If anyone could pull this off, Connor knew, they could.

It was Tunney who officially put it into words.

"We'll be ready," he said.

"Then let's get to it," Connor said. "Tunney, David: get your teams and gear together. Leave any spare equipment or food you were saving for later—we're traveling light. Final coordination run-through in ten minutes."

He gestured to Barnes.

"As for you, your mission's just been changed. Collect your team and meet me in the corner."

Orozco was outside Moldering Lost Ashes, walking the building's northern perimeter, when he heard the sound of distant gunfire.

And there was no doubt—none at all—as to what it meant.

Oh, God, he pleaded silently. *Please, no. Not Kyle and Star.*

He stood motionless, a cold breeze whipping dust through his hair, listening as the single gun became many, then none, then became three explosions that he knew had to be the bombs he'd given Kyle.

And then, silence.

Ninety seconds later, Orozco was back inside, hurrying across the lobby toward Grimaldi's office.

Wadleigh and Killough were standing outside the door, talking together in low voices. They looked up as Orozco approached.

"The chief's busy right now," Wadleigh said, holding up a hand.

Without slowing down, Orozco strode between the two men, deflecting Wadleigh's hand with his forearm as the other made a belated grab for him. Twisting the knob, he shoved open the door and stepped inside.

Grimaldi was busy, all right. He was talking very quietly, very earnestly, and *very* closely with Candace Tomlinson, the seventeen-year-old girl from the food dispute that morning. Both of their heads snapped around as Orozco stormed into the room, identical expressions of chagrin flashing across their faces.

Grimaldi, at least, had the grace to blush. Or maybe it was a flush of anger.

"What the *hell* do you think—?"

"Candace, get out of here," Orozco cut him off. "The chief and I need to talk."

The girl, incredibly stubborn when it came to her possessions and her rights, nevertheless knew when not to argue. She scrambled out of her chair, gingerly circled Orozco, and fled the room.

Orozco swung the door shut behind her.

"First of all, this wasn't what you think," Grimaldi growled, managing as usual to get in the first word. "I was talking to her about her habit of snooping into—"

"Forget Candace," Orozco again cut him off. "Forget everything. The Terminators are coming."

Grimaldi seemed to draw back a little.

"Really," he said, his voice back on balance again. "And you know this how?"

"Nguyen and his men left earlier this afternoon," Orozco said. "I was just outside, and I heard gunfire—a *lot* of gunfire—coming from the direction they would have taken."

"Did you hear any T-600 miniguns?" Grimaldi asked.

Orozco blinked. It was an obvious question, but not one he would have expected to come from Grimaldi.

"No," he conceded. "But they hardly need to use their guns to kill people."

"Not exactly my point," Grimaldi said. "But fine. My next question would have been who shot first. But if there wasn't any T-600 gunfire I guess that one's already been answered, hasn't it?"

Orozco grimaced. It was obvious where Grimaldi was going with this.

"Chief, I know you believe the Terminators don't attack unless someone attacks them first," he said, fighting hard to keep his voice calm and reasonable. "But that's just not true. I've seen it happen. They block off a neighborhood, then come in—"

"Yes, we've all heard your little horror stories," Grimaldi interrupted. "Correct me if I'm wrong, but I don't remember you ever showing us any actual proof."

"What sort of proof do you want?" Orozco demanded. "A pile of bodies riddled with minigun rounds? I've already told you that Skynet usually sends in scavengers afterwards to collect the bodies, for God only knows what purpose."

"And anything they miss becomes coyote and rat food, I suppose," Grimaldi said with a maddeningly patient nod.

"It's an interesting story. I, on the other hand, have ten years of experience that says if you leave the Terminators alone, they'll leave you alone."

"Your experience is worthless," Orozco snapped. "Skynet's left us alone here because it was busy elsewhere. But now it's our turn. The Terminators are coming. *We have got to get everyone out.*"

Grimaldi shook his head.

"No."

Orozco took a step toward the desk.

"We're getting everyone out," he said, resting his hand on his holstered Beretta. "Give the order, or I'll give it for you."

To his credit, Grimaldi didn't even flinch.

"Mutiny, Sergeant?"

"Replacing a superior who's shown himself unfit for command," Orozco countered. "Now give the order."

"Suppose I do," Grimaldi said. "How do we get all the food and plants and equipment out? More importantly, where do we all go?"

"South," Orozco told him. "Fewer people that direction, which means we should be able to find shelter without having to fight for it."

"And the food?"

"We take everything we can carry," Orozco said. "After the Terminators leave, we may be able to come back and retrieve anything we had to leave behind."

"Just abandon everything?" Grimaldi shook his head. "No."

Orozco squeezed the grip on his Beretta. "Give the order," he bit out.

Grimaldi gazed unblinkingly into his eyes. "And if I don't?" he countered. "Are you going to shoot me?"

For a few seconds Orozco glared at him. But the chief was right. Orozco couldn't just shoot him down. Not in cold blood. Not for this.

"In that case," Grimaldi said calmly into the tense silence, "you're invited to leave."

Orozco hesitated another few heartbeats. Then, without a word, he turned and strode out of the room.

Wadleigh and Killough were still loitering outside the office. Wadleigh started to say something, got a look at Orozco's face, and instead stepped back out of his way.

Only not far enough. As Orozco passed, he grabbed Wadleigh's arm and half pulled, half dragged the man across the lobby, ignoring his protests until they were nearly to the fountain. Then, bringing them to a sudden halt, he swung Wadleigh around to face him.

"That drainage tunnel Kate Connor mentioned," Orozco ground out. "Did you find it?"

Wadleigh's eyes flicked to the office door, where Killough was standing slack-jawed as he watched their little drama.

"Yeah, we found it," he said, lowering his voice. "And no, we didn't seal it. Just covered it with a few bricks, like you said."

"Good." Orozco let go of his arm, giving him a little push as he did so. "Show me."

Wadleigh gulped and shot one more look toward the office. Grimaldi, Orozco knew, wouldn't be happy with either of them if word of this got back to him.

Orozco didn't give a damn.

"Sure," Wadleigh said. "Follow me."

Kyle and Star had made it to within a block of the line of rusting cars that marked the northern edge of Death's-

Head territory when one of Kyle's backward glances finally spotted the Terminator striding down the street toward them.

"It's coming," he panted to Star, gripping her hand tighter and trying to push a little more speed out of his legs. The Terminator still hadn't opened fire, but it wouldn't be long now. Not with the lead they had on it.

Unless it was counting on the Death's-Head Gang not to let them through.

Kyle eyed the barrier looming ahead of them: ten cars turned up on their sides with their undersides facing him. They mostly formed a single solid line, but they'd been offset enough to create a single zigzag gap near the center, just big enough for one person at a time to get through.

There were no sentries on guard, or at least none that Kyle could see as he steered Star toward the gap. If the Terminator behind them was going to open fire, he knew tensely, this would be the time for it. They reached the car, and with a quick sideways two-step Kyle ducked around the hood of the front vehicle and then around the trunk of the rear one, pulling Star along behind him.

They skidded to a sudden stop. Facing them ten feet away was a line of men with rifles and shotguns, all of them pointed squarely at Kyle and Star.

"Freeze it!" one of the men snapped.

"Terminators!" Kyle gasped, fighting to catch his breath. "Terminators—coming."

"He's right, Rats," someone called from his right. Kyle turned and saw another man with a shoulder-slung rifle peering up over the cars with a slender periscope. "Got one heading straight toward us."

"Ah, *hell*," Rats bit out, glaring at Kyle. "What the

friggin' hell did you do? Huh?" He stepped up to Kyle
and pressed the barrel of his rifle into the center of his
chest. "Huh? What the hell did you *do*?"

"We didn't do anything," Kyle protested. "It's just
after us, that's all. Look, just let us go through and we'll
be gone."

"Friggin' hell with *that*," Rats snarled. He shoved on
the rifle, and Kyle winced as the muzzle dug into his
skin. "Back out the way you came. Now."

Kyle stared at him.

"But—you can't. Please."

"Back out on your own feet, or we shoot you and toss
your carcasses out to the machine," Rats said tightly.
"Your choice."

Kyle looked down at Star. She was watching him
closely, her face calm with the assurance that he had
some plan.

Only he didn't.

"Can't we at least talk about it?" he pleaded, looking
back at Rats.

"Yeah, that's a smart idea," Rats said sarcastically.
"You go out there and talk." He jabbed with his rifle
again. "Last chance to do it breathing."

Kyle took a deep breath. It was clearly no use.

"Come on, Star—"

He broke off as a screech of metal on pavement came
from *behind* Rats, from the upended cars that formed
the compound's southern barrier a hundred feet away.
Rats and his men spun around at the noise, their
weapons tracking in that direction. One of the cars near
the middle of the barrier teetered and then toppled over,
slamming to the pavement with a teeth-rattling crash.

And through the gap in the barrier strode three T-600s.

Rats' men were nothing if not fast on the uptake. The Terminators had barely come into sight before a thunder of gunfire erupted from all across the compound, including the buildings on both sides of the blocked-off street. The Terminators twitched violently as round after round slammed into them.

But they kept coming.

Something arced across and down from one of the upper windows on the eastern building, and the machines were abruptly engulfed in a blazing wash of fire.

And then Star was tugging on Kyle's arm, pulling him urgently backward toward the upended car they were standing in front of. Kyle glanced at the car, noting for the first time that all of the vehicle's glass was gone. She tugged again, pointing toward the open gap where the windshield had once been.

They had just slipped inside the car when across the way there was a violent triple explosion.

Star turned wide-eyed to Kyle as they pressed themselves back into the wide cavity where the car's seats had once been. *Their guns?* she signed.

Kyle nodded. *The fire must have blown their ammo,* he signed back.

But if the Terminators' miniguns were gone, it was clear from the intensity of the gunfire still hammering across the compound that the Terminators themselves were far from defeated. Putting his arm around Star's shoulders, Kyle eased them both down into sitting positions, trying to make them as small and invisible as possible.

Star took off the jacket Kyle had given her, handing it to him. Kyle nodded his thanks and draped it across their torsos, then changed his mind and pulled it up over their faces as well, covering them from head to chest. The more they could look like a pile of discarded rags, the better the chance that the Terminators and Rats' own people would miss them in all the confusion out there.

He'd barely gotten the jacket arranged, and his eye pressed against a small rip in the material, when the Terminator who'd been behind them strode through the gap between the cars. It passed them and headed in to join the battle.

Kyle grimaced. So that was why the machine hadn't shot them in the back. It had known the other three T-600s were coming up on the compound from the south, and had merely been herding its prey toward this new group of hunters. If Rats had let them go like Kyle had wanted, he and Star would probably both be dead now.

And even as the narrowness of their escape shivered through him, it occurred to him that Skynet's little neighborhood containment setup had suddenly been blown to hell. Between the Terminator he'd shattered in the alley and the four now embroiled in this battle with the Death's-Heads, there had to be a huge open gap in their sentry line.

He could only hope that Orozco would figure that out, and would take advantage of this chance to get the residents of the Ashes to safety.

The gunfire was intensifying, and acrid smoke was starting to drift in through the car's missing windows. Pulling Star closer to him, trying not to choke or sneeze, he settled down to wait it out.

Orozco stared at the pile of broken concrete and dirt stretching three-quarters of the way up to the drainage tunnel's ceiling.

"So that's it," he said, his words echoing oddly in the confined space.

"I guess so," Wadleigh said. "Sorry."

Sorry. Orozco felt a surge of unreasoning anger. *Sorry.* Like the two of them had lost a race, or a bet, instead of losing the one chance the people of the Ashes had of surviving the night.

He took a deep breath. *Stop it*, he told himself firmly. He had more urgent things to do than be annoyed at someone else's poor choice of words.

He turned around, lifting his torch higher, studying the tunnel roof. If there were any other manhole shafts up there that might offer a way out, this could still work.

But there weren't. The only shaft that was visible in the flickering torchlight was the one they'd come down, fifty meters back from the blockage.

"We could try heading northwest," Wadleigh suggested hesitantly. "That has to be the direction Connor and her people came in from."

"Which is exactly why we can't use it," Orozco said. "I don't believe for a minute that they came here just to recruit new talent. They were hunting Terminators; and if they came in from the northwest, that's probably where they were hunting them."

Wadleigh grunted. "In that case, we'd damn well better seal the place down, but good. Just in case the Terminators start hunting back."

"You're probably right," Orozco conceded, eyeing the pile of debris. If he and Wadleigh tackled it together...

But no. Several of the pieces of broken concrete were bigger than even the two of them could handle, especially in such a cramped space. There was no escape for anyone here.

Or anywhere else. All that was left now was to dig in as best they could and prepare for war.

"Time to get back," he said, nudging Wadleigh back along the tunnel.

"So after we seal the cover, what then?" Wadleigh asked as they picked their way carefully over the curved concrete.

"We start by getting the fire teams together," Orozco told him. "That'll be your job. Break out all the weapons, including the ones in the reserve cache, and get them into the hands of people who know how to use them. Pull out all the ammo, too. If Grimaldi gives you static over any of this, you send him to me."

"Don't worry, he won't," Wadleigh said grimly. "What about you?"

"I'm going to set up a few booby traps," Orozco said. "If I have any time left after that's done, I'll see about making some more bombs."

They reached the shaft and climbed carefully up the rusted rungs to the rabbit warren of broken steel and concrete that lay just outside the northern edge of Moldering Lost Ashes. Zigzagging their way over and through the debris, they climbed through the empty window that led back into the building.

After his confrontation with Grimaldi, Orozco had rather expected there to be a reception committee waiting for him in the lobby. He was right. Grimaldi and Killough were standing near the corridor entrance, flanked by Barney and Copeland. The latter two were holding rifles at the ready.

"Sergeant Justo Orozco," Grimaldi said in his most pompous corporate CEO voice, "as the leader of Moldavia—"

"Stuff it," Orozco said shortly, striding past the group.

Grimaldi was apparently expecting him to do that. He took a quick step forward as Orozco passed and grabbed the sergeant's arm. "You are ordered confined to your room until—"

The speech cut off with a yelp as Orozco reached over with his other hand and grabbed Grimaldi's arm, prying it off and twisting it over at the wrist.

"Let him go," Copeland snapped. He started to lift his rifle.

And froze. "No," Wadleigh said quietly.

Orozco turned to look. Wadleigh's face was pale and his throat was tight, but the Smith & Wesson 9mm he was pointing at Copeland was rock-steady.

"He's right," Wadleigh continued. "The Terminators aren't going to give us a pass. They're machines. They're programmed. They're going to kill us all."

"That's enough, Wadleigh," Grimaldi bit out. "Sergeant Orozco—"

Orozco twisted his arm a little harder, and again the chief broke off with grunt. "Here's what we're going to do," Orozco said, keeping his voice low. "We're going to prepare for an attack. The fire teams are going to be assembled, and they're going to answer to me. You can either help, or you can stay out of our way. Is that clear?"

"And if I don't?" Grimaldi gritted out. "What are you going to do, shoot me?"

"That's twice you've offered me that choice," Orozco reminded him. "Keep it up, and one of these times I may take you up on it."

For a half dozen heartbeats the lobby was silent. "All right, Sergeant," Grimaldi said at last. "You go ahead and make your preparations. Take anyone you need;

take any resources you need. *But.*"

He let the word hang in the air a moment. "If we're still here in the morning," the chief continued, "*you* won't be. Is that understood?"

"Yes," Orozco said.

Letting go of Grimaldi's arm, he stepped back. Grimaldi straightened back up, and once again briefly locked eyes with Orozco. Then, without another word, he gestured to his men, and the four of them headed back across the lobby toward Grimaldi's office.

Orozco turned to Wadleigh. "Thanks," he said.

"No problem," Wadleigh said as he holstered his gun. "Just remember this when they kick *me* out, too."

"I will." Orozco turned back again.

And for the first time noticed Reverend Sibanda seated on the rim of the fountain where Grimaldi and the others had blocked Orozco's view of him. "Can I help you, Reverend?" he asked.

"I understood there was trouble brewing," Sibanda said, standing up and walking over to them. "I see it was more serious than I thought."

"Actually, no matter how serious you thought it was, it's worse," Orozco told him.

"So I gather," Sibanda said soberly. "What can I do to help?"

"At this point, I really don't know," Orozco said.

"Chief Grimaldi said you were to use all resources," Sibanda said quietly, his dark eyes burning into Orozco's. "I'm one of those resources. Please tell me what I can do."

Orozco eyed the man, trying to think. There was a huge amount of work to do, but with the preacher's hands half crippled with arthritis he was out of the running for most of it.

"Do what you can to keep the people calm, I guess," he said. "About the only thing that would make this situation worse would be mass panic."

"I can do that," Sibanda promised. "And when the time comes, I'll help you lead them to the Promised Land."

Orozco looked away, his mind flicking back to the dark thought of a couple of days ago. The thought that the truly chosen ones of Judgment Day had been those who'd been granted a quick death.

"We'll be going to the Promised Land soon enough," he agreed quietly. "I'd be honored to have you along for the journey."

"I'll be there," Sibanda said, his voice calm and assured. "If you'll excuse me, I'll go begin my preparations."

He turned and walked off across the lobby.

"So will we," Orozco murmured after him.

Because he, for one, had no intention of going to this particular Promised Land without a fight.

He slapped the backs of his fingertips against Wadleigh's chest.

"Break time's over. Let's get to work."

The gunfire in the Death's-Head compound seemed to go on and on, punctuated by the occasional thunder of explosions and the whoosh and reflected glare of more of the gang's napalm firebombs. One of them hit the ground close enough to Kyle and Star's sideways car that the fire blazed through both the windshield and rear window openings, heating the roof three feet in front of them hot enough to glow a dull red.

There were probably screams and curses amid all the commotion, too. Fortunately, perhaps, the hammering of the gunfire drowned out all such sounds of human agony.

But in the end, neither the gang's weapons nor their stubbornness did them any good. One by one, the guns fell silent, and the running footsteps came to a halt, and silence again descended on the world.

Slowly, Kyle eased his eye back to the rip in the jacket that still covered their faces. Very little of the compound was visible through the open windshield of their sanctuary car, but even that was enough to turn his stomach. There were dead bodies everywhere, some of them mostly whole, some looking like they'd been ripped apart where they stood.

He was still gazing at the carnage when one of the Terminators stepped into his field of view.

The machine was a mess. Its skin and clothing had been almost entirely burned away, exposing not only its entire metal body but also dozens of small dents and blackened scorch marks. It was limping badly, hardly able to walk, its right leg bending oddly with each step. Its left leg wasn't much better, and its entire right arm up to the elbow was a twisted mass of torn metal.

The Death's-Heads might have lost the battle, but they'd given a good account of themselves along the way.

Kyle felt a stirring inside him. With its weapon gone, and with that limp, this was one Terminator that wasn't going to be chasing down anyone any time soon. This might be his and Star's one chance to make a run for it.

He was still trying to decide whether or not they should try when three more Terminators strode into view. Two of them were in the same shape as the first one, nothing but skinless machines with broken leg servos and mangled right arms.

But the fourth Terminator stood in sharp contrast to its fellow machines. It still had most of its skin and clothing, with no perceptible limp and all its limbs intact. More importantly, it still had its minigun.

Kyle grimaced. It was just as well that he and Star hadn't tried to run.

Star touched his arm. Carefully, Kyle turned his head beneath the jacket to look at her. *What's happening?* she signed, her face drawn and anxious.

They're still there, he signed back.

Her lip twitched. *So we stay here?*

For the moment, Kyle signed, trying to smile reassuringly. *Don't worry, we'll get away soon enough. Just be patient.*

He turned back to the Terminators. The three damaged ones had opened up a pack of tools they must have found somewhere in the compound, and in complete and eerie silence each was starting repair work on itself.

Kyle felt his lip twist. *What, were you expecting them to sing?* he told himself sarcastically. Of course they were fixing themselves in silence. They were machines, not living beings.

More to the point, they were machines that could be damaged—and even destroyed.

And *that* was what Kyle needed to focus on. Not on all the dead bodies lying on the ground out there, but on the fact that the Terminators themselves could be killed.

No battle plan, Orozco had once told Kyle, *ever survives contact with the enemy. That being said, though, a plan is always the place to start.*

Reaching beneath the jacket to take Star's hand, Kyle settled down to watch the Terminators making their repairs, and began working out his plan.

CHAPTER THIRTEEN

Dusk had faded to full night when Orozco finally heard the distant sound of minigun fire.

He stood up from the fountain rim where he and Wadleigh's fire team had been sitting and crossed to the archway. The Terminator fire was coming in short bursts, he noted grimly, the rhythm that would typically be used to clean out a house after a successful breach. So far he hadn't heard any answering fire, but maybe that was just being swallowed up by the louder sounds of the miniguns.

Or maybe all the victims were dying before they had a chance to shoot back.

There was a movement at the corner of his eye, and he turned to see Grimaldi come up beside him.

"So it's started," the chief said quietly.

Orozco nodded. "So it would seem."

"Yes." Grimaldi paused as another burst of minigun fire split the night, this group coming from a different direction. "So you were right."

"Yes," Orozco said flatly. "I was."

"So that's it," Grimaldi said, an agonized ache in his voice. "We're all dead. Because of me."

Orozco looked at him. The chief was staring out the

archway, his face drawn, his eyes wet with tears of regret or anger or frustration. And for a long moment Orozco wanted to tell the other that, yes, this *was* all his fault.

But he couldn't. He couldn't kick a man who was watching his world-view crumbling right in front of him. "We're not dead yet," he said instead. "If you're finally ready to help, you could go check on the fire teams on the balcony. Make sure they're ready."

Visibly, Grimaldi pulled himself back together. "Yes, I can do that," he said. "Do you want me to go look at the loading dock area, too?"

"Sure," Orozco said. There wasn't much to do back there that hadn't already been done, but he could understand Grimaldi's sudden burning desire to do *something*. "Then come back here and I'll set you up with one of the flanks. Any more of your allies sitting it out?"

Grimaldi winced at the word *allies*. "Probably," he admitted. "I don't know how good most of them will be in a fight, though."

"Trust me, there'll be plenty of work for them to do," Orozco assured him. "We need people to carry ammo, patrol the inside perimeter, carry messages, move and assist the wounded, build and repair barricades and fire stations, and eventually move the dead."

A muscle in Grimaldi's cheek twitched. "You want all the children here, too?"

"Anyone who can help, yes," Orozco said. "No one gets a free pass tonight."

"I understand," Grimaldi said. "I'll go get them."

He moved away.

Orozco watched him go, then turned back to the darkened street outside the archway. Listening hard to the minigun fire, he tried to estimate the position of each of the groups of Terminators. And to estimate when one of those groups would arrive at the Ashes.

Full night had fallen, and the team was indeed ready, when Connor finally heard the distant sound of mini-gun fire.

"That's it, people," he said. "Time to move."

The other men and women in the room didn't need to be told twice. Already they were grabbing their packs and guns and doing their final weapons checks.

"One minute," Connor said.

Sixty seconds later, they were ready. He cracked the door and took a careful look outside. All seemed clear.

"Remember: radio silence if at all possible," he said. "David?"

David nodded, and he and his demolition squad slipped past, disappearing into the night as they headed out toward the access shaft where they would enter the tunnel that ran alongside the Skynet warehouse. Tunney was next, his squad slated to follow David's group as rearguard until they split off to approach the staging area from the west.

The newcomers were with the latter group, Callahan and the Iliakis and young Zac. They had wanted to go with Barnes's squad, but Connor had judged Tunney's to be the one where they would be in the least danger, as well as where their inexperience was least likely to get someone else killed.

Ideally, of course, he would have preferred to leave them here with Kate in the relative safety of the temp base. But they'd made it clear that they were going to go out there, either with Connor's people or by themselves. Better they at least go with someone who could look out for them.

The Iliakis were the last of the squad out the door, and Connor felt a twinge of guilt as he watched them go. Carol had quietly insisted on going into danger with her husband, exactly as Kate had wanted to do with *her* husband.

Only in her case, Connor had said no.

And then it was Connor's turn. He gave Kate a silent nod good-bye, got one in return, and led his team out into the night. Distantly, he wondered if Kate was thinking about the Iliakis, too.

The gunfire had slackened somewhat, he noted as he and his four teammates moved quickly but cautiously through the deserted streets on their way to the staging area's southern edge. The Terminators must have finished off one of their targets and were in the process of moving on to the next one.

Fortunately, the recruitment tours they'd made of the neighborhood had marked most of the inhabited buildings, where the Terminators were going to be gathering. Hopefully, the routes Connor and Tunney had mapped out would get them all where they needed to be with a minimal chance of running into trouble along the way.

"Shh-shh!" Someone behind Connor hissed a warning.

Instantly, Connor dropped into a crouch, the rest of the squad doing likewise. *Minimal*, the thought flashed through his mind, *doesn't mean zero.*

Half a block to their right, striding away from them down the street, were a pair of T-600s.

Connor eased his hand away from his rifle and onto one of the blast grenades at his belt. The Terminators were facing away from his squad, their attention clearly elsewhere. But that didn't mean they might not suddenly decide to look behind them.

Especially given that Skynet's spotters were already in the air. The HKs drifting over the city were playing it cool, running with spotlights off and minimal turbofans. But Connor could hear their rumble as they watched for any refugees who might try to slip past its ground forces.

But like the T-600s themselves, the HKs were evidently focusing for the moment on their own map of targeted buildings, leaving the neighborhood's uninhabited areas alone. The two T-600s came to the end of the block, turned the corner, and vanished from sight.

Still watching the corner, Connor rose from his crouch.

"Damn, that was close," Tony Tantillo muttered. "Where's our air support, anyway?"

"It'll be here," Connor assured him.

Somewhere down the street, from the vicinity of the Moldavia, the miniguns opened up again. *All those children*, Kate had said earlier, troubled by the thought of leaving them to die. *All those children....*

But it was out of Connor's hands now. Signaling to his team to follow, he continued on into the night.

Yoshi was strapping into his A-10 when Blair finally made it to the hangar.

"Come on, come on—the call came three minutes ago," Yoshi called impatiently. "What's the holdup?"

"Ninety seconds," Blair promised as she sprinted toward her own fighter. "Wince? Yo—Wince?"

"Right here," the old man said, popping into view around her plane's nose. "You're all set. I think."

"What do you mean, you *think*?" Blair asked as she stopped beside him.

"I got you an extra 150 rounds for your GAU-8, just like you wanted," he said, patting the Gatling gun protruding from the plane's nose. "But I have to tell you: there's a chance—a really small chance—that the gun will jam up first thing off the chocks."

"Really," Blair said. "Let me get this straight. My options are either I get to completely snooker the HKs with extra firepower, or else I get to be flying toast?"

Wince made a face.

"Something like that."

"Good enough," Blair said, grabbing the cockpit ladder and heading up. "I'll let you know what happens."

The hangar doors were open, and Yoshi was jockeying his A-10 out into the wide street beyond by the time Blair got her engines up to power. She gave Yoshi a thirty second head-start, then followed him out.

To her mild surprise, both planes reached the end of their avenue airstrip and made it into the night sky without any HKs appearing overhead to argue the point.

"Hickabick?" Yoshi's voice crackled in her headset. "How you doing?"

"Smooth and hungry," Blair replied, glancing over her board. The GAU-8's counter, she noted, still indicated her ammo load at 1100 rounds, which implied that Wince's extra one-fifty weren't being registered. She would have to remember that as she watched her fire count. "Ready to kick some?"

"You bet," Yoshi said. "You're on cleanup—follow me in."

His A-10 turned left toward the Skynet staging area. Blair matched the maneuver, falling back far enough off his tail to make sure he had all the fighting room he might need. There were four HKs in the air over there, running dark and probably quiet, drifting along over the multi-block region like vultures waiting for something to die.

Little did Skynet know.

She and Yoshi had covered about half the distance when the HKs suddenly seemed to notice that they had company. Two of them veered suddenly out of their lazy search pattern and turned toward the A-10s, jumping like scalded frogs as they kicked their turbofans to full power.

"Watch it—two more coming in from the north," Yoshi warned.

Blair peered in that direction, to find that the two new bandits were also coming in dark. Big surprise there.

"I see them," she confirmed. "Which ones do you want?"

"You know how my vertigo is," Yoshi said.

Blair smiled tightly.

"Happy hunting," she said. Twisting her stick over, she sent the A-10 into a hard turn north toward the incoming HKs, a turn that would certainly exacerbate the imaginary vertigo of any pilot.

The two newcomers were coming in fast she noted as she settled into an intercept course. Way too fast for a typical dogfight. Had Skynet analyzed her performance over the years and concluded its best bet was a high-speed skimmer attack?

Or had it conceded the point of her combat record and decided to simply ram her and be done with it?

There was one way to find out. Aiming her A-10 squarely between the two incoming aircraft, she nudged up her speed.

The hardest part about playing chicken, the old saying went, *is knowing when to flinch.* But the HKs didn't seem to have heard that one. Neither aircraft veered so much as a degree off their intercept course as they all rushed toward each other. Blair gave it three more seconds, and then it was time to flinch.

But not the kind of flinch she would normally do in this situation. Not her usual tight evasive turn to left or right. Doing the same thing over and over against Skynet was a guaranteed way of getting yourself killed. Instead, she jammed the stick forward, dropping her nose and throwing her A-10 into a power dive toward the streets below.

She was instantly vindicated as the two HKs split formation, twisting to right and left as they shot past overhead. Had she turned in either of those directions, she would have ended the evening inside a massive fireball.

Which might still happen. For the second time in three days, the dark streets were rushing up at an ungodly speed. *Gotta stop doing this*, she told herself firmly as she hauled back on the stick, twisting her fighter up again just in time to avoid splatting herself all over the landscape. Setting her teeth as her plane switched from power dive to power climb, she waited to the near-stall moment and rolled over into her signature Immelmann turn.

She leveled off, eased back on the throttle, and searched the sky for her opponents.

She'd half expected the HKs to try to take advantage of her vulnerability during the dive by turning around and attacking. Instead, the two aircraft were speeding away from her at full speed, curving around toward the northeast and continuing to angle apart to keep her from taking both of them in a single one-two shot.

In the absence of a one-two shot, a one-one shot would do just as well. Lining up her nose with the HK on the right, she keyed for the GAU-8 and squeezed the trigger.

Wince had been concerned that his upgraded system would jam. Blair hadn't had any such doubts, and as usual she'd been right. The Avenger roared to life with all its throaty glory, spitting a river of 30mm destruction at the enemy aircraft. The river reached the HK, and in the fiery light of the machine's explosion Blair continued her turn and nailed the second one as well.

The two groups of flaming debris rained down on the long-suffering city. Blair put her A-10 into another curve back around toward the west. There was a third bonfire on the ground in the distance over there, where Yoshi had apparently taken out the first of his two targets, and Blair could see the faint flickers of gunfire flashing back and forth as he engaged the second. Beyond the dogfight, the two remaining HKs were still gliding over the staging area neighborhood, playing spotter duty for the mass slaughter going on in the streets below.

She gave the sky a quick scan, and then a more careful look. Far to the south, faintly silhouetted against the moonlit clouds, were two more HKs, probably part of Skynet's Capistrano radar tower defense. Either the neighborhood slated for tonight's destruction was a particularly important one, or else the computer figured it could afford to spend a few HKs for the chance to take out a couple of Resistance A-10s.

Blair smiled tightly. If burning through HKs was Skynet's plan for the night, she would be more than happy to accommodate it.

Turning her A-10 onto an intercept vector with the newcomers, she headed in.

The Terminators who had destroyed the Death's-Head compound were finally on the move.

Though not very well, or very quickly, Kyle noted. Even after a couple of hours' of running repairs, the three skinless machines were still limping badly as they headed toward the gap in the north barrier where he and Star had entered the compound earlier. Limping badly enough, in fact, that the three machines were actually shuffling along together as a group, with the two outer ones supporting the third. Their red eyes glowed bright in the moonlight, the faint sheen from their metal bodies looking strangely like human sweat.

But if those three no longer posed a serious threat, the fourth Terminator most certainly did. It walked a few paces behind them, matching their speed but with no trace of their limping. Its own eyes swept the compound alertly as it herded the damaged machines toward the gap, its minigun poised and ready.

Kyle tensed, holding himself as still as he could. If any one of the four Terminators happened to look into the cars they were passing...

But none of them did. One by one, they maneuvered through the gap and disappeared into the night.

Kyle took a deep breath, feeling the tension running out of him like rainwater off a collector gutter.

"They're gone," he whispered to Star.

There was a pause, and then she tugged gently on his sleeve and started signing.

"Wait a second," Kyle said, pulling the jacket away from their faces so that he could see her better in the dim light. The full chill of the night air struck him like a slap across the face. "What did you say?"

Where did they go? Star signed.

"I don't know," Kyle said. "They're gone. Isn't that enough?"

And right on cue came another burst of minigun fire, from somewhere west or northwest of them.

Somewhere in the general direction of Moldering Lost Ashes.

Kyle listened to the gunfire, his throat tightening. His people were under attack, people who had taken him and Star in when they didn't have anywhere else to go. And Orozco was there, too, who'd been their teacher, their guardian, and their friend.

But there was nothing he could do to help them. Besides, he'd promised Orozco he would stay away from the place.

And he had a responsibility already. A responsibility named Star.

"Come on," he said. He eased himself up out of his sitting position, wincing at the sudden twinges of pain in muscles that had been too still for too long. Getting a grip on the edge of the windshield frame, he pulled himself out of the car.

From inside, only the very edges of the compound had been visible. From outside, though, the full extent of the carnage could be seen. Kyle stared at the bodies littering the street, his stomach churning, a small part of his stunned mind grateful that the darkness hid most of the details.

He turned back as Star emerged from the car.

"Over here," he said, putting an arm around her shoulders and turning her away from the bodies and toward the gap between the cars. "We need to make sure Fido's still with the broken ones."

She frowned up at him. *Fido?*

"The Terminator who chased us after they killed Vuong and the others," Kyle explained, grimacing at the memory. The traders had made their own promise to Orozco, a promise to protect him and Star. And had been murdered for their efforts. "It's just something to call it."

What does it mean?

"I don't know," Kyle said. "I heard once that it was a name people used to call dogs. Family dogs," he added as her eyes widened. "Not the wild ones." Stepping to the edge of the gap, he looked carefully out.

The damaged Terminators hadn't made it very far. They were not quite a block away, plodding along together like gangers drunk on homemade wine. Fido was still walking behind them, its head turning back and forth. Probably looking for fresh targets, now that Skynet's killing spree had begun.

Star caught his arm. *Where are we going?*

"Somewhere away from here," he told her, giving Fido one last look and then stepping back into shelter around the front of the car. "We'll head east, the direction we were going when...you know."

What about Orozco and the people at the Ashes?

Kyle grimaced. Star had that *look* about her, the one that said she was about to go all stubborn on him. "There's nothing we can do to help them," he told her firmly. "Besides, Orozco told us not to come back."

The *look* darkened a little more. *We can't just leave them.*

"Orozco told us not to come back," Kyle repeated, starting to get angry.

We can't just leave them, Star signed again, and crossed her arms across her chest.

Kyle clenched his teeth hard enough to hurt. Couldn't she see he was trying to help her?

And then he took a closer look at her face. Behind the angry defiance, he could see the trembling lower lip and the tears in her eyes.

He sighed. She knew what he was trying to do, all right. But running away...she wouldn't be able to live with herself afterward.

Actually, come to think of it, Kyle wasn't sure he could, either.

"Fine," he said, giving up. "Stay here a second. I'll go find a couple of guns and we'll go back to the Ashes and see what we can do to help."

Steeling himself, he headed into the compound.

There were dozens of guns lying around the street among the dead bodies. Kyle chose a rifle with a nearly full clip, gingerly removing an extra clip from the body of the man whose fingers were still wrapped around the weapon. A pump shotgun was next, along with a small pouch full of extra shells. Additional ammo for his Colt wasn't quite as simple, but it took only four tries to find someone carrying rounds of the right caliber.

He was stuffing the extra cartridges into his pockets when Star suddenly appeared at his side, her face taut. *It's coming back*, she signed.

Kyle didn't need to hear any more. "Let's go," he muttered, throwing a quick look behind him as he looped the shotgun over his shoulder and grabbed the rifle. Nudging Star ahead of him, he headed toward the line of cars at the southern end of the compound.

Star had ducked through the wide gap the other Terminators had made, and Kyle was starting to follow, when the roar of automatic fire split the night and a crackle of shots slammed across the car beside him.

Kyle threw himself behind the car as a second burst

shredded the rusting metal. "Go!" he shouted at Star, looking around. "That building—there," he added, pointing to a dilapidated four-story structure just to the west of them. "Go on—I'll catch up."

Star's eyes were wide with fear, but she nodded and sprinted toward the building. Lifting the rifle to his shoulder, Kyle eased back to the end of the car and looked around it.

Fido was striding across the compound, its glowing red eyes sweeping the area as it looked for something to kill. Sighting carefully along the barrel of his rifle, Kyle squeezed off a shot.

The round slammed into the Terminator's hip, and for a moment its stride faltered as it worked to regain its balance. Kyle fired another shot, this time at the machine's knee. It again staggered slightly, then sent another burst from its minigun into Kyle's shelter. Kyle fired twice more, then ducked back from the gap and headed after Star.

The girl had made good headway, but Kyle had longer legs and he caught up with her before she was more than halfway to their target building. "Come on," he said, grabbing her hand and pulling her along with him. If they could get into the building before the Terminator made it through the line of cars, they had a chance.

If they couldn't, they were both dead.

CHAPTER FOURTEEN

John's team slipped out into the night, and Kate was all alone.

For a few minutes she paced around the narrow building, pausing occasionally to arrange or rearrange the stacks of extra clothing, food, and weapons that the attack teams had left behind, just for something to do. Outside, she could hear Skynet's slaughter working its way through the neighborhood, and she found herself wincing with each burst of minigun fire. Sooner or later, if they hadn't already, the Terminators were going to reach the Moldavia building.

All those people. All those children....

She stopped by the door, glaring at it as if it was the door's fault she was stuck in here. *It isn't fair*, she groused to herself. The new recruits had gotten to go with the teams. Even Leon and Carol Iliaki, and she knew John was aware of his blatant hypocrisy on that one. Leon's wife was allowed to fight alongside *her* husband, but Kate wasn't allowed to fight alongside hers.

She took a deep, ragged breath. *Stop it*, she told herself firmly as guilt momentarily eclipsed her anger. This was ridiculous, and disgustingly out of character besides.

She didn't much care for mood swings in others, and she liked them even less in herself.

But damn it, it wasn't *fair*. She should have stood up to John. She should have done something about this.

And abruptly, she decided she would.

Slinging her medical bag over her shoulder, she picked up her rifle and cautiously opened the door. No one and nothing was moving out there. Listening to the deadly clatter of minigun fire and the pounding of her own heart, she headed out into the darkness.

The sounds of the distant explosions faded away, and as they did so another burst of minigun fire rattled across the cold night air. Balancing precariously on one of the skeletal seats in the overturned bus he and the others had moved into an hour ago, Barnes raised his head up through one of the glassless windows. Maybe this time there would be something out there to see.

Not yet. Wherever the Terminators were operating, whoever they were killing, they hadn't yet made it to this part of the neighborhood. Lowering his head, he dropped back into the bus's interior and looked at Dozer and Reynolds.

To find them looking right back at him.

"Something wrong?" he asked.

The two men glanced at each other. "Just wondering if us being here is really such a good idea," Dozer said.

Barnes grimaced. The man did have a point. When a team was as outnumbered and outgunned as theirs was, standard military doctrine was to stay together, taking advantage of mutual support and overlapping fields of fire. Connor had already gone out on a limb by sending David and Tunney out on their own, even if all three of those squads would eventually end up converging on the same target.

But to then split off Barnes's squad this way, especially given how isolated they now were from everyone else, was pushing the doctrine to breaking point.

But he wasn't going to tell Dozer that. You never second-guessed your commander in the middle of an operation. You especially didn't second-guess John Connor. "Connor knows what he's doing," he told the men brusquely.

"Sounds like they're getting closer," Simmons murmured. He was crouched at the wide opening where the bus's rear doors had once been, peering out into the night.

Barnes focused on the sound of the minigun bursts. Simmons was right. It wouldn't be long now.

"We have a specific plan?" Reynolds asked.

Barnes shrugged.

"We wait till they get near Moldavia's archway, then we blow 'em to splinters."

"I like it," Simmons commented dryly. "Simple, direct, and effective."

There was a sudden sound of feet on gravel, and Pavlova ducked in beside Simmons.

"They're coming," she said, panting as she holstered her .45 and picked up her rifle. "I make it five T-600s, heading in from the west on the second cross street to the north."

"Walking straight down Orozco's throat," Barnes growled. "Okay, take your—"

"Movement!" Simmons cut in. "Someone—human—coming around the first corner to the north. Heading our way."

Barnes cursed under his breath as he hurried toward

the rear of the bus. One of Orozco's people trying to make a run for it? Some lunatic ganger out for a stroll? He reached Simmons' side—

Just as Kate Connor slipped past Simmons into the bus. Barnes felt his mouth drop open in surprise. "What—?"

"John changed his mind," she said, breathing a little heavily as she unslung the rifle from her shoulder. "He thought I'd be safer with you than back there alone."

"Right," Barnes said, gazing hard into her eyes.

But she returned his gaze steadily, and after a moment Barnes gave a little shrug. If you didn't second-guess John Connor, you also didn't second-guess John Connor's wife.

"Fine," he said, pointing to the middle of the bus. "There's your station, right below mine and Simmons'. You'll be on reload and backup duty."

"Got it." Giving a brisk nod, Kate stepped past him and headed for the pile of ammo bags.

Barnes glanced around at the others. None of them looked particularly happy that Kate had crashed the party. But somehow, none of them looked all that surprised, either. "What are you all staring at?" he growled. "Get to your stations. We've got some Terminators to kill."

There was another burst of minigun fire, this one much closer than the last few had been. Orozco peered over the fountain wall toward the archway, resetting his grip on his M16.

It wouldn't be long now.

He took a moment to look to his left, across the line of men and a few women who were crouching with him along the back side of the fountain's wall. Half turning, he scanned the balcony, where the rest of the teams were lined up. With the building's rear and sides blocked and booby-trapped, the main entrance was now the only way for the Terminators to get in.

This was where the war for Moldering Lost Ashes would take place.

Everyone else knew that, too. And they were scared. Some of them were scared enough to be well on the way to being terrified.

But they were still there. None of them had dropped his or her weapon and scurried away to try to find somewhere to hide.

They were good people Orozco knew as he let his eyes drift across each of their faces. It had been a privilege to live here among such people for the past two years.

It would be an honor to die among them.

A figure moved in the shadows at the very edge of the archway, and Orozco turned back to see Grimaldi hurrying across the lobby toward them. The chief rounded the fountain and dropped into cover beside Orozco.

"They're coming," he said as he snatched up his rifle, his own fear under tight control. "Five Terminators, heading down the street straight toward us."

Orozco peered through the archway. He could see them now, too, dark figures moving against a slightly lighter background, striding through the shadow of the sniper nest building toward them.

"Five targets," Orozco confirmed, resting the barrel of his M16 on the fountain wall. By all rights, he knew, he should have been the one up there at the archway, exposing himself to danger as he watched for the enemy to make its appearance. But Grimaldi had insisted that Orozco was too valuable to their defense, and had taken that duty himself.

"Remember: aim for the heads and necks," he called softly to the rest of the fire team. "As they get closer, shift fire to hips and knees and try to cripple them. They'll be firing, too, very hard and very fast, so keep yourselves as much under cover as you can. Grenadiers, stay under cover until they trigger the traps and I call for you. And do *not* light your fuses until I give the word.

"Everyone understand what you're supposed to do?"

There was a flurry of tense acknowledgments.

"Good," Orozco said, thumbing off the M16's safety. "Hold your fire until they're past the building and start across the street—we might as well take advantage of what little light is out there."

He watched as the figures approached, lining up his sights on the head of the one in the center. The Terminators reached the edge of the building's shadow and stepped out into the pale moonlight, their rubber faces impassive, their right arms crooked at the elbow, their terrible miniguns pointed straight down the Ashes' throat.

Holding his breath, Orozco tightened his finger on his trigger—

And without warning, a brilliant flash of light erupted in the very center of the Terminators' formation. Two of the machines were instantly slammed flat on the ground by the impact. The other three staggered but managed to stay on their feet.

And as the shockwave from the blast echoed through the lobby, all hell broke loose outside.

For the first few seconds all Orozco could do was stare in disbelief as the Terminators lurched and jerked under the withering fire coming at them from somewhere to the south. The two that had gone down attempted to get back up, but their efforts were stymied as they came under the same pummeling attack. All five Terminators were firing back now, their miniguns stuttering with an angry bull-hornet buzz, but the return fire didn't seem to be having any effect on their attackers.

The hail of lead continued unabated, tearing away the machines' rubber skin and sending clouds of metal splinters into the air. Another grenade exploded in their midst, and one of the Terminators twisted violently as its right arm was blown completely off its body.

And with that, Orozco abruptly unfroze.

"Grenadiers: follow me," he shouted over the gunfire. Dropping the butt of his M16 onto the floor beside the fountain, he snatched up his lighter and two of the pipe bombs from beside him and sprinted for the archway.

His squad of bomb throwers were clearly even more befuddled by the sudden change in the situation than Orozco himself had been, and only two of them managed to unfuddle themselves fast enough to take him up on his invitation. But two were enough. With their full attention on the other attack, the beleaguered Terminators probably never even saw the three figures running toward them through the gloom.

Orozco lit one of his fuses as he ran, his peripheral vision confirming that his two companions were doing likewise. As he reached the archway he came to a halt and carefully lobbed his bomb directly beneath the feet of one of the machines. The others' bombs were right behind his.

Shouting a warning, Orozco turned his back and threw himself flat on the floor.

The three bombs went off nearly simultaneously, the multiple shock waves lifting Orozco a couple of centimeters and slamming him back down again. Rolling over, he looked behind him.

The barrage and the bombs had done the trick. All five Terminators were down, with severed metallic body parts strewn every which way across the pavement.

Through the ringing in his ears, Orozco suddenly realized the other gunfire had ceased. Focusing hard, he was just able to hear some running footsteps coming toward the archway.

He shifted his second bomb to his left hand and got a grip on his holstered Beretta. Better to be cautious, even though he was pretty sure he already knew who it was who had just saved their bacon for them.

Sure enough, a few seconds later the running footsteps slowed to a more cautious walk, and Barnes and two other men came into view.

For a moment the big black man and the Hispanic Marine locked eyes in the mutual look of men who knew what had just gone down, and therefore had no need to actually mention it. Then Barnes jerked his head toward the mass of metallic body parts that had recently been five of Skynet's killing machines.

"Don't just stand there," he growled to Orozco. "Split up the pieces before they try to put themselves back together."

"Right," Orozco said. Looking back at the fountain, he gestured to Grimaldi and the others to stay put, repeated the gesture to the two grenadiers beside him, then made a wide circle through the very northern edge of the archway and out into the street. A moment later he had joined Barnes and the others in their task of throwing chunks of smoking metal to the four winds.

He did note, though, that Barnes made a point of

examining the Terminators' five miniguns, putting aside the two that still seemed functional.

"I guess that'll have to do," Barnes said as he surveyed their handiwork. "Nice little bombs you got there."

"They're not bad," Orozco said. "All things being equal, I'd rather have a few bricks of C4. Thanks for the assist."

"Glad to help," Barnes said, his face hardening. "Yeah, a little C4 or thermite and we could do a *real* job on the damn things. Too bad. If Skynet can collect all the pieces, it can probably hammer one or two of 'em back together."

"Does Skynet even bother with retrieval?" Orozco asked. "I thought it had automated factories putting these things out."

"And we're doing every damn thing we can to put *those* out of business, too," Barnes said with grim satisfaction. "Yeah, it's been picking up wrecked Terminators wherever it can. Especially these T-600s."

"Nice to know Skynet has to scrabble for resources just like the rest of us," Orozco said with a grunt. "Maybe we can keep it too busy to bother with this particular batch of parts."

"We'll get the busy part, anyway," Barnes said, cocking his head to the side. "Hear that?"

Orozco frowned. As far as his still only half-functional ears could tell, the streets around them were completely silent.

"I don't hear anything."

"You got it," Barnes agreed. "All the T-600s that were out killing people have stopped."

Orozco's stomach tightened. "And have all been retasked to us."

"Yeah," Barnes said. "Fact, that's kind of what we had in mind."

"Wonderful," Orozco growled. "Does the bait get to hear more about this plan? Or do we just get to be bait?"

"Hey, pal, you were already dead," Barnes pointed out. "If this batch hadn't taken you out, the next wave would have."

Orozco glared at him. But the man was right.

"Point taken," he acknowledged reluctantly. "Let's try it again: you mind sharing the plan with the rest of the class?"

"Better," Barnes said, lowering his voice. "Here's the deal. We think we know where Skynet's staging area is for this operation. Most of our people have moved in and are ready to attack it."

"Only you need to make sure no one's home to spoil the surprise," Orozco said, nodding as it all became clear. "So we make noise and trouble out here so that all the machines will come out to play."

"Yeah, but don't worry—we'll be doing everything we can to help you," Barnes promised. "Thing is, if we can clear the staging area and then hold it so that the T-600s can't get back in to reload, we should have enough breathing space to take them out permanently."

"Until Skynet sends in more, anyway," Orozco said.

"Shouldn't be any," Barnes said. "That's what a staging area's for. Skynet moves a bunch of Terminators in so it can mass them for a major op—"

He broke off as, without warning, a Hunter-Killer abruptly shot into view around the corner, its Gatling guns roaring.

Orozco dived for cover beneath the edge of the archway's overhang, Barnes and the other two men right behind him. The HK angled itself upward, braking to a hovering halt in front of the building. It swiveled around, bringing its weapons to bear on the four sitting ducks.

And made a hard skid to the side as a shredding volley of automatic fire slammed up into it from down the street. The HK spun around, its quarry suddenly forgotten as it clawed madly for altitude and distance. It reached the end of the block and disappeared from sight, fire hammering it the whole way.

"Damn," Barnes muttered as he and Orozco got cautiously to their feet again. "Thought we had that one for sure. Skynet's usually smart enough not to send them down into city streets where someone with a high-power weapon can—"

"Barnes!" one of the other Resistance men snapped. He was kneeling over the other man, and in the dim starlight Orozco could see a dark stain spreading across the downed soldier's chest.

Barnes stepped over to them, grabbing at his combo earphone/wire-mike. "One down," he snapped. "Kate, Pavlova—get over here."

Orozco looked south as two women appeared from the overturned bus and headed toward the Ashes at a dead run. "What can I do?" he asked.

"If you've got a medic handy, send him over," Barnes said, squatting down beside the injured man. "If not, we got it covered."

The two women arrived and deftly shouldered the men aside as they broke out medical kits. Orozco watched them work, and it was only as one of them turned briefly into the glow of a small flashlight that he realized it was Kate Connor, the woman who'd made that dramatic appearance earlier on the Ashes' balcony.

"Snap it up," Barnes said, looking around them. "We need to get under cover."

"You're not going to try to use that bus again, I hope," Orozco said. "Skynet knows you were in there. It's probably already got a T-600 or two on the way."

"You got any suggestions?"

"Right there," Orozco said, pointing to the building across the street. "We've got a sniper's nest up on the second floor overlooking our entrance. We knocked out the walls so that it runs all the way along the building's eastern side, including the two corner apartments. We also put in a bunch of extra shielding, mostly scavenged stone and brick."

"Sounds good," Barnes said, running a quick eye over the building. "We'll take it."

Turning toward the bus, he waved. A moment later, a man loaded with heavy machineguns and ammo boxes slipped out of the front and headed toward them, staggering under his load. A grunted order from Barnes, and the other uninjured Resistance man headed back to help him.

Orozco looked down at the wounded man. The two women had finished with him, at least for now, and were packing up their gear. "Is he going to make it?" he asked.

"He should," Kate said. "He's stable, at least for now."

"You need any help carrying him inside?" Orozco asked.

"We got it," Barnes said.

"Okay," Orozco said. "Oh—very important. If you decide you need to come in here for any reason, stick to the edges of the archway, the places where it's too low for a Terminator to get through without ducking."

Kate's eyes flicked upward to the archway.

"Understood," she said.

The two men arrived, puffing under their load of munitions. At Barnes's hand signal, they headed across the street and disappeared into the sniper nest building. "I guess this is it," he said, nodding to Orozco.

Orozco nodded back. "See you on the other side."

Barnes slung the two captured T-600 miniguns over his shoulders with his other weapons. Then, stooping down, he carefully lifted the injured man in his arms.

Orozco must have looked as astonished as he felt, because Kate chuckled. "Clean living," she explained dryly. "Good luck, Sergeant."

"And to you, Ma'am."

She and Barnes headed across the street. Orozco checked both directions, then made his way carefully back through the archway and returned to the fountain.

"Who were they?" Grimaldi asked. "It was too dark to see."

"Nobody special," Orozco said. "Just the people you drew down on this morning."

He had the minor satisfaction of seeing Grimaldi's eyes widen.

"Oh, hell," the chief muttered.

"Yeah, well, don't panic," Orozco advised him. "They're here to help."

Grimaldi looked over at the building across the street...and for the first time, Orozco saw some actual hope creeping into the other's eyes.

"I hope you thanked them," he said.

"I did," Orozco said. "You'll get a chance later to do that yourself."

"I hope so," Grimaldi said. "You want me back on watch?"

Orozco shook his head.

"No need. When the next batch gets here, we'll know it."

There had been a couple of bad moments along the way, the worst being when Fido made it through the Death's-Head barrier before Kyle and Star had quite reached the building they were heading for. The Terminator managed to unload a couple of bursts of fire before they could get inside, but the distance and piles of rubble protected them.

And then they were through the sagging doorway, Kyle pulling Star to the side as the machine behind them uselessly hammered a third burst of fire into the concrete wall.

"That was close," Kyle muttered, breathing heavily as he eased back to the doorway for a look.

The Terminator was still coming, of course. If there was one thing about Terminators, it was that they didn't give up.

He stepped back out of the doorway and looked around. He and Orozco had checked out this place a few months ago, hoping to increase their farming area. But the structure had turned out to be too dangerous, with the flooring in particular badly decayed in far too many places.

One of the worst of those places was right here on the first floor.

He returned to where Star was huddled against a sagging wall, wheezing a little as she panted, an uneasy look on her face as she glanced around. She'd stepped though one of the floor's weak spots on that last visit, and would probably have fallen all the way to the sub-basement if Orozco hadn't grabbed her arm in time to pull her out.

"Come on," Kyle whispered, taking her hand. "Don't worry—I remember where the safe paths are."

Star looked doubtful, but she nevertheless allowed Kyle to help her to her feet and lead the way around flaking concrete pillars and decaying wooden walls.

The building's wide central corridor was just as Kyle remembered it: a single two-foot-wide line of solid tile running above an under-floor girder, with five feet on either side of equally solid-looking tiling that rested on utterly rotten joists and floorboards. Kyle led Star along the safe path to the far end of the corridor and settled her behind a rusting stove.

"Stay here," he told her, taking the shotgun and handing her the rifle. Grabbing a length of half-shredded copper tubing that lay partly buried in dust beside the stove, he returned to the corridor.

He walked back to the middle of the central path and poked a couple of holes into the flooring, one on either side, with his knife. Bending the tubing into a U-shape, he pushed the ends into the holes he'd made, turning it into a sort of copper rainbow and what had to be the world's most obvious tripwire. He returned to the corridor's far end and then worked his way through the row of half-shattered rooms flanking the corridor until he'd reached a spot directly across from the tubing.

Settling himself near a large hole that looked out into the corridor, he pressed his eye against a much smaller hole and waited.

He had barely gotten in position when the Terminator appeared.

For a long moment the machine stood motionless at the end of the corridor, its head panning back and forth as its blazing red eyes assessed the situation. Kyle watched, wondering whether the machine might just walk carelessly ahead onto the rotten floor and end the problem right there.

But no such luck. Either the Terminator had sensors that warned it of the floor's hazards, or else the presence and positioning of the copper tubing in the middle of the floor was enough of a clue for it to come to the logical conclusion. With one final sweep of its head, it stepped forward onto the safe path. The tiles creaked ominously under its weight, but held. Holding its minigun ready, the machine started forward.

Keep going, Kyle urged it silently, fingering his shotgun as he watched it picking its way carefully along. It reached the tubing—

And stopped.

Kyle held his breath, knowing there were two ways it might choose to deal with the obstacle facing it. The most obvious would be for it to merely reach down and pluck the tubing out of the floor. In that case, Kyle and Star were in big trouble.

But the machine—and the Skynet computer that controlled it—had no way of knowing how long the tubing had been there. For all Skynet knew, it might have been there for hours or days, connected to some immensely clever, immensely destructive booby trap.

Which left option number two...and as Kyle watched, the Terminator lifted one foot high and started to carefully step over the tubing.

It was in mid-step, its entire weight balanced on a single foot, when Kyle lined up his shotgun with the hole in the wall and fired two shots squarely into the machine's massive torso.

The Terminator reacted instantly, dropping its airborne

foot back to the floor in an attempt to reestablish its balance. Unfortunately for it, the only floor within reach was useless for the purpose. With a loud snapping of broken wood and tile, the Terminator crashed through the floor and vanished from sight.

Kyle retraced his steps as quickly as he safely could, to find that Star had abandoned her refuge by the stove and was standing at the end of the corridor, peering at the huge hole in the floor.

Is it dead? she signed.

Her answer was a burst of machinegun fire from the subbasement below them.

"Not unless there are miniguns in hell," Kyle said grimly, grabbing her arm and pulling her out of the line of fire. "Let's get out of here."

And go back to the Ashes? she signed, looking closely at him.

Kyle grimaced. He'd hoped the run-in with Fido might have changed her mind, that she would realize how useless they would be in a straight-up fight and let him take her away from the death and hell their neighborhood had become.

But if the look on her face was anything to go by, she was more determined than ever.

Star's instincts regarding Terminators had never been wrong yet. He would just have to trust that she was right this time, too.

"Sure," he said, taking the rifle from her and slinging the shotgun over his shoulder. "Let's go."

"Tee two: first swing double eagle." Barnes's voice crackled through Connor's earphone. "Teeing up for swing two."

The earphone went silent, and Connor took a careful breath. So Skynet's first assault on the Moldavia had been beaten back, and Barnes's team was getting ready for the Terminators to try again. That was good.

But all the preliminary success in the world couldn't help soothe the churning in his gut.

One of Barnes's team had gotten hit...and Barnes had called both Pavlova *and* Kate in to help him.

Which implied that Kate had been right there with them, despite Connor's specific instruction that she was to stay in the temp base.

The question was why the hell *had* she been there?

But he couldn't ask her that question. Even if it hadn't been vital that he and the others lurking near the staging area maintain radio silence, he couldn't put a question like that on an open channel.

Because he knew full well why she'd sneaked off and joined Barnes's squad. He'd seen the expression on her face when she realized he was letting Leon and Carol Iliaki go into danger together while Kate herself had to stay behind.

The children of the Moldavia, and her need to prove herself a worthy leader, had apparently been stronger than the constraints of obedience to her commander. *And* husband.

He took a deep breath, forcing his anger away. There was a time for emotion, and the middle of combat wasn't it.

But assuming they all survived the next few hours, he and Kate were going to have a long, serious talk.

"Movement," McFarland murmured from beside him. "East door."

Connor peered between the broken boards that shielded

his squad's position, gazing across the patch of open ground at the sagging warehouse. The east door, which had been shut a minute ago, was now open. A moment later, two T-600s strode out into the moonlight, heading southeast at full speed across the open area.

Connor watched as they headed toward the protective mounds of rubble ringing the warehouse, feeling an unpleasant tingle of suspicion. The Terminators weren't heading anywhere near his squad, and were showing no indication that they were even paying attention to anything in this direction. But there was always the chance that Skynet was playing it cute, that the T-600s were planning to climb over the rubble, circle south, and come up on them from behind.

Bishop was the squad member currently farthest to the rear. Connor caught her eye and nodded his head behind her. She nodded an acknowledgment and silently slipped away to play scout and rear guard.

"Funny," McFarland murmured in his ear. "I'd have thought Skynet would have had to lose at least one more round before sending in the reserves."

"And then send more than just two of them," Connor agreed. "Maybe those two are on some different errand."

McFarland grunted. "My condolences to whoever's at the other end."

Connor nodded. "Agreed."

The last of the HKs spun around, its starboard engine sending up clouds of thick smoke, and crashed to the ground, bursting into flames on impact.

Blair checked the rest of the sky around her, just to be sure, then once again turned her A-10 back toward the beleaguered neighborhood where she was supposed to be helping out.

Still, all things considered, it had been a remarkably quick battle. She'd dealt very efficiently with the first two Capistrano HKs, destroying both before the four in the follow-up wave were close enough to join in. The sheer number of opponents had made that second dogfight trickier, but whatever Skynet's knowledge of aerial tactics, the HKs' physical limitations simply didn't give the computer much to work with.

In the end, Blair had turned all four machines into blazing scrap metal, and Skynet had apparently decided it had taken enough losses for one night.

But the victory had been costly. Her single Sidewinder missile was gone, and the counter on her GAU-8 showed only five rounds left.

Which, thanks to Wince, meant she actually had 155 rounds. Enough to deliver one good sucker punch, maybe two, before Skynet woke up to the fact that its own count was seriously off.

That ought to be enough for Yoshi and me to take out the final two HKs and give Connor the clear air space that he needs—

Blair's train of thought froze. The two HKs were still there, still meandering their watch over Skynet's mass slaughter.

But in the distance to the north another HK had appeared from somewhere and was engaged in a savage dogfight with Yoshi's plane.

And Yoshi's A-10 was on fire.

"Hang on, Jinkrat," she snapped as she twisted her fighter toward them. "I'm on my way."

"Stay there," Yoshi ordered, his voice nearly inaudible

over the staccato beat of the shells slamming into his cockpit and the roar of the flames blazing around him. "You've got a job to do. Do it."

"Damn it all, Jinkrat—"

"So long, Hickabick," Yoshi interrupted her, his voice calm with the quiet serenity of someone who sees death approaching. "Kill a few for me, will you?"

"I will," Blair promised, her stomach twisted into a hard, nauseated knot. "Good-bye, Yoshi."

"Good-bye, Blair."

And with that, Yoshi spun his crippled fighter around in an impossibly tight turn and rammed its nose full speed into the HK's side.

The vehicles were still locked together in their death embrace as they tumbled in a blazing fireball to the earth.

Blair blinked sudden tears from her eyes, her throat aching. The odds had finally caught up to Yoshi...and Blair had lost yet another friend.

But at least this time she'd been able to say good-bye.

She turned her eyes back to the two hovering HKs, forcing down the pain and grief and fury. Allowing those emotions to control her would only get her killed, too. Yoshi wouldn't want that, nor would any of the rest of the long line of ghosts of her late comrades, a line forever haunting the back of her mind. They would all want her to live, and to keep fighting, and to send Skynet and its damned killing machines to hell.

"Skynet, this is Hickabick," Blair said softly into her radio. "Ready or not, here I come."

CHAPTER FIFTEEN

The first attack had been, in Orozco's opinion, arrogantly casual, almost to the point of carelessness.

Skynet had learned from its mistake. It had learned all too well.

The second attack was brutal. There were at least ten of the hulking T-600s involved this time, their miniguns blasting away in a brute-force approach that tore at least three centimeters off the stone of the archway, pockmarked every one of the lobby walls, and destroyed most of the fountain wall that the first-line defenders were using as cover.

When the dust finally settled, five of those first-line defenders were dead.

"Damn every one of them to hell," Grimaldi snarled as he and Orozco stood next to what was left of the archway, peering cautiously outside as the frantic clatter of barricade rebuilding went on behind them. The street looked even worse than the building itself, Orozco noted, with fragments of at least five more Terminators lying among the bullet scorings and grenade pits.

Some of those pieces were already trying to pull themselves back together.

"Damn it—look," Grimaldi snapped, jabbing a finger

toward one of the quivering pieces. "It's—"

Snatching the chief's arm, Orozco yanked him back under cover just as a burst of minigun fire burned through the air where his hand had been.

"Careful," Orozco warned mildly. "You may need that hand later."

"Not likely, the way things are going," Grimaldi muttered. "But thanks." He nodded toward the Terminator parts. "How many of them do you think will reform?"

"No idea," Orozco said. "They've certainly got plenty of raw material to work with, though. Especially since all the parts from that first assault are also still there."

"I hadn't thought about those," Grimaldi admitted, shaking his head. "Damn it. You can't kill them; and even when you do, they don't stay dead."

"They die permanently enough if you blow up their skulls or cook their electronics," Orozco said. "Otherwise, no, they don't go easy."

The chief ducked his head to peer out at the building across the street, which looked in worse shape than the street and the Ashes' lobby combined.

"You suppose any of those folks survived?"

"If I had to bet on any of us getting through this, I'd bet on them," Orozco said candidly. "The real question is whether they'll be able to do anything more to help us, what with those Terminators that seem to have moved into the bus down there. Between that bunch and the ones to the north, Skynet pretty well owns the street right now."

Grimaldi grunted. "Damned stupid bus," he said sourly. "We should have blown the thing up years ago."

"You're right, we should have," Orozco agreed. "A little too late now."

Grimaldi sighed. "Yeah, I know. I'm not blaming you, you know."

"I know," Orozco assured him. Some men dealt with danger by swearing, or praying, or clamming up completely. Others, like Grimaldi, opened their mouths and babbled.

"Wait a second—maybe it *isn't* too late," Grimaldi said suddenly, leaning a little farther out toward the edge of the archway, though not far enough to draw any fire. "We've still got some of your pipe bombs left, right? Could we toss one into the bus from the southwest sentry post?"

Orozco shook his head. "The second-floor overhang would block the toss. Ditto for anywhere else we can get to in the building."

"Damn," Grimaldi muttered. "So what *do* we do?"

Orozco looked back into the lobby, where Wadleigh and Killough and the others had nearly completed the replacement barricade.

"We finish getting the barricade set up, make sure our guns are loaded, and wait for the next wave," he said.

"Yeah." Grimaldi looked up at the archway. "Who knows? Maybe they'll actually make it through the archway this time."

"It could happen," Orozco said.

"Tee two: second swing eagle," Barnes's voice came again in Connor's ear. "Lobster remains, green eight, Gulliver, maybe hole four. Estimate all other greens cleared."

Connor shook his head, in relief and amazement both. Judging by the level of gunfire he and the others had heard coming from that direction, Skynet had cleared out the area, all right. It had cleared all its Terminators out of the other buildings and alleys and sent them straight at Barnes and the people in the Moldavia.

And it was almost for certain that the six T-600s that had just emerged from the staging area warehouse were heading out to join in the next wave.

The big question was whether those six were everything Skynet had kept in reserve, or whether there were more of them in there. Unfortunately, there was no way to know other than to walk inside and do a head count.

Meanwhile, some of the Terminators that had been wrecked would be pulling themselves back together, and those that were still whole would be running short of ammunition. Sooner or later, the machines would start coming back for reloading and field maintenance.

Connor and his men had to be inside and in control of the warehouse before that happened.

He watched the six Terminators as they climbed the wall of rubble, an idea niggling at the back of his brain. It would be risky, but it might be the way to force Skynet's hand.

He motioned McFarland close.

"Pass the word," he whispered in the man's ear. "As soon as those Terminators are clear, we're following them."

McFarland threw him a quick look.

"How far?" he asked.

"All the way," Connor told him. "Skynet probably thinks it's got Barnes pinned down, at least on a north-south line. I'm guessing this bunch is going to come in from the west, which means that if we come up behind them we'll be able to pin *them* down."

"Okay," McFarland said slowly, clearly still working

through this sudden change in plans. "What do we do about the warehouse?"

"*We* don't do anything," Connor said. "If we can help force Skynet to clear it out, David and Tunney should be able to take and hold it without us."

McFarland still looked doubtful, but nevertheless gave a brisk nod.

"Right," he said. Moving over to Joey Tantillo and his brother Tony, he began whispering the new orders.

Connor looked upward. Nothing was visible, but from the low rumble vibrating across the city he could tell that at least one HK was still moving around on spotter duty. Possibly more than one.

Resolutely, he looked away from the sky. Every leader faced the temptation of getting bogged down with all the details of an operation, and giving in to that urge was a sure way for the operation to end in disaster. The HKs were Blair's assignment, just as demolition was David's and decoy was Barnes's.

And all of them were damn good at what they needed to do. Connor had given the orders, assigned the best people to the tasks at hand, and now he had to sit back and let them do their jobs while he concentrated on doing his.

McFarland eased back up to his side.

"Ready," he murmured.

Connor nodded. "Nice and easy, and don't let them spot us," he said. "Let's go."

The HKs didn't change position as Blair drove in on them, but continued to hover over the battle zone, dark and silent, like a pair of overconfident street toughs inviting her to take her best shot.

But she wasn't fooled. There was no bravado in Skynet's programming—only cold, hard calculation. It knew Blair's GAU-8 was down to its last few rounds, and it was deliberately holding its HKs steady, probably hoping they could shoot her down into the neighborhood that she and the others were trying so hard to save.

She held her vector steady, once again playing chicken with the HKs. Unlike the last time they'd done this, though, Skynet apparently decided there was no point in sacrificing any of its killing machines by attempting to ram. She had barely reached the edge of their range when both HKs opened up with their Gatling guns, filling the air around her with lead.

Blair maintained her vector, wincing with the thud that came each time one of the rounds found its target. The single impacts became pairs and then triads as Blair closed the distance and the HKs fine-tuned their aim.

And as the triads became quads and suddenly blossomed into a hailstorm of impacts, Blair twisted the stick hard to the right, curving out of their line of fire and heading east.

"I'm hit!" she shouted into her mike. "I can't stay with you."

"Get clear, Hickabick," a voice came promptly in her headset. "You can't do any more back there."

Blair frowned. It was indeed the correct coded response to her coded fake distress announcement.

But that had been *Connor* giving the reply, not Barnes. Connor, who was supposed to be maintaining radio silence, lest Skynet figure out there was trouble lurking in its private little paradise. Could he have launched the warehouse attack already?

It seemed way too early for that. But then, the ground

operation wasn't Blair's concern. *Her* concern was clearing out the sky over Connor's head.

She was still in the middle of her evasive turn when one of the two HKs broke formation, revved its turbofans to full power, and turned onto an intercept vector.

Blair smiled grimly. Skynet had taken the bait.

Time to make it regret that decision.

It was one of those times, and there had been many in their life together, when John had done something Kate wasn't sure whether to be proud of, stunned at, or furious over.

"Hole four probable; forward bad lobster fifty; clear lobster duo," John's situation report ran through her earphone, the field jargon nearly as opaque to her as it hopefully was to Skynet.

"Check," Barnes replied crisply. "Tee two; Gulliver hole three; dogleg tee nine."

"Check," John said. "Clear lobster duo."

"Check."

The radio went silent again, and Barnes looked at Kate.

"You get all that?" he asked.

"Most of it," Kate told him, still struggling through the translation amid her swirling emotions. "I know he's left his position to come help us, or he wouldn't have used the radio."

"Yeah, but it's not just for us," Barnes said. "*Lobster* means five to ten T-600s coming in on a pincer."

"From the west," Kate added, visualizing the holes of the imaginary golf course that John had created for their position reports.

"Probably along that north cross street," Barnes said. "With T-600s north of us, and the damned busload to the south pinning us down—"

"That was the Gulliver reference," Pavlova put in helpfully.

"Yes, I got that," Kate told her.

"—the only retreat we had was out the back of the building," Barnes continued, throwing a brief scowl at Pavlova. "So now Skynet's trying to close that one off, too."

"Which then puts it into position to hit us from three sides," Kate said, her annoyance fading. *As long as he's concerned for the whole squad's safety, and not just mine.*

"Right," Barnes said. "But what Skynet doesn't know is that Connor's squad is coming up *behind* this new bunch. When they get within range, a couple of us'll pop open the back door and hit them from the front while Connor hits them from the back."

"Movement," Simmons called from the north-facing wall, his eye pressed to one of the holes the Terminators' last attack had opened up in the brick and stone. "Five T-600s, middle of the street, moving in."

Barnes barked a laugh.

"Yeah, right. Middle of the street. That must be the ones who're out of ammo, or just about. Simmons, wait'll they get into Orozco's line of fire before you take them. Might as well cross-fire 'em. Pavlova, Dozer; you're out the back door with me."

There was a brief shuffling of weapons and feet, and then the three of them were gone.

"Where do you want me?" Kate asked, crossing to Simmons' side.

"Thanks, but I can handle these," Simmons told her. "You just stay with Reynolds."

"There's nothing more I can do to help him," Kate said. "Tell me what I can do to help *you.*"

Simmons' lip twitched. "I guess you could go back there and keep an eye on the bus," he said, gesturing behind him at the south wall.

"You know, I *can* shoot," she pointed out.

"I know," Simmons said, just a little too quickly. "But Barnes is right—this bunch is probably out of ammo, which means they're coming in mostly to distract us. We don't want the ones in the bus blindsiding us while we're potshotting clay pigeons."

"Fine," she fumed, and retreated across the room to the position Simmons had indicated. The assignment made sense—it really did. And if she wasn't here to handle that job, Dozer or Pavlova, one of the more experienced fighters, would have had to take it.

But logical or not, it still felt like Simmons was babying her. And she hated being babied.

She squeezed her rifle hard. *Stop it*, she ordered herself. What was *with* her these days, anyway? Anger at perfectly legitimate orders, her strange mood swings, this near-obsession she'd suddenly developed for the Moldavia's children, when people were dying all around her? Maybe she was just grouchy because she seemed to start every morning these days feeling nauseated...

She froze. *Oh, no. No. Not now.*

"You okay?"

She looked back at Simmons. He was eyeing her oddly. "I'm fine," Kate assured him as calmly as she could, fighting the sudden impulse to run somewhere safe and hide.

There wasn't anywhere that was safe. Not here in the middle of a fire zone.

Besides, she had a job to do.

She searched for a moment until she found a spot

where she could watch the Terminators in the bus and also keep an eye on the wide archway leading into the Moldavia. If she was going to protect her squad from a sneak attack from the south, she might as well do the same for Orozco and his people, too.

Wiping the sweat from her hands, trying to settle the sudden horrible fluttering in her stomach, she got a firm grip on her rifle and settled in to watch.

CHAPTER SIXTEEN

Blair had dodged and jinked and run and been as panic-stricken as she could possibly manage, taking fire on her beloved A-10's tail the whole way.

But all the crap had been worth it...because she'd finally succeeded in drawing the pursuing HK away from Connor and over a completely uninhabited part of the city.

Payback time.

She pulled back on her stick, guiding her fighter up and over into yet another of the Immelmann turns that Skynet probably had memorized by now. But that was fine, because she knew that the quickest and most straightforward way for the pursuing HK to counter the maneuver would be to simply lift straight up, wait for Blair to turn toward it, and then pour point-blank fire down her throat.

Sure enough, as she finished her roll and leveled off, she found the HK hovering a hundred meters directly in front of her.

And as its Gatlings opened up, Blair squeezed her GAU-8's trigger.

The HK had no chance to even try to dodge away from the utterly unexpected attack. It disintegrated into a huge fireball right where it was, sending pieces of itself flying in all directions. Blair twisted her stick again, guiding the A-10 around the worst of the explosion.

"Hickabick: one down," she called into her radio as she curved back toward the main combat zone. "Number two in my sights."

Or maybe not, she amended to herself. In the distance ahead, the last HK suddenly poured power into its turbofans and headed south. Trying to get to the relative safety of the Skynet forces at Capistrano, or else hoping Blair would chase it within range of those forces.

Which was pretty much what Blair had expected Skynet's response to be. It was willing enough to send one of its two remaining HKs to take her down when it thought she was out of ammo and an easy target. But now that it realized it had no idea what her weapons status really was, it wasn't willing to risk losing its last eye in the sky. Especially in the midst of a battle that was obviously not going the way Skynet had expected it to.

But whether or not that last HK survived was no longer Skynet's decision. If Blair put on a burst of speed, she ought to be able to get to the fleeing aircraft before it got anywhere near safety.

"Ready or not, here I come," she said softly into her radio.

"Hickabick, I need a Tonto," Connor's voice came.

Blair swore under her breath. She had been looking forward to sending that last HK into the dirt. But business before pleasure.

"Hickabick: check," she said, veering reluctantly away from her pursuit.

Blair found some of Connor's code-talk to be obscure in the extreme. But this particular one was something for which she at least had a vague memory: Tonto, wingman to the Lone Ranger, who always got sent on ahead to scout the territory.

But he did it carefully and subtly, she reminded herself. She wasn't sure what was happening on the ground, but if Skynet still didn't know that they'd spotted its staging area, it wasn't going to be Blair who gave the show away. She swung her A-10 around, tracking out a wide circle that would take her back toward the combat area and only coincidentally bring her within sight of the warehouse.

That single glimpse was enough to show that Connor had been right to send her in for a look. Four T-600s had left the warehouse and were in the process of climbing the south edge of the ring of rubble.

"Location?" she called.

"Tee four," Connor's voice came back, barely audible over the noise of intense automatic weapons fire.

Most likely the weapons fire Blair could see lighting up one of the streets ahead. Adjusting her vector again, she headed over for a closer look.

It was Connor, all right, hunkered down about two blocks west of the Moldavia. His team was currently in the process of blowing the stuffing out of three T-600s, who were fighting back from among the blackened pieces of at least two more of the machines. Another line of fire was coming from the building across from the Moldavia, trapping the T-600s in a crossfire.

Blair frowned. Given their basically hopeless situation, why hadn't the surviving Terminators tried to make a run for it? Skynet was usually reluctant to simply waste its machines these days, and it could send the T-600s in practically any direction right now without exposing them to more fire than they already were receiving.

Unless Skynet wanted them there for a reason.

She swung the A-10 around again, ostensibly for another look at the battle, in fact for a second look at the four T-600s that had just left the warehouse.

That second look was all she needed. She'd been right: the three Terminators in the crossfire weren't just standing around waiting to be demolished. They were standing around waiting for the four newcomers to sneak up behind Connor and catch him in a crossfire of their own.

"Hole four: crab," she called urgently into her mike.

"Hole four: crab," Blair's voice came through Connor's earphone.

He frowned even as he lined up another shot on the T-600s he and McFarland were currently keeping off balance. *Crab* was the code for one to four Terminators moving in on a pincer.

But only four? Surely his attack on this six-machine group was serious enough to warrant a bigger force than that.

Unless it was the biggest force Skynet was still able to send.

"Timing?" he called into the mike curving around his cheek.

"Two minutes," Blair reported. "Maybe less."

"Check," Connor acknowledged. "David: go. Tunney: stand ready. Barnes: boil lobster."

"Check," Barnes's voice came, and there was a sudden intensification of fire from the other end of their shooting gallery as he and his squad settled down to the serious task of destroying the remnants of the six-Terminator force.

Leaving Connor and the others free to handle the four T-600s currently trying to sneak up behind them.

"All right, people, we have a crab coming," he called. "McFarland, you're ghost. The rest of you, follow me."

Connor had already picked out a good rear-guard position across the street. He headed off toward it with Bishop and the Tantillo brothers on his heels. McFarland stayed behind, trying to lay down enough fire by himself to keep Skynet from realizing that the rest of the group had just disappeared.

The position turned out to be not quite as good as it had looked. But it was good enough.

"Grenades," he ordered Joey Tantillo as the others deployed for cover fire. Connor hadn't wanted to risk using the squad's two C4 grenades so close to Barnes and the Moldavia defenders, but lofting them into a group of Terminators coming in from the opposite direction shouldn't be a problem.

He peered in the direction of the cross street where the four T-600s should soon be appearing. The staging area warehouse was hopefully emptied of Terminators and minutes away from a breach, while the machines here on the streets were pinned down or ripe for destruction. Skynet's only remaining HK was in no position to observe and report on any of it until it was too late. The operation was going very well.

It was going *too* well.

He looked around, half expecting to see a group of Terminators they hadn't yet tagged bearing down on them from the rear. But there was nothing. All the evidence pointed to a quick and complete victory.

He didn't believe it for a minute.

"Everyone keep a sharp eye," he called into his mike. "Skynet's up to something." He grimaced. "I just don't know yet what it is."

CHAPTER SEVENTEEN

Orozco's first warning was the sound of a distant double blast coming from somewhere behind him, a pair of hammerfalls loud enough to penetrate even the heavy gunfire he and his teams were pouring into the two Terminators still fighting to reach the archway.

"Grimaldi!" he shouted.

"I heard it," Grimaldi shouted back, slinging his rifle over his shoulder. "I'll go check."

He rose up into a crouch, paused for a moment, then took off in a broken run that got him safely across the lobby and into the main corridor heading back through the building.

Orozco turned back to the archway, a fresh wave of tightness knotting his stomach as he continued to pour fire against the attacking machines. Grimaldi and his men had sealed off the rear of the building years ago, and several teams had worked for hours earlier that day to inspect and reinforce those barriers. The building was as secure as they could make it, and Orozco himself had added a few booby traps to help keep out any unwelcome visitors.

But those explosions a minute ago had sounded a lot like two of his home-made pipe bombs. The question was, had one of the guards back there accidentally set them off, probably killing him or herself in the process?

Or had Skynet created a way inside?

The Terminators in the street were starting to pull back, their rubber flesh tattered, their appearance now more akin to mummies than human beings. Orozco watched warily as they backed out of view and out of range, then shifted his attention to the street leading past the sniper's nest. There were two or three more Terminators down there, slowly disintegrating under an outpouring of fire from the rear of the nest. Barnes and Kate and their team, protecting all of them from what had obviously been Skynet's idea of a flanking maneuver.

Meanwhile, the fire coming from the Ashes' own defenders had stopped now that their primary targets had retreated.

"Right flank: new target," Orozco called, pointing down the street at the other Terminators. Rather than just sitting around, he and his people might as well give Barnes's squad a hand. "All marksmen move to this side of the barricade."

It was amazing, he reflected, what an hour and a couple of small victories could accomplish. The same men and women who'd been quaking in their shoes earlier now nearly fell over each other getting to the right-hand side of the barrier just for the chance to target a few more of their attackers.

They were firing away when Grimaldi skidded to Orozco's side, his face white.

"They're coming in!" he gasped, panting for breath.

"Where?" Orozco snapped, shooting a look over the other's shoulder. The hallways, at least as far down as he could see, were still clear.

"Ventilation shaft beside the loading dock," Grimaldi said. "They breached the wall back there and are working their way in."

Orozco cursed. The two explosions he'd heard must have been the two pipe bombs he'd set inside that shaft, the first designed to blow up the intruder, the second to blow up the wall over the shaft and hopefully seal the gap.

"Did the bombs stop them?" he asked.

"Didn't you hear me?" Grimaldi demanded. "I said they're *working their way in.* I could see their eyes in the ducts. And not just the ducts—they're hammering at the whole wall back there."

"Damn." Orozco spun around. With a ductwork breach, at least the machines would have to come in one at a time. But if they managed to take down the wall, the whole back of the building would be open to them. "Cease fire!" he shouted. "All teams, cease fire! We have a breach."

The guns instantly stopped.

"Where?" Wadleigh demanded.

"Loading dock vent shaft and duct, and they're working on the wall," Grimaldi said. "Everyone, back there, on the double."

He broke off, looking with sudden uncertainty at Orozco. "Everyone?" he repeated, making it a question.

"Yes, everyone," Orozco confirmed, looking up at the fire teams on the balcony and gesturing them down to the lobby.

"Right," Grimaldi said. "Come on."

He sprinted back toward the hallway, his rifle bouncing across his back, the rest of the fire teams right behind him.

Orozco looked out through the archway, wondering

belatedly if this was really the right decision. If the attack on the building's rear was a feint, leaving the main entrance undefended this way could be the last mistake any of them ever made.

But he had no choice. If Skynet was hitting them in the rear with any significant force, it would take every gun and gunner Orozco had simply to stand against it. He would just have to hope that Barnes and his people could cover them up here.

The fire teams from the balcony were streaming down the stairway now, looking at Orozco for orders. Pointing them toward the building's rear, he slung his M16 over his shoulder, grabbed his last two pipe bombs, and hurried to join them.

Something was wrong.

Kate gazed out on the street below, trying to figure out what it was that had suddenly set off alarms in the back of her head. The two Terminators to the north were still retreating from their latest attack on the Moldavia, their miniguns silent and possibly dry. Simmons was encouraging their departure with deliberately placed shots, his rounds slamming into their heads and hip joints. A couple of T-600s a block farther north of the retreating machines were offering some cover fire, but their shots were sporadic and ineffective.

The gunfire coming from behind Kate, off to the west, was still going strong as Barnes and the others hammered the first wave of reserve T-600s that Skynet had sent into the battle. In contrast, the Terminators in the bus to the south hadn't moved at all, and were only firing occasional shots, as if content with making sure there was no traffic on the street.

And then, suddenly, Kate had it. The Terminators to the west and north were firing, Barnes and Simmons were firing, and even farther to the west John and his squad were firing. Everyone who had a target to shoot at was doing so.

Except the people in the Moldavia.

And up until a minute ago they'd been firing down the street at Barnes's target T-600s.

Why had they suddenly stopped?

"Hickabick, I need a sitrep at tee two and hole nine," she said into her mike.

"Check," Blair's voice came back. "On my way."

At the other end of the room, Simmons turned around, reaching up a hand to cover his mike.

"Trouble?" he asked.

"Orozco's people have stopped firing," Kate told him.

Simmons turned back to his peephole.

"Huh," he said. "You're right. I hadn't even noticed."

Overhead, the roar of an A-10 briefly drowned out the chattering of gunfire as Blair shot over the Moldavia.

"Tee two looks clear," the pilot reported crisply. "Turning to hole nine."

"Maybe they just ran out of ammo," Simmons offered as he squeezed off a couple more rounds at the retreating T-600s.

"Maybe," Kate said.

The front of the building looked all right, at least as far as Blair could see from the air. There were a couple of T-600s to the north firing at the building and Barnes's squad, with two more retreating in that direction, plus the remnants of another group to the west that Barnes and Connor were hammering.

She also caught a glimpse of the foursome still hoping to sneak up on Connor from even farther to the west.

There was other movement, too, beside the staging area warehouse's south wall. Shadowy figures—David and his demolition team—had come out of the drainage tunnel and were busily setting their explosives in preparation for the squad's breach. From what Blair could see, it looked like Connor had decided to bring the whole wall down, and Blair made a mental note to try to get back in time for the show.

Massive explosions were always entertaining to watch, especially explosions involving Skynet property.

For another moment she held her course, studying the area. So far, the only T-600s that Skynet had sent against the Moldavia had been that first wave plus some reinforcements from the area around it, followed by the groups of six and four from the warehouse.

But that couldn't be all of the T-600s that Skynet had in the area. Were the rest of them still on border patrol?

Blair hoped so. As long as Skynet held to the assumption that it could contain the area, Connor's team would be able to take out the machines in twos and fours and sixes instead of having to face all of them at once in a single massed attack.

Of course, once Skynet realized its staging area had been breached, its strategy would undoubtedly change. And quickly.

Giving the area around the warehouse one final check, she swung back around the block, clearing the broken structures around the Moldavia and coming in along the service alley that ran behind the building.

And as she came within sight of the building's rear, she felt her jaw drop in stunned disbelief.

Skynet's reserve of Terminators weren't standing idly by along the neighborhood's borders, trying to keep everyone inside the kill zone. They were right here—twenty of them at least—single-mindedly pounding at the building's back wall and ventilation structures, breaking their way inside.

"Hickabick," she called tautly into her mike. "Double lobster at hole nine. Repeat: double lobster at hole nine.

"And they're going in."

"Oh, hell," Tony Tantillo said.

"And then some," Connor agreed grimly. A double lobster—ten to twenty T-600s—about to breach the Moldavia. And from the tone of Blair's voice, he guessed the number was probably closer to twenty than ten. Skynet was throwing an incredible number of resources at the beleaguered building.

"Hickabick, are there any tee times still available?" he called into his mike.

There was a brief silence.

"Yes, but I was hoping to save the last one of the day for Curly," she replied.

Connor's eyes flicked toward the south. The last HK had fled several minutes ago and was nowhere in sight, but it would be back the minute Blair ran out of ammo. She couldn't afford to be caught in that position. Neither could Connor and the breach teams, for that matter.

But the option was for them all to sit back and do nothing, and let Orozco and his people die.

"Tee time at hole nine," he ordered. "Bring the whole set of clubs."

"Check," Blair said.

And with that, the die was cast.

"Barnes?" Connor called.

"I heard," Barnes said. "Soon as we're finished here, we'll see about giving them some support."

Connor frowned. Getting into the building from Barnes's position would mean crossing a street that he'd thought Skynet was holding. Had the Terminators abandoned their positions there?

"What about Gulliver?"

"No change," Kate's voice put in.

"Yeah, but they gotta be running low on ammo," Barnes said. "Don't worry, we'll make it."

"Not until Gulliver's neutralized," Connor told him firmly. "There's still that group at green eight, and I don't want you running through a crossfire. As soon as we're finished here, we'll deal with it."

Barnes muttered something.

"Make it snappy," he said.

"Here they come," Joey Tantillo murmured.

Connor peered down the street to the west. The first of the four T-600s had rounded the corner and were starting to move toward McFarland, who was still pelting the remnants of Barnes's set of targets.

"Easy," he warned Joey quietly. "Make sure they're all in view, with nowhere to go."

"Don't worry," Joey murmured back, his hand hovering over the grenade launcher's trigger. "The only place they're going is hell."

Blair hadn't been in either of the groups who had scouted the neighborhood earlier that day. She'd never met any of the people of the Moldavia. She also knew that with an HK still armed and flying, spending the last of her ammo on that crowd of T-600s would probably be the last thing she accomplished before her own death.

But it would be worth it. It would very much be worth it.

She roared down the service alley at full speed, ignoring the clatter of minigun fire slamming suddenly into her A-10's belly. At point-blank range she opened up with her GAU-8, spending her last eighty rounds in a single glorious burst that went through the T-600s like a mowing machine, shattering them into shards of twisted metal and scattering heads and limbs and torsos across the pavement. The roar of her fire abruptly cut off as the gun went dry, and she pulled up and out, circling back around for a visual assessment of the carnage.

She'd accomplished a lot with that strafing run. But not enough. Eight Terminators were still on their feet... and even as she watched, the first of them broke through the wall and disappeared into the building.

"Hickabick," she said with a sigh. "Tee time over. Lobster going in at hole nine."

"Check, Hickabick," Connor's voice came back, glacially calm as the man always was in combat. "We'll deal with it. Get clear."

"Check," she said.

But she wouldn't be clear for long, she knew. She'd blown the last of her ammo, and if the surviving Terminators had spotted that half second of dry shooting before she could let up on her trigger, Skynet knew she was empty.

Far to the south, she could see the last remaining HK rising from the refuge where it had gone to ground. No longer cowering from its attacker, it was coming now for vengeance.

Blair took a deep breath, the line of ghosts in the back

of her mind shivering with anticipation. She had cheated death far longer than she'd had any right to, and the bill had finally come due.

But if she was going out, she was going out with flair. One way or another, she was going to keep that HK off Connor's back. She owed the man that much. The machine was going down.

Even if Blair went down with it.

The Terminator in the ventilation duct had stopped moving and was starting to disintegrate under the withering fire from Orozco's team when the wall twenty meters away sudden exploded inward. Orozco had just enough time to see a pair of glowing red eyes before the machine shoving its way through the remaining sheetrock opened fire.

Five men died in that first blast, men who with bitter irony had only been over there in the first place so that they would be out of the way while they reloaded their guns. The next salvo took out three more, mostly those who were quick enough to turn their guns against this new threat. More guns turned toward the Terminator and opened fire, rattling it with multiple impacts but not seeming to cause any serious damage.

And then, behind the Terminator, Orozco saw more red eyes moving in from behind.

"Fall back!" he shouted. "Teams one and two, regroup at the corridor fire stations. *Move!*"

The men and women scrambled to obey. But for many it was already too late. The minigun bursts became a roar as the Terminator held down the trigger, filling the area with flesh and blood and bodies. Beside Orozco, Wadleigh gave a sudden agonized cough and started to fall. Orozco grabbed his arm and hauled him bodily around the corner into a corridor filled with fleeing people. Behind him, the fire ceased as the Terminators temporarily ran out of targets, and Orozco could hear the sound of more tearing sheetrock.

And with that, he knew it was over. With the Terminators still held at bay outside the Ashes, there had still been a chance. With them inside the building, there wasn't a hope in hell of stopping them.

But that didn't mean they should just give up. If he and the others were going to die, they were going to make Skynet pay as dearly for its victory as they could.

Only two of the men of Team One had made it to the fall-back positions when Orozco arrived, and only Bauman of Team Two was at the second. Orozco dropped beside the latter, swinging Wadleigh around behind the barrier and taking a moment to lower him as carefully as he could into a sitting position with his back to the wall.

Only then did he see that Wadleigh's shirt was drenched in blood.

"Hang in there," Orozco urged him. "As soon as we get a few more people here to help, we'll get you back to the medics."

"Never mind that," Wadleigh said, his voice gurgling a little, bubbles of blood flecking the corners of his mouth. "Where's my rifle? What happened to my rifle?"

"Here, take this," Orozco said, drawing his Beretta and pressing it into the other's hand.

Wadleigh smiled weakly in thanks, and Orozco turned back to the barrier.

"Where's everyone else?" he asked Bauman.

"Run out or dead," Bauman said, his voice sounding

more weary than bitter. "Not here, anyway." He looked sideways at Orozco. "So why are *we* here?"

"Because someone needs to slow them down while everyone who's left gets back to the lobby and regroups," Orozco told him.

Bauman snorted.

"Why? So they can die up there instead of back here?"

"So they can have the best possible chance to live," Orozco told him brusquely. "Because protecting them is our job right now." He looked Bauman squarely in the eye. "Because if we're going to die, that's how *men* die."

Bauman took a deep breath.

"Yeah," he said. He took another deep breath. "Okay. As long as there's a good reason."

Behind Orozco came a sudden gasp, and then silence, and he turned to find that Wadleigh was dead. Reaching down, he closed the man's eyes, then gently retrieved the Beretta from his limp hand.

"But we're not doing a Little Bighorn here, either," he told Bauman as he holstered the pistol and pulled out one of his two remaining pipe bombs. "As soon as the first metal bastard sticks his nose around that corner, you and the others are going to lay down enough fire to hold him back while I blow the floor out from under him."

"Okay," Bauman said. "Sure. Let's give it a try."

The sound of breaking sheetrock faded away. *They must all be inside*, Orozco guessed.

"Steady," he told his men as he got out his lighter. *If this was a Western*, the thought whispered through his mind, *this would be the time Barnes would lead a cavalry charge to the rescue.*

But this wasn't a movie. And no one came charging to the rescue anymore.

But this was still how men died.

Through the floor he felt the faint vibrations as heavy footsteps approached. Flicking the cap on his lighter, he held the bomb ready and waited.

Connor had noticed the bus that morning as Barnes's group was having their confrontation at the Moldavia. Had not only noticed it, but had gauged its usefulness as a bunker, and had also done a quick mental inventory of all the possible ways it could be successfully taken out.

Which was why he and his squad were currently making their approach along the street just north of the bus instead of taking the time to go an extra block south and come up behind it. Just ahead, on the southwest corner of the street, was the burned-out remnant of what had once been a corner store, with glassless windows that looked out onto both the bus's north-south street and Connor's own east-west street.

Once the squad reached the store, it would be a straightforward matter of slipping through the windows on their side, crossing under cover to the other side, and sending their last C4 grenade directly into the bus.

At which point Barnes and his squad should be able to duck through the more distant and less effective fire from the north end of the street and go to Orozco's aid.

Connor just hoped they would be in time to do something useful.

They were nearly to the store when some instinct made Connor glance over his shoulder. There, striding silently toward them along the far side of the street, were a brand new set of four T-600s.

Before Connor could even open his mouth to shout a warning, they opened fire.

McFarland took the brunt of that first salvo, his body all but disintegrating under the hail of bullets, dead long before he hit the pavement. Connor swung his MP5 around, flicking the selector to full auto and opening fire, striking the Terminators and sending their next salvo wide.

"Through the window!" he shouted at the rest of his squad.

Peripherally, he saw them charging toward the corner store as he continued to fire. His clip ran dry, and he slammed in a fresh one, ignoring the bullets hammering into the wall behind him.

"Clear!" he heard Tony's shout as a hail of cover fire opened up at the Terminators from behind him. "Connor!"

He turned and sprinted toward the store. Bishop and Tony were crouched by the window, their rifles blazing as he dived headlong through the opening. He hit the floor and rolled onto his shoulder and back, coming awkwardly up into a crouch.

"Everyone okay?" he called.

"For now," Joey said grimly. "But that may not last much longer."

And only then did Connor's brain catch up with his combat reflexes, and he recognized the trap Skynet had maneuvered them into.

Because if those ambushing T-600s had attacked while Connor's squad was still in the middle of the block, they would have stopped right there, hammering the machines with enough gunfire to keep them off balance long enough for Joey to take them out with their last C4 grenade.

Instead, by waiting until the squad had this convenient

bunker to retreat to, Skynet had put them within range of both the T-600s on the street *and* those in the bus.

Two targets. Only one grenade.

It wasn't really a choice, Connor knew with a sinking heart. Tactically, the only viable move would be to ignore the bus, use the grenade against the group to their west, and then slip out that way. Taking out the bus wouldn't be of any help, since Skynet could still pull in the Terminators from the north end of the street to block any exit in that direction, leaving Connor and his squad still pinned.

But if Connor did it that way, if he left the bus alone, Skynet would maintain its control of the street, blocking all access to the Moldavia.

And the people in there would all die.

Joey was crouching beside him, the grenade launcher in his hands, his eyes steady on Connor's face. Probably he'd run through the same train of logic, and knew that the people in the Moldavia were doomed.

"Get the launcher ready," Connor told him evenly. "We're taking out the bus."

The hallways were filled with smoke and the thunder of machinegun fire, the screams of the wounded, and the bodies of the dead.

Orozco continued backing slowly down the hall, firing at every pair of red eyes he could make out through the drifting smoke. There were a lot of them, at least five sets he could see at the moment. The Terminators were working their way toward him, pausing at each doorway along the hall to check for potential victims.

Sometimes the room was empty, and the Terminators would continue their march forward. Far too often, though, there was someone hiding in there. Then there would be yet another burst of minigun fire, and another person would join the ranks of the dead.

Orozco was alone now. All those who'd once stood with him had either been killed or had turned and fled. He still nursed some frail tendrils of hope that at least some of those who'd run hadn't actually deserted, but had instead headed back to the lobby to regroup for a counterattack.

He wasn't really expecting that. But he also didn't blame them. The Terminators had brought a living, pulsating hell to their home, and men and women who'd never before been through such sound and fury and death could hardly be expected to stand against it for long.

In fact, Orozco hoped that some of them had made it out of the building alive, and would find a way to slip through Skynet's cordon and escape. Sending a few survivors back to the world would at least give his death some meaning.

A death that wouldn't be much longer in coming. His left arm was wet with blood, and he knew he'd taken a round somewhere up there. He couldn't feel any pain, thanks to the adrenaline pumping through his system. But all the adrenaline in the world couldn't plug leaking skin. Even if he managed to avoid taking any more damage, he would eventually collapse from loss of blood.

But not yet. Not yet. Not as long as there was hope for any of his people.

A pair of glowing red eyes loomed up through the smoke in front of him. Orozco squeezed his M16's trigger, the impact of the round sending the head bouncing backward.

Clenching his teeth, firing again and again, Orozco continued his slow, steady, lonely retreat.

The exit from the sagging building led through a maze of back alleys and ruins. Kyle and Star moved through them, staying in shadow as much as they could, both of them alert to the probability that there were other Terminators somewhere in the area.

But though the night was filled with the thunder of gunfire, and the broken clouds above reflected an eerie glow from the multiple fires going on across the city, Kyle didn't spot a single one of the red-eyed killing machines.

His plan had been to head due west, then turn north when they got to the street that passed by the building's main entrance. They were nearly to the service alley that ran along the rear of the Ashes building when a much louder hammering of nearby gunfire suddenly rolled across him.

Reflexively, he pulled Star down beside him into the partial shelter of a ragged waist-high wall, wincing at the sheer thundering power of the blasts. He'd heard similar barrages on and off throughout the long night, but they'd always been coming from somewhere in the distance, and up in the sky. To hear it up close like this was brain-rattlingly terrifying.

But it was over quickly. Wishing he knew whether that was a good thing or a bad thing, he started to stand up—

And dropped back down as a jet aircraft shot straight out of the alley in front of him, followed by a blast of hot air that knocked both him and Star flat on their backs. He caught a glimpse of an angry red-yellow glow blazing from the inside of the plane as it climbed sharply back into the sky.

The roar faded as the plane headed somewhere else.

"You okay?" Kyle asked as he took Star's arm and got the two of them back on their feet.

She gave him a quick nod, her eyes tense, her hand gripping his tightly.

"Yeah, I know," Kyle agreed, peering ahead down the street. It looked clear. "Okay, here's the plan. We cross the alley and go one more block, then turn north and head back to the Ashes. Right? Let's go."

Somewhat to Kyle's surprise, they made it to the next street without incident. Stepping up to the corner of a small makeshift shanty that someone had long ago built out of scrap wood and brick, and then abandoned, he looked carefully around it.

His worst fears had envisioned a dozen Terminators marching on the building. But again to his surprise, he found that the street stretching out in front of him was completely deserted.

Mostly deserted, anyway. Four or five blocks to the north he could make out a couple of figures in the middle of the street, figures too distant for him to tell whether they were human or machine. But otherwise the path looked clear.

"Okay, here we go," he whispered to Star. Taking her hand, he started to ease around the corner.

As the shanty wall above his head exploded in a shattering hail of gunfire.

He took the rest of the corner in a dive, pulling Star with him as the stream of lead raked down the wall of the shanty from somewhere behind them, raining bits of wood and brick across his back and legs.

Kyle winced, squinting against the dust as the rounds began tracking back and forth, methodically perforating the walls of the makeshift structure. He risked a quick look, and through the disintegrating walls spotted two T-600s marching stolidly toward them, miniguns blazing.

Their only chance now was an all-or-nothing run for the archway. Getting a fresh grip on Star's hand, Kyle prepared himself.

And then, to his stunned surprise, a head and torso rose into view through one of the upper windows of the overturned bus half a block away.

It was another Terminator. Only this one was between them and the Ashes.

Kyle froze, the roar of the miniguns in his ears drowning out the painful thudding of his heart. So that was it. He and Star were caught in the open between two groups of killing machines.

They were dead.

Unbidden, tears welled up in his eyes. Not tears of fear or anger, but of frustration and shame. He'd failed. He'd failed himself, and he'd failed Orozco.

Worst of all, he'd failed Star.

He frowned, blinking away the tears as something strange caught his attention. The Terminator in the bus wasn't looking at him and Star. In fact, it was looking in almost exactly the opposite direction.

He studied the machine, his flash of shame fading as he tried to figure out what was happening. Orozco had told him all the Terminators were linked together through Skynet, so that what one Terminator saw or heard could be passed on to any of the others.

The Terminators shooting up the shanty beside him knew that he and Star were here. So how could the machine in the bus *not* know it?

And then the Terminator in the bus opened fire, its minigun raking the side of the old corner store half a block further north.

. And abruptly, Kyle understood. The Terminator knew he and Star were there, all right. It just didn't care. All it cared about right now was trying to kill the people he could see cowering inside the store.

And when it had accomplished that, *then* it might have the time to deal with these two annoying kids who had refused to simply lie down and die.

Kyle hissed out a breath, a surge of anger driving out the last remnants of his momentary panic. He didn't know who the people in the store were, whether they were a fire team Orozco had sent or just a group of civilian refugees running from Skynet's slaughter.

But who they were didn't matter.

What mattered was that Kyle still had two bombs left, and a good throwing arm.

"You think we were annoying before?" he muttered as he reached into his shoulder bag. "Let me show you what annoying *really* is."

CHAPTER EIGHTEEN

Connor had moved to the north-facing window and was assisting Bishop and Tony in their efforts to keep the group of T-600s there at bay when he heard the explosion from behind him.

"You get it?" he shouted over his shoulder to Joey.

"It's got," Joey called back, sounding bewildered. "But not by me."

"What?" Connor demanded, turning around and looking through the other window.

The bus was a shambles, all right. Its edges had been splayed outward by a seriously healthy blast, its empty windows and other openings flickering with light from the small fires the explosion had ignited inside it.

And Joey was, indeed, still clutching the squad's last grenade.

Connor had no idea what had happened, but this wasn't the time to try to figure it out. From the look of the bus, the explosion had been strong enough to rattle the Terminators' electronics and temporarily stun them. But unless it had been powerful enough to dismember them, they would soon be up and running again.

Someone had to get to them before that happened, and put them out of action permanently.

"Joey, Tony: take them out," Connor ordered, jerking his head back at the other four T-600s who had suddenly stepped up the tempo of their attack. "Bishop: you're with me." Without waiting for acknowledgment, he zigzagged through the debris of the store, dived through the east-facing window, and sprinted toward the bus.

He was nearly there when he suddenly realized he and his team weren't alone. Half a block away, at the next street to the south, he could see two figures: a child and young adult or teen, cowering against a building that was being steadily demolished around them. More Terminators on their way into the battle zone, with the two kids caught in the middle of it.

He had reached the bus and was leaning in for a closer look when Bishop caught up to him.

"How many?" she asked, panting.

"Two," Connor told her. The word was barely out of his mouth when the crunching blast of a C4 grenade came from behind them. "You take close," he added, "I'll take far." Ducking his head, he stepped inside the vehicle.

The two Terminators were lying on the ground, unmoving, their miniguns momentarily silenced. Great sections of their rubbery skin had been torn away by the blast, and a couple of joints on each one were no longer looking quite right.

Mentally, Connor threw a salute to whoever it was who'd put together this particular explosive. Even considering the concentrating effect the confined space would have had on the blast, it had still been one hell of a bomb.

Stepping over the first Terminator, he placed the muzzle of his MP5 against the dented skull of the second and squeezed the trigger.

It took two three-round bursts to batter through the tough metal. But when the echoes had died away, the last hint of red glow had faded from the machine's eyes.

Terminated.

Connor looked back at Bishop, gave her a thumb's-up and got one in return, then grabbed hold of one of the skeletal seat frames and climbed up to the top side of the bus. Hoping it wasn't too late to save the two kids he'd seen out there, he eased his head cautiously through one of the windows.

He had had long experience with the kind of fire-power Skynet had put into the hands of its T-600s, and he'd seen what that firepower could do. But even Connor found himself in awe at how the scene outside had changed during the handful of seconds he and Bishop had been inside the bus.

The structure the kids had been huddling beside was gone. All of it. There were still a few sections of wall standing, but nothing taller than half a meter and most considerably shorter. The roof, what was left of it, had collapsed into the house, and was lying in broken pieces across broken furniture and other unidentifiable bits of material.

And with the building no longer in the way, Connor could now see the two T-600s approaching from fifty meters away.

"There," Bishop said from the next window, jabbing a finger over Connor's shoulder.

Connor looked where she was pointing. Sure enough, the two kids were still there, hugging the ground in front of one of the few remaining pieces of wall.

"Can we take them?" Bishop asked.

Connor grimaced. Bishop was experienced enough to

know that the answer to that was no. Not just the two of them, not with the weapons they had available.

But if they didn't do something, those two kids were dead.

"Let's find out," Connor said. Hauling his MP5 up through the window, he pointed the muzzle at the approaching T-600s and opened fire.

He hadn't expected the fire from their two guns to stop the T-600s, and he had been right. But he *had* expected that the disruption in the machines' balance would throw off their aim, and he was right again. The Terminators jerked from the multiple impacts as Connor's and Bishop's slugs slammed into them, the machines' own fire going wild.

"Come on!" Connor shouted toward the two kids. "Come on—*now!*"

The older of the two, the teen, eased up onto his side and looked cautiously over the remains of the wall at the two T-600s. He looked back at Connor and Bishop, peered north along the street, then leaned over and said something to the child beside him.

The two gathered their feet beneath them and bounded up.

But to Connor's surprise, instead of running for the bus they instead dashed straight across the street and disappeared behind some ruins on the northwest corner there.

"What in—?"

An instant later he got his answer as a hail of gunfire slammed into the bus from the north.

Instinctively, he dropped back down, Bishop hitting the ground a quarter second behind him.

"You all right?" he asked her.

She nodded, then jerked her head and gun around

toward the rear of the vehicle. Connor swung his MP5 around as well—

Just as the Tantillo brothers dived in through the opening.

"Sorry we're late," Joey said, breathing hard as he gave each of the dead T-600s a quick look. "They'd moved too far apart for the grenade to take them all out together. I had to drop the wall on them instead, but then we had to go blast each of them before they could dig themselves out. What did we miss?"

"Never mind what you missed," Connor said. "What's going on at the other end of the street?"

"More company," Tony said, peering cautiously out the rear doors. "Probably not happy about losing their handy City Transit bunker here." He rapped his knuckles on the side of their flimsy sanctuary.

Connor mouthed a curse. Which meant Barnes was still being blocked from going to Orozco's assistance. He hadn't expected Skynet to be able to get fresh Terminators into position that fast.

"Kate?" Connor called into his mike. "What's your sitrep?"

"We can't get across," his wife's voice came back tautly. "Not unless we can par-six it."

"Not a chance," Tony murmured, covering his own mike. "They're standing right in the middle of the intersection. No way to sneak up on them without being spotted."

And meanwhile, there were probably Terminators slaughtering their way through the Moldavia. Connor looked around the bus, thinking hard. Barnes was pinned down; Connor's team was pinned down; David and Tunney had their hands full dealing with the warehouse.

And then, Connor's eyes fell on the miniguns still clutched in the T-600s' hands.

"Hickabick?" he called into his mike. "Hickabick?"

"Hickabick," Blair's voice came back. "Sorry—been a little distracted."

"No problem," Connor said. "Where are you?"

"Off the course," Blair replied. "Got invited to a game of Brooklyn tag."

Which meant she was somewhere way south of the mission grid Connor had set up.

"I need you and your game here," he said. "Tee two off Gulliver."

There was a brief pause.

"Check," Blair said. "You *do* realize the course is closed, right?"

"Understood," Connor said. "Soonest."

"Check," Blair said again.

Connor looked over to see the rest of the squad eyeing him with varying degrees of bafflement.

"You thinking she can bluff them off the street?" Tony asked.

"Slipstream won't take them out, will it?" Bishop offered doubtfully. "They're supposed to be too heavy for that."

"No, to both of you," Connor said as he started climbing toward the top of the bus again. "Tony, Joey: you have two minutes to get those miniguns free and ready to fire. Bishop, up top with me—we need to find out where those other two T-600s went."

He reached the line of windows and eased his head up for a look. But for once, caution was unnecessary. The Terminators at the north end of the street were evidently saving their ammo to keep Kate and Barnes out of the

Moldavia, and the machines that had been firing on the two kids had disappeared.

Disappeared back onto their tail, no doubt. But there was nothing Connor could do about that now. Turning toward the south, he looked upward.

Nothing.

He checked east and west, then south again. Still nothing.

Had Blair lost her macabre game of tag with that last remaining HK? Connor checked east and west again, and even north, just in case she had gotten disoriented.

And then, there they were: a pair of shadows framed between the city's broken buildings to the south, heading toward them across the moonlit sky.

Abruptly, Connor tensed. Blair was coming toward him, all right, exactly as ordered. But she was coming in way too high for what he needed. He had to get her to drop to strafing level.

Only there wasn't anything in the mission code for that.

Beside him, Tony popped his head out of the next window over.

"Got 'em," he announced, tapping the muzzle of the minigun he was holding just out of sight. "Still got plenty of ammo—they must have figured they were here for the long haul." He peered up into the sky. "If you're thinking what I think you're thinking, aren't they coming in too high?"

"Yes, they are," Connor said through clenched teeth. There had to be a way for him to clue in Blair without tipping his hand to Skynet at the same time.

And then, he had an idea. A completely crazy idea.

"You and Joey get ready," he told Tony. "You're only going to get one shot at this."

* * *

They had made it two blocks past the corner with the bus when Star suddenly grabbed Kyle's arm and staggered to a halt.

"What's wrong?" Kyle asked sharply as he grabbed her around her waist. "Were you shot? Are you hurt?"

She shook her head. *Tired*, she signed.

"Oh," Kyle said, relief flooding into him. After all that shooting back there, he'd feared the worst. "Over here," he said, leading her to an angled piece of broken concrete and helping her sit down. She was worn out, all right, her chest heaving as she gasped for breath, her face shiny with sweat, her legs trembling with fatigue. He should have noticed that earlier, he told himself guiltily.

Still, under the circumstances, there hadn't been a lot he could have done differently.

Though he had the discomfiting sense that Star had a different opinion on that one. The look on her face was one he'd seen before.

"What?" Kyle asked warily.

Why didn't we go with the people in the bus? she signed.

Kyle grimaced. What could he say? He'd seen the line of Terminators moving into the street to the north, clearly preparing to march on the people who'd blown up their buddies. The man and woman in the bus were as good as dead. If he and Star had joined them, they would have been dead, too.

No, he couldn't tell her that. Not after those people had saved their lives.

"We need to get back to the Ashes," he said instead. "Orozco needs our help, and the people on the bus had it under control. Besides, we don't even know who they were."

He really should have known that Star wouldn't buy that one. *We didn't know Nguyen or Vuong, either*, she reminded him pointedly. *But we went with—*

Abruptly, she broke off, her face going rigid.

Kyle froze, his eyes darting through the pale moonlight around them. Had the Terminators back there caught up with them already?

But no. That pair should still be somewhere to their east. The lone figure he could see striding along the street toward them was coming instead from the west. It seemed to notice the two kids sitting on the slab and changed its course to head toward them.

Kyle whipped his rifle up to his shoulder, uncertainty flicking through him. The figure was big, but he'd seen humans who were nearly that size. And so far, it hadn't opened fire on them.

And then, as it passed through a patch of moonlight, he saw the glint of metal from the minigun in its right hand.

"Go north," Kyle muttered at Star. "*Go.*"

The girl nodded and took off, her legs pounding the pavement as fast and hard as they could. Aiming at the Terminator's leg, Kyle squeezed the trigger.

The machine staggered with the impact, pausing as it fought to regain its balance. Kyle fired a second shot, and a third, each one briefly stopping the machine in its tracks. So far, the barrage seemed to be keeping it back.

He frowned suddenly.

Or was that what Skynet *wanted* him to think?

He squeezed off one final round, then abruptly leaped to his feet and took off after Star.

And as he did so, a burst of minigun fire slashed through the space he'd just vacated.

The other two Terminators had caught up.

Kyle threw a quick look over his right shoulder. They were both still half a block back, but they were taking every opportunity to fire at him as he darted in and out of their view past rusting vehicles, piles of rubble, and clumps of weeds.

But though they were firing, neither Terminator seemed to be making any effort to close the distance between them. In fact, they were actually retreating, backing toward the street they'd just passed.

Kyle looked over his other shoulder. They weren't chasing him for the simple reason that Skynet had already put the other Terminator on that job. It was striding toward him, all traces of its earlier unsteadiness gone.

He turned forward again, putting everything he had left into increasing his speed as he realized what Skynet was up to. Guessing that Kyle and Star were on their way to the Ashes, it had pulled the three Terminators from somewhere with the hope that the two from the east would drive him and Star straight into the arms of the one to the west.

Now that the plan had failed, Skynet was going to try the same thing, but in a slightly different way. The single Terminator was now going to chase him and Star until they either dropped from exhaustion or else turned east and tried to get back home. Only they would never make it, because the other two Terminators would be paralleling their run along the next north-south street over, which would put them in position to intercept him and Star if and when they tried to turn in that direction.

It was a good plan, and with anyone else it probably would have worked with lethal efficiency. But there was something Kyle knew that Skynet didn't. Something that might just get him and Star out of this alive.

He glanced over his shoulder again. Terminators weren't all that fast, and the one back there was starting to fall behind. But he wasn't falling behind fast enough. Reaching into his shoulder bag as he ran, Kyle pulled out his last pipe bomb. He'd hoped he could save at least one of them, but he needed to slow the machine down and there was no other way he could think of to do that without having to slow down himself.

Lighting the fuse, he let it run down to just the right length, then hurled the bomb behind him.

It exploded with the usual thundercrack, lighting up the cityscape and peppering Kyle with bits of shrapnel. He looked back again, to see that the blast had knocked the Terminator off its feet. The few extra seconds it would cost the big machine to haul itself back up and continue the chase ought to be enough.

They would *have* to be enough.

Star had made it nearly to the next corner when Kyle caught up with her.

"Come on," he told her, grabbing her hand. "I've got a plan."

The bursts of minigun fire echoing through the hallways had become more and more sporadic over the past few minutes. Either the Terminators moving through the building were running low on ammo or, more likely, were running low on people to kill.

And as Orozco reached the lobby he discovered why. Everyone who had managed to evade the killing spree up to now had apparently gathered here, those with guns crouching on the far side of the barricade the fire teams had put together, those without huddling together behind them. Some of the people were whimpering or crying, and Orozco could hear at least one quiet stream of curses being repeated over and over.

They were facing death, and they were terrified. But they were still holding.

Grimaldi rose from the center of the barricade as Orozco approached.

"Thank God—I thought they'd gotten you," the chief said. His eyes dropped to Orozco's blood-soaked sleeve—

"I'm fine," Orozco said, forestalling the obvious question. "What have we got?"

"A dead end," Grimaldi replied, his voice glacially calm. "Terminators have moved into position on the street about half a block north. Some of our people made a run for it, but were cut down before they got even halfway across. I was wondering if we might be able to set up enough cover fire to let at least some of them get out."

It was a pretty futile hope, Orozco knew. But it would be better to try something than just sit here and wait to be cut down.

He was opening his mouth to say so when the roar of miniguns erupted from behind him, and Grimaldi's chest exploded in a spray of blood and bone and flesh.

Orozco threw himself to the side, the bullets that were tracking along the top of the barricade stitching a line across his left shoulder and sleeve as he fell. He hit the ground and rolled over, trying to pull his M16 out from beneath him, where it had landed. Another burst slammed into the barricade just above his head, and with a gurgling scream the man standing behind it toppled forward, dropping his rifle across Orozco's ribs and clutching at his own shattered legs.

For a second he teetered, and then pitched forward to

sprawl across Orozco's head and shoulders.

Orozco gasped in pain as the man's weight slammed against his injured left arm. His right arm was pinned beneath the man's torso, and he fought furiously to work free enough to at least shove him off.

Another burst of fire jerked the man's body sideways, cutting off his screams forever.

And with that, the end had finally come. The Terminators would shoot everyone, Orozco knew, and then would systematically go around the room and put another couple of slugs into each of the bodies, just to make sure. After that they would probably go through the entire building on the off-chance that they'd somehow missed someone.

There was nothing Orozco could do to stop them. He couldn't even get to his gun.

The tumult of screams and scattered return fire was fading away now, leaving only the bursts of minigun fire to intrude on the silence. Closing his eyes, wishing he could also close his ears, Orozco waited for death.

There were three entrances to the Ashes' secret underground gasoline stash. Kyle took the closest, pushing Star in ahead of him and ducking in quickly behind her. He didn't know whether the pursuing Terminator had been in position to see where they'd gone, but he had to assume it had.

They would have to work fast.

Star got the hidden door open in record time. Kyle slipped past her to the tank and twisted the tap all the way over, starting the gasoline spilling onto the ground.

Spilling way too slowly. Pulling out his knife, Kyle jabbed at the side of the tank, poking hole after hole in the tough fiberglass until the gasoline was flowing freely.

"Go out the second way, but stay out of sight," he told Star, his eyes watering a little. The smell of the gasoline was overwhelming. "Wait for me just inside the exit."

She nodded and disappeared out the door and up one of the sloping decoy tunnels. Sliding the bag Orozco had given him off his shoulder, Kyle held it under one of his knife slashes, letting it fill about a third of the way up with gasoline. Then he backed out of the room, carefully pouring a trail of gasoline as he went. He walked about halfway up the tunnel he'd sent Star to, then returned to the main chamber.

Dropping the bag in the steadily deepening pool, he headed up the third tunnel, the one facing the Ashes. He reached the entrance and carefully looked out.

And quickly ducked back in again as the two Terminators who'd been trying to flank them from the east spotted him.

At least, Kyle hoped they'd spotted him. Hurrying down the tunnel, making just enough noise to let them confirm where he'd gone, he splashed through the pool of gasoline and ran up the tunnel he and Star had entered by.

Again moving carefully, he looked out.

The single Terminator was actually farther back than the other two Terminators had been. But unlike them, it wasn't just standing there trying to reacquire its target. It had already heard from the other two, and was striding toward Kyle at full Terminator speed. He held his position just long enough to make sure the machine had spotted the hidden entrance, then again ducked back inside.

Again he ran to the chamber and splashed through the pool of gasoline. But this time, he turned to the side and headed up the third tunnel, the one with the trail of gasoline soaking into the dirt and Star waiting for him at the far end. He reached the end of the trail, crouched down, and pulled out his lighter.

The wait wasn't very long. Short enough, in fact, for him to realize just how close he'd cut this one. Less than fifteen seconds after he'd gotten the lighter into his hand, he felt the thud of heavy footsteps as the Terminators entered the hidden tunnels. Counting off the seconds, trying to visualize their progress, Kyle waited for just the right moment.

And as the first Terminator reached the chamber Kyle ignited the lighter, threw it onto the gasoline trail, and turned around for a mad dash to the end of the tunnel. He'd gotten maybe two steps when there was a deceptively soft *whoosh* from behind him—

And suddenly he was blown nearly off his feet as a shockwave of wind and fire slammed into his back.

Desperately, he tried to get his feet under him again. But the burning air was swirling like a dust storm all around him, twisting him around, keeping him off balance as he staggered his way onward.

He gasped in a breath of air that seemed to itself be on fire—

Behind him came a thunderous explosion, and the swirling air became a huge flaming hand that picked him up and threw him straight down the tunnel.

An instant later, the world went black.

Blair was still a kilometer out from the Moldavia when she began to see the individual muzzle flashes from the T-600s' miniguns on the street half a block north of the besieged building.

There were a *lot* of flashes, too. Skynet was definitely turning up the heat down there. Either the civilians were trying to escape, or else Barnes had launched a sortie against the machines.

Either way, it was the sort of situation that begged for air support.

Only Blair was out of ammo, and everyone down there knew it. Including the man who'd given her the order to come back here in the first place.

Was Connor hoping the Terminators would raise their fire toward her A-10 as she overflew them, temporarily easing some of the pressure on the ground troops? If so, he was going to be disappointed. The T-600s didn't need to shoot at her. Skynet's last HK was still on her tail, and apparently had gotten a reload for its Gatlings while it was hiding out at Skynet's Capistrano tower. So far its fire hadn't connected with her in any serious way, but even Blair's luck couldn't hold out forever against this much firepower.

The radio crackled, and she cocked an ear, wondering if Connor had reconsidered and had new orders for her. And the voice that came through her headset was definitely John Connor's.

But it was *not* the cool, calm set of new orders she had expected.

Connor was singing.

"Dum dum, dum dum de-da-dum," he said, his voice falling and rising and falling again. "Coming for to carry me home. Dum dum, dum dum de-da-dum. Coming for to carry me home."

Blair stared at the landscape stretched out in front of her. Had the man gone *insane*?

"Dum dum—" he launched into the song again.

Blair opened her mouth...

Closed it again. Men like Connor didn't go insane.

Not like this. Whatever he was doing, it was for a reason. Something about the song itself? The tune, or maybe the words that he wasn't saying? She searched her memory, listening with half an ear, trying to chase down the song's name.

And then, suddenly, it clicked.

It was an old, old song, one she could remember her mother singing to her as a lullaby on warm summer nights. *Swing Low, Sweet Chariot.*

Swing low...

It still didn't make sense. But at least now it was an order she could understand.

"Check," she murmured, and shoved her stick forward.

She'd had a faint hope that the screaming power dive might take the pursuing HK by surprise. But no, the damn machine was sticking to her like one of Wince's noxious glue concoctions.

Was Connor expecting her to do a sudden pull-up and try to smash the HK all over the landscape? It was worth a try, anyway. Waiting until the last second, Blair pulled out of her dive, leveling off at barely fifty meters above the street.

But again, her shadow matched the maneuver perfectly. Worse, with Blair's maneuverability now constricted by the buildings rising up on both sides, the HK was taking the opportunity to pour some serious fire into her tail. Ahead, Blair could see the bus lying on its side in the middle of the street south of the Moldavia building—

She caught just a glimpse of the two miniguns opening up from atop the bus as she flashed past, their twin lines of destruction focused behind her.

The HK never had a chance. It tried to dodge, but the same canyon of buildings that was hemming in Blair was doing the same to it. The streams of lead caught the machine in its nose, belly, and turbofans, and as Blair watched in her mirrors the HK exploded in midair.

"Pull up!" Connor snapped.

That was an order Blair didn't need to hear twice. She hauled back on her stick, pulling her fighter out of the path of the flaming debris now arrowing toward the ground from behind her. She reached building-top height and turned west, looking down out of her cockpit in time to see what was left of the HK crash onto the street and sweep across the line of T-600s that had been firing at Barnes and the Moldavia.

"We have breach!" David's voice came suddenly in Blair's ear. "Repeat, we have breach. We're going in—"

"Watch it!" Tunney's voice cut him off. "T-1 on guard! Make that *two* T-1s."

"I got east," David snapped over the crackle of machinegun fire. "Fire in the hole!"

"Fire in the hole!" Tunney echoed.

There was a violent thud in Blair's ear, followed half a second later by a second one.

"T-1 neutralized," David reported, his voice tight. "Two men down."

"T-1 neutralized," Tunney said. "No casualties. Moving in to assist."

Blair swung her fighter around toward the warehouse. The wall she'd seen David's people mining was all but gone, the roof sagging badly over neat stacks of equipment and on top of what was left of the two T-1 watchdogs that the C4 grenades had just finished off.

Blair sighed. "Damn," she muttered under her breath.

She'd *really* wanted to be there to see that wall come down.

CHAPTER NINETEEN

"Well done, everyone," Connor said into his mike, feeling the first trickle of hope he'd had all night. "David, set up a defensive line; Tunney, move in to support him. We'll be heading in immediately as backstop. And remember, even T-600s who are low or out of ammo are nothing to be treated lightly."

"Don't worry about us," David responded, his voice sounding grimly pleased. "I count at least twelve spare miniguns, plus four crates of ammo belts." He paused. "I mean, *damn*, there's a lot of stuff in here. Skynet was definitely planning a big night."

"It was probably going to hit another neighborhood after it finished with this one," Barnes said gruffly. "What about us, Connor?"

Connor grimaced. He knew what Kate and Barnes wanted to do. He also knew that it would probably be a heartbreaking waste of their time. The Terminators that had breached the Moldavia had had a lot of time in there. More than enough time to kill everyone in the building.

But the squad had come this far, and they'd put their lives on the line to do it. If there was anything that could be salvaged from the ruins across the street, they deserved the chance to try.

"Go ahead," he told Barnes. "But tread lightly. Any Terminators still in there will probably be heading straight through you to try to get to the warehouse. Hickabick, do what you can to fly cover for everyone."

"Check," Blair's voice came back. "Nice singing voice, by the way."

Connor smiled tightly. "Thanks."

And with that, it suddenly occurred to him that he finally had an answer to the question Kate had asked him in the middle of the night, just two days ago. The question born of fatigue and tension and momentary hopelessness.

Even in this dark and dismal world, there *were* still reasons for people to sing.

All at once, the firing stopped.

Orozco frowned, his view blocked by the body lying on top of him, trying to listen through his ringing ears. Surely the Terminators hadn't stopped their attack already. Or had the battering of the gunfire—combined with his slow but steady loss of blood—merely made him deaf?

And then, as the ringing in his ears faded; he heard the thudding of heavy machine feet. He wasn't deaf, and the Terminators were still here.

Only they seemed to be moving away from him.

Away from him?

It would be a risk, Orozco knew. Movement of any sort was pretty much a guaranteed way of attracting Terminator attention. But he needed to see what was happening out there. Gathering his last reserves of strength, he leaned his shoulder against the body lying on top of him and pushed.

For a moment nothing happened. Orozco kept at it,

clenching his teeth against the throbbing pain in his arm, and suddenly the body rolled over onto its back.

He tensed. But no miniguns roared, and no slugs hammered into his body. Blinking the sweat and the other man's blood from his eyes, he craned his neck and looked around him.

The Terminators were leaving. All of them, lumbering at full speed toward the archway.

They stepped beneath it—

The multiple explosions were actually quieter than Orozco had expected them to be. But the visuals were every bit as spectacular as he'd hoped. Just above the archway, the ten pipe bombs he'd drilled into the decorative facing went off simultaneously, lifting two floors' worth of stone a foot straight up into the air. The facing reached the top of its rise and fell back down, the impact shattering the archway below it and dumping the entire mass of stone onto the Terminators.

Orozco squinted as a wave of dust blew threw the lobby, tasting the bitterness of this last twist of irony. He'd set up the booby trap to hopefully eliminate some of the attackers before they could get inside the building. Instead, they'd come in through the rear, and had missed the trap entirely.

Now when everyone was already dead and destroying the Terminators gained nothing for anyone, they had finally triggered the damn thing.

Just the same, he was glad he'd lived long enough to see it.

The roar of tumbling rock faded away, and with it the last sound Orozco knew he would ever hear.

Resting among the dead, he closed his eyes and prepared to join them.

***

The Terminators were coming.

Blair watched them as she circled as slowly as she could without stalling out. There were sixteen in all, marching in from the west and northwest, probably the last of the T-600s that had been on containment duty at that edge of the neighborhood. With the steadiness and determination of an incoming tide, they were converging on the warehouse.

And unlike the remnants of the earlier attack force, this group almost certainly was still heavily armed.

Blair shifted her attention to the warehouse itself. David and his team had unlimbered two of the spare miniguns, and Tunney's team was busy uncrating extra ammo belts. It was shaping up to be quite a fight.

Though it could have been a lot worse, she knew. Between her own strafing run on the crowd behind the Moldavia, Connor's and Barnes's squads blowing away T-600s in job lots, and the entryway crash that Kate Connor had described—and which Blair *again* hadn't seen, *damn it*—the Terminator count was way down from what Skynet had started with that evening.

The gasoline fire west of the Moldavia might have taken out a couple, too—one of Barnes's team had reported spotting two T-600s in that area just before that particular balloon went up.

Still, there was no getting around the fact that there were sixteen fresh troops moving in.

So far none of them had tried taking a potshot at Blair's A-10, but that might just be because Skynet wanted them saving their ammo for the main event.

She grimaced, wishing she had a few rounds left in her GAU-8. Just a few. A strafing run now with 30mm explosive shells would be so soul-satisfying.

"Incoming!" David's voice snapped.

Blair jerked her head up, swearing at herself under her breath. So intent had she been on the approaching T-600s that she'd neglected her primary duty of watching the skies. She darted her eyes around the horizon.

And felt her blood freeze. Approaching rapidly from the north were no fewer than seven shadowy aircraft.

All of them bearing down on the warehouse.

"Oh, hell," she murmured, automatically turning her fighter to intercept. Though what she could do against that many HKs, with an unarmed fighter—

"Hickabick, isn't it?" an unfamiliar voice crackled suddenly in her ear.

Blair frowned. Since when did Skynet program its HKs with folksy voices?

"Hickabick here," she acknowledged cautiously.

"Snarkster here," the voice said. "Commander of Squadron Five. No offense, but you might want to pull up just a bit."

Blair frowned even harder...and then, as she peered out at the approaching shadows, their shapes suddenly clarified. She saw the slender bodies, the side-mounted weapons pods, and the flickering of the rotating blades above them.

They weren't Skynet's Hunter-Killers. They were Resistance Apache combat helicopters.

"About time, Snarkster," she chided, pulling up out of their way. "Got some targets for you about half a klick west."

"Excellent," Snarkster said grimly. "You just point 'em out, step aside, and enjoy the show."

Two minutes later, the sixteen T-600s had been turned

into blazing mounds of scrap metal.

And Blair had very much enjoyed the show.

CHAPTER TWENTY

Kyle woke up to the very strange sensation of being hot and cold at the same time.

Carefully, he opened his eyes. He was lying on his side on the ground, his head propped up on Star's lap. One of her hands was resting on his cheek, the other clutching his shoulder like she was afraid he was going to leave her.

"How long?" he asked, startled by the croaking sound of his own voice.

Half an hour, Star signed. Her expression, Kyle noted, was seriously worried. *How do you feel?*

"Cold," Kyle told her. "*And* hot. What—?"

And then it all came flashing back to him. The fire and explosion he'd set off, the wall of flame that had thrown him clear out of the tunnel...

He reached a hand to his cheek. It was warm, but sunburn warm, not at all like skin that had been burned to a crisp. The image he'd had of being bathed in flame must not have been nearly as bad as it had seemed at the time.

His back, on the other hand...

He started to reach behind him, but stopped as Star caught his hand. *Gone*, she signed. *Your jacket. Gone.*

"Ah," Kyle said. So that was where the cold part of the sensation was coming from. The wall of flame that had kicked him out of the tunnel had burned the jacket clean off his back.

Hopefully, it had left most of the skin behind. At least Kyle couldn't feel any particular pain coming from back there.

Maybe the pain would come later. Propping himself up on one elbow, he blinked his eyes a few times and surveyed the damage.

It was pretty impressive, if he did say so himself. The broken-building camouflage that had disguised the three entrances to the gasoline stash was completely gone, though pieces of it were still smoldering with foul-smelling black smoke. Where the chamber and stash itself had been was now a deep crater.

And lying in the middle of the crater were three unmoving metal bodies.

So it had worked. He hadn't been completely sure it would, not even with something as hot as a gasoline fire. But it had worked.

"Come on, we'd better get moving," he said. Pressing one hand to the ground, he heaved himself to his feet.

And nearly fell over again. Star was instantly at his side, holding him up as he fought against the sudden light-headedness that had sent the whole world spinning around him.

The spinning faded away, leaving behind a terrible weakness. There was no way they were going to make it back to the Ashes, he knew. Not yet.

But there might be another option.

"The ganghouse," he told Star, nodding his head in that direction. "The one where they tried to jump us yesterday."

But there's someone still in there, she objected.

So she'd also seen the face looking out when they'd passed by earlier with Nguyen's people.

"I doubt it," he said. "If they had any brains they took off as soon as the Terminators started shooting."

And even if they hadn't, he added to himself, there was still no choice but to risk it.

It took them five minutes to pick their way around the smoldering rubble and get to the ganghouse. Gripping his Colt—somehow, in all the chaos around the gasoline stash he'd lost the rifle and shotgun—he pushed the door open.

To his relief, the place was deserted.

"This'll do," he declared, glancing around and spotting a chair that had been conveniently left beside the door. "Hang on—I have to sit down for a minute."

He eased himself down on the chair, relieved that he'd made it here without collapsing. His legs were trembling, and there were white spots dancing in front of his eyes. Taking deep breaths, keeping his eyes on the floor in front of his feet, he concentrated on not passing out.

And started as a ration bar and a bottle of water suddenly appeared in front of him.

He looked up. Star was holding them out to him, a worried look on her face.

"Where'd you get these?" Kyle asked, frowning as he took them from her.

Over there, she signed, and pointed across the room.

"Whoa," Kyle murmured, gazing in surprise at the pile of clothing and the small boxes stacked neatly on one of the room's other chairs. "Where'd *that* come from?"

Star gave him the kind of exaggeratedly patient look that she did so well.

"Right—you don't know," Kyle said. "Well, I don't

suppose whoever left it is coming back any time soon."
He peered across at the clothing. "You suppose there's a
jacket over there that would fit me?"

Star's answer was to make a beeline for the stack.

Kyle had finished the ration bar and half the water by
the time she returned, triumphantly carrying not just a
new jacket, but a new shirt and new jeans as well.

"That's great," Kyle said, setting down the water and
trying not to wince as he stripped off the tattered
remains of his own clothing. The new outfit was a little
big for him, but it was warm and—most importantly—
not half burned away.

"Just like Christmas, huh?" he commented as he sat
down again. "I don't suppose there was any more water
over there?"

Connor had met General Olsen a couple of times over the
past few months, and hadn't been particularly impressed.
The man had a casual way of talking, and an air of easy-
going charm that Connor found gratingly at odds with
the deadly seriousness of life in Skynet's shadow.

But if Olsen the man wasn't anything remarkable,
Olsen the soldier and commander was. Connor had seen
only a partial list of the man's accomplishments, but that
was more than enough to have earned him humanity's
respect, and Connor's as well.

And so it was without a single twinge of resentment or
cynicism that Connor threw Olsen a salute as the general
stepped out of the last of the five Black Hawk troop car-
riers to land on the warehouse grounds.

"General," he said. "Glad you could make it."

"Nice to be here," Olsen replied. He glanced around
at the swarm of men and women lugging the crates and

boxes to the line of cargo helicopters, then looked back at Connor. "'Course, I expect you'd've been even gladder if we'd shown up, say, an hour earlier?"

"It could have been helpful," Connor agreed, choosing his words carefully.

Olsen grinned tightly.

"I'll just bet it would've." The grin faded. "I wish I could've, too. But I 'spect you know how it is."

"Command needed to know you weren't risking men and resources for a hopeless cause?"

Olsen grunted. "You never have been much of one for spackling over your words, have you, Connor?"

"Not really," Connor said. "Did we pass the test?"

"Passed it and then some," Olsen said, nodding. "Enough that Command's ready to take you and your team on full-time."

"You mean like the last time they took us on?" David put in as he came up to them. His voice was respectful enough, but Connor could see the slow simmer going on behind the other's eyes.

Connor could sympathize. Having their hard-earned prize suddenly and casually taken over this way wasn't an easy thing to swallow.

But then, getting Command's attention *had* been the chief goal of the mission, after all.

"No, I think you've actually convinced them this time," Olsen said. If he had noticed David's anger, he was pretending he hadn't. "This isn't some new probation or any of that crap. You're being offered a full slot in the Resistance structure, no strings, and all the goodies that go along with it."

"Funny," David said, throwing a pointed look at all the crates making their way into Olsen's helicopters. "I thought we'd already found ourselves a stack of goodies."

"Oh, that you did," Olsen said, his genial voice hardening just noticeably. "But if you'll look closely, you might notice it's mostly goodies you can't use."

He pointed to a pair of crates being manhandled into one of the Black Hawks. "That ammo, f'rinstance. Fits HK Gatlings. You have anything that caliber?"

"Probably," David said stubbornly.

"Probably not," Olsen countered. "Might figure out a way to adapt it to an A-10's GAU-8, but it'd be real tricky. Be a lot simpler to just take out the GAU-8 and shove an HK Gatling in its place." He raised his eyebrows. "You have any spare HK Gatlings lying around?"

"Our pilots don't usually leave much worth salvaging," David said with a touch of pride.

"True enough," Olsen acknowledged. "'Course, even if you had one, swapping it out would take a heap of work and a crapload of equipment you probably don't have. And as for the rest of the stuff…"

He looked back at Connor, a frown creasing his face.

"You really don't know what you've got here, do you?"

"I only arrived just before you did, General," Connor told him. "I haven't had a chance to look around."

"Then let me enlighten you," Olsen said, his folksy manner suddenly gone. "This here wasn't just a neighborhood-sweep staging area. It was that, too, but it wasn't mostly that." He waved a hand behind him. "This here was gearing up to be a brand spankin' new maintenance center."

Connor shifted his eyes over the general's shoulder, an unpleasant tingle running through him. No wonder Skynet had been so hell-bent on defending the place.

"Really," he murmured.

"Really," Olsen assured him. "And maybe not just maintenance, either. There are whole crateloads of electronics and minicomputers in there, plus some weapons we're going to want to look into reverse-engineering. I could be wrong, but I'm guessing Skynet was planning a serious upgrade for pretty much everything it's got in this sector. And all that was slated to happen right here."

He smiled lopsidedly.

"Except you and your team have just single-handedly stopped it. You think Command's going to be fussing over probation protocol?"

"I see your point," Connor said.

"I would damn well hope so," Olsen said. "They've got a base all picked out for you to move into—nice and big, well protected, and out of this mess that L.A.'s become."

"Sounds enticing," Connor said. "And the catch?"

Olsen shrugged. "You learn to take orders." He grinned. "'Course they're all *good* orders. That goes without saying."

David snorted. But the sound was more thoughtful than resentful, and he was no longer glowering as he watched the crates being loaded aboard the Black Hawks.

"Okay, it's a deal," Connor told Olsen. "We'll need to get the rest of our people back, and there's some food and random equipment we left at our staging area."

"Call the people; forget the clutter," Olsen said briskly. "I got a report just before I landed that Skynet's got more HKs burning their way up from San Diego. It is *not* happy with you and your crew right now."

"Understandable," Connor said, flipping on his transmitter. "Barnes: get your squad together and bring it in, double-time. Don't bother stopping by the staging area—we're leaving whatever's there behind."

"Got it," Barnes said briskly. "On our way."

Connor flicked off the transmitter and turned to David.

"Go gather your squad and Tunney's," he told him. "We'll be traveling—" He raised his eyebrows at Olsen.

"In my personal choppers, yes," the general confirmed with a nod. "Oh, and I got another report on the way in. The other choppers have finished cleaning out the rest of your base, people, and whatever else they could load aboard. Soon's we're done here, we're out."

Connor nodded. "And double-time it," he added to David.

The other nodded and moved off.

"What about our pilot?" Connor asked. "Last I heard she was being escorted out, but had been ordered to shut down her radio."

Olsen nodded. "Security measure," he said. "Our airstrip is still secret, and we'd like to keep it that way as long as we can."

"Of course," Connor said. "I just want to make sure she's taken care of."

"Oh, she will be," Olsen promised. "We treat our pilots very well, and from what we saw tonight she's definitely one hell of a pilot." He shook his head. "One hell of a plane, too. That has got to be the damnedest patchwork job I've ever seen on an A-10. I'm surprised the thing's still flying. Whoever your mechanic is, he's a wizard."

"He is all that," Connor agreed. "And before you ask, you can't have him."

Olsen grinned. "We'll see. Anyway, like I said, we're on tight numbers, so grab your people, grab your butt, and get all of it aboard the choppers."

"Yes, sir." Connor turned and started to walk away.

Olsen's hand snaked out to touch his arm.

"You did good today, Connor," he said quietly. "Right now, everyone knows that. But they'll forget. People always forget."

"That's fine," Connor said. "I'm not in this for the glory."

"I know you're not," Olsen said. "I'm just saying that when the rest forget, don't you forget, too."

Connor gazed out at the quiet city around them. The city where so many people had died tonight.

"Don't worry, General," he said quietly. "I won't forget. Ever."

It took Kate a good half hour of work, plus nearly a third of the medicines and bandages in her field kit, to put Sergeant Orozco back together. But when she was finished, she had the satisfaction of seeing his eyes flicker open.

"Sergeant?" she called gently. "Sergeant Orozco? Can you hear me?"

The eyes closed, flickered again, and then opened all the way. For a long moment he stared up into her face, his forehead furrowed with questions or confusion or disbelief.

"It's Kate Connor, Sergeant," Kate said, wondering how much the morphine was fogging his brain. "We were here this morning."

"I know," Orozco said, his voice weak but with no signs of disorientation. "What are you doing here *now*?"

"We came to help," Kate said. "I'm sorry we couldn't get here sooner."

Slowly, Orozco turned his head, his eyes taking in the devastation and death around them.

"How many?" he asked.

Kate felt her stomach tighten.

"You're the only one we've found alive."

For a long moment Orozco lay silently. Kate watched him, wondering if he was going to slip off into unconsciousness again. Then, finally, he stirred.

"I'm not feeling much pain," he said. "Morphine?"

Kate nodded. "I have more if you need it."

"Maybe later," he said. "What's the damage?"

"Not as bad as it could have been," Kate assured him. "You had a through-and-through in your upper left arm and another slug in your shoulder. I got it out. There were also several grooves in your left forearm, which I sewed up, and you took a grazing shot across your right hip."

"Right hip, huh?" Orozco said, frowning. "I didn't even know about that one. How mobile am I?"

"Well, you won't be going on any long hikes for awhile," Kate said. "Fortunately, you won't have to. Now that you're stable enough to move, I can call for a litter to get you to the chopper. A few weeks in rehab—"

"Whoa," Orozco interrupted. "Chopper?"

"The Resistance has arrived in force," Kate told him. "We're going to be taken to one of their bases."

"A base with generals and admirals and everyone?" Orozco asked.

"Probably," Kate said. "And that's good. It means they should have everything we'll need to get you on your feet again."

"Glad to hear it," Orozco said. "I hope they find someone they can use it on. You'd better get going. Thanks for patching me up."

Kate stared at him.

"What are you talking about?" she asked carefully.

"We're taking you with us."

"I don't think so," Orozco said, a sudden bitterness in his voice. "It was people like your precious generals and admirals who brought Judgment Day down on the world in the first place. It'll be a cold day in hell before I'll ever work for them again."

"But you can't just stay here," Kate protested. "Where will you go? What will you do?"

"I'll survive," Orozco said. "I'm a Marine. That's what Marines do. If you can spare me a little food and water, I'd appreciate it. If you can't, that's fine, too."

"Sergeant, you're not thinking clearly," Kate said, putting some firmness into her voice. "You're alone, you've lost a lot of blood—"

"Your generals are waiting, Ms. Connor." Orozco cut her off.

"Then look at it from my position," Kate said, switching tactics. "I'm a doctor. How can I just walk away and leave you here alone? Or never mind me. What's John going to say when I tell him I left an injured soldier behind?"

"You'll tell him first that I'm not one of his soldiers," Orozco said. "And you'll tell him second that you didn't have a choice." His right shoulder twitched.

And Kate looked down to see the man's bloodied hand gripping the butt of the Beretta belted at his side. "You wouldn't," she said, looking him squarely in the face.

For a moment he held her gaze. Then, almost reluctantly, his eyes drifted away.

"No," he admitted. "But you never know what a crazy man's going to do, do you?" He looked over her shoulder, toward the huge mound of stone rubble she and the others had had to climb over to get into the building.

"Did a good job on that archway, didn't I?"

"Yes, you did," Kate said, conceding defeat. If he truly didn't want to come with them, there really wasn't any way she could justify forcing him to do so.

Her earphone crackled.

"Barnes: get your squad together and bring it in, double-time," John's voice came. "Don't bother stopping by the staging area—we're leaving whatever's there behind."

"Got it," Barnes said. "On our way."

"Time to go?" Orozco asked.

"Yes," Kate said, unfastening her ration pouch from her belt and laying it beside Orozco. "This is all the food and water I've got with me, but there's more in a sort of long house two blocks west of here. It's on the street where—"

"I know the place," Orozco said. "Passed it once or twice."

Kate nodded and stood up.

"Last chance."

Orozco nodded. "Better get going."

"Right." Kate hesitated, then unclipped her medical bag and set it beside the ration pouch. "Good luck."

"One other thing," Orozco called after her.

She paused and turned back.

"Yes?"

"There were 280 people who died in here tonight," Orozco said, his voice dark. "I'd consider it a personal favor if you and Connor would take out a Terminator for each of them."

Kate swallowed, her throat feeling tight. "We'll do our best," she promised. "And we'll think of you with every single one of them."

"Good enough," Orozco said. "*Vaya con Dios*, Ms. Connor."

***

Kate had been waiting by the pile of stone for about two minutes when Barnes and the rest of the squad returned.

"No one else?" Kate asked. A silly question, she knew—they would certainly have called her if they'd found anyone else still alive.

"No," Barnes said, making it official, as he gestured everyone to start climbing the rubble. "You got a litter coming for Orozco?"

Kate shook her head as she started up the treacherous footing.

"He's not coming with us."

A couple of the other heads turned at that one. But Barnes just grunted.

"You get attached to a place like this, I guess."

They were over the rock pile and walking down the empty streets before Barnes spoke again.

"I found that preacher—Sibanda—over in the hallway off the lobby," he said. "Still had his arms around a couple of kids."

"Thin black guy?" Simmons asked. "North hallway by one of the windows?"

Barnes nodded. "That's him."

"I saw him, too," Simmons said grimly. "Looked like he was huddled over the kids, trying to protect them, when they shot him in the back."

Kate felt a fresh wave of sadness and guilt flow through her. All those children...and neither she nor anyone else had been able to save a single one of them.

"Any particular reason you brought that up?" she asked Barnes.

"Not really," he said with a shrug. "Just making conversation."

* * *

For nearly half an hour Kyle and Star just sat there in the abandoned ganghouse, quietly eating and drinking, Kyle on the chair, Star on the ground at his feet. It was the first time since they'd left the Ashes, Kyle reflected soberly, that he'd felt at peace.

But it wasn't real, he knew. Peace was only an illusion these days.

And it was time for them to go.

To Kyle's relief, there was no lightheadedness this time when he stood up. Maybe he hadn't really been injured in the blast, but had mostly been just hungry and thirsty. Adjusting his new shirt and jacket across his shoulders, he fastened his holster around his new jeans.

"Ready?" he asked Star.

She nodded, then pointed questioningly at the packages of ration bars and water bottles.

Kyle pursed his lips. If this stuff had belonged to the gang that Orozco had chased out, he would have no particular qualms about taking it all. It wasn't really stealing to take something from a thief.

But his new clothes didn't look like the stuff the gang had been wearing. It was too clean, for one thing. And the water bottles seemed way too well taken care of, too. He had the feeling that someone else had moved in after the gang had cleared out.

And he and Star couldn't steal from ordinary citizens. Even if all the stuff really had been abandoned.

Or at least they couldn't steal *everything*.

"Go get two bottles of water and four of the bars," he instructed Star. "Somebody might still come back for the rest."

Star wrinkled her nose, but nodded and went over to

the stack. She was sorting through the packages when something behind the clothing seemed to belatedly catch her eye. Reaching down, she lifted a shotgun into view.

This time, Kyle didn't hesitate.

"Yes," he said firmly.

A minute later, shotgun in hand, food and water in his new jacket's pockets, Kyle opened the door and they once more slipped out into the night. *Where are we going?* Star signed.

"Back to the Ashes," Kyle told her, frowning as they set off along the street. Was that the sound of helicopters just fading away in the distance? Probably his imagination.

"We need to see if there's anything we can do there to help."

The streets were eerily quiet, with only the sound of their own footsteps breaking the silence. Kyle looked around carefully as they walked, wondering if any of the people they'd seen earlier were still lurking around here somewhere.

But they all seemed to have left. Could that have been what the sound of the helicopters had been about?

Too bad. He would at least have liked to find out who they'd been, and whether they'd really been with the Resistance or just faking it. He might have been able to find out whether the people in the bus who had saved him and Star had made it out alive, too. Now, he'd probably never know.

But at least when the men and women had left, the Terminators had left with them.

The Ashes building, when Kyle caught his first glimpse of it, was a shock. The distinctive stone archway was gone, as was most of the front of the building just above it, the whole mass having collapsed into a shattered heap of stone blocking most of the entrance.

Star clutched suddenly at Kyle's arm.

"It's okay," he soothed her. "Remember how Orozco told us that if there was ever an attack he could put bombs in the archway to bring it down on them?"

Star shook her head violently, her fingers digging into Kyle's arm. Kyle frowned...and then, his fogged brain got it.

He pushed Star against the building beside them, pressing himself there next to her as he fumbled his new shotgun to his shoulder. Heart thudding in his ears, he gave a quick look around them, then turned back to the Ashes building.

There it was, digging diligently through the rocks at the far end of the pile, lifting huge chunks of stone and concrete off the stack and setting them down on the street beside it.

Apparently, not all the Terminators had left.

Kyle frowned, wondering what the machine was doing. Was it looking for other Terminators that had been trapped in the collapse? It was using both hands, he noticed, and he looked briefly for where it had set down its minigun.

But there was no weapon to be seen. It must have lost the weapon, Kyle decided, or else had run out of ammo and dumped it. The Terminator pulled out another block of stone and set it aside.

Then, without warning, it turned directly toward Kyle and Star.

And as Kyle got his first clear look at the torn skin on its torso, skin torn away by a close-range shotgun blast, he suddenly realized who this was. Not some random Terminator, but their old enemy Fido.

For a long moment the machine gazed toward them. Kyle froze, his shotgun still pointed even as he realized how utterly useless the weapon was at this range.

And then, to Kyle's surprise and relief, the Terminator merely turned back to the rock pile. Leaning over, it reached both hands into the hole it had dug.

Kyle started breathing again. Maybe the machine hadn't seen them. Maybe its optics had been damaged by its tumble through the rotten floor near the Death's-Head compound.

The Terminator was still working at something in the hole, perhaps a stubborn stone that didn't want to be moved. Then, with a massive tug, it pulled a half-crushed metal arm out of the hole.

Only it wasn't just an arm. It was an arm that was still clutching a minigun, the weapon's ammo belt trailing down into the hole behind it.

Fido hadn't given up on hunting them. It also wasn't simply looking for broken Terminators or scrap metal to take back to Skynet.

It was looking for a new gun.

"Time to go," Kyle murmured, taking Star's arm and backing them along the wall again. They reached the corner, and just as they eased around it out of the Terminator's sight the machine once again turned its red eyes toward them.

It had seen them, all right. And as soon as it got its new weapon free, it was going to come after them.

"Come on," Kyle said. Still holding Star's arm, he broke into a dead run back toward the ganghouse.

Where? Star signed frantically as her feet pounded against the pavement.

"Not sure yet," Kyle told her. "Let's first just get some

distance between us and it. Distance *and* buildings," he added as he pulled her around the corner onto the next street heading north.

He took a deep breath, consciously settling his pumping legs into a steady rhythm, feeling a trickle of frustration run through him. He'd thought the terror of the night was over. He'd *needed* the terror of the night to be over.

But it wasn't. Maybe it never would be.

But it didn't matter. What mattered was that he and Star were still alive.

And they would stay that way, too. No matter what happened, no matter what the universe and Skynet threw at them, they would get through it. If and when that Terminator back there found them, Kyle would find a way to destroy it. Then he'd do the same to the next one Skynet sent after them, and the next one, and the one after that.

Because Star was counting on him.

The street stretched far ahead of them, fading away into the darkness. Watching Star out of the corner of his eye, making sure she was keeping up, he began studying the ruined buildings they were passing. Somewhere along here, he knew, he'd find something he could use.

The quarters General Olsen's aide took Connor and Kate to weren't a lot bigger than some of the other places they'd called home over the years. They weren't all that much better furnished, either.

But it wasn't bitterly cold, there was space for them to stow their weapons and other gear, and the floor was mostly nice and flat. More importantly, it was safe.

And that was a far rarer and more precious commodity than anything else the Resistance could have offered them.

"Yes, I could live here," Connor commented as he set down his MP5 and started taking off his gun belt.

Kate didn't answer. Crossing the room to a table beside the bed, she began divesting herself of her own load of weapons and equipment.

She'd hadn't said much on the helicopter ride out of Los Angeles, Connor had noticed. Virtually nothing, in fact, except for her brief assurance that she wasn't injured.

"You hungry?" Connor asked. "There's supposed to be a twenty-four-hour mess tucked away somewhere."

"Not right now," Kate said, her voice low.

Connor watched her, his own heart aching in sympathy. No matter how well an operation went, there never seemed to be any truly solid victories against Skynet. And even those partial victories always had to be paid for in human lives.

But seldom was the price as high as it had been tonight.

Kate finished unpacking her equipment and hung her jacket on top of her rifle. Then, not bothering to undress any farther, she climbed into the bed, rolling up onto her side and turning her face toward the wall. Setting down the rest of his own gear, Connor climbed into bed behind her.

"You want to talk about it?" he asked gently.

"Yes." She hesitated. "But first I need to apologize. I shouldn't have sneaked off against orders to join Barnes's squad. Apart from the fact that you're my husband, you're also my commander. It was inexcusable, and it jeopardized the whole mission."

Connor shrugged. "I don't know about the *jeopardized* part. I gather the only person who knew I hadn't actually sent you was me."

"Which could have been more than enough to get everyone killed," she reminded him soberly. "No, I was right the first time. Anything that distracts you affects your judgment, and damages your ability to be who you need to be. And if my presence on a mission is that distraction, then I just have to stay home."

"Or I need to adjust to you being who *you* need to be," Connor pointed out, resting his hand on her shoulder. "And the fact remains that if you *hadn't* been there, Reynolds would probably have died. You did good, Kate."

Her shoulder seemed to tighten beneath his hand. "Not good enough," she said in a low voice. "All those people...Orozco..."

"I know," Connor said. "I wish we could have saved them, too. But we don't always get what we wish for. We gave it everything we could. It just wasn't enough."

"But Orozco," Kate objected, some fire finally coming back into her voice. "Why would a strong, competent military man *do* something like that? Can someone real ly hate authority *that* much?"

"It's possible." Connor hesitated. "Or maybe it's that he hates *us* that much."

Kate rolled over to face him, her eyes wide.

"*Us?* But we tried to help."

"But we're part of the official Resistance now," Connor reminded her. "The people who didn't show up to help until it was too late."

Kate's face went rigid.

"You mean Orozco thinks—? Oh, John."

Connor nodded, forcing back a surge of frustration of his own.

"I know," he said. "And there's nothing we can do

about it, either. Except try to make sure it never happens again."

He ran his fingers gently across her cheek. "But don't worry about Orozco," he added. "He's a survivor. He'll be okay."

"I hope so," Kate said, laying her hand on top of his. "And as long as I'm apologizing, I also need to apologize for the way I've been lately. I think I'm—well, I need to check, of course, but all the signs are that—I mean—"

"Hey, relax," Connor said gently, smiling at her sudden babbling. He'd seen that a lot after missions, and it was a lot healthier than her earlier silent act. "Like I said, you did good out there. Barnes and Simmons both told me that, and you know how hard it is to get those two to agree on *anything*."

"I'm glad it worked out," Kate said. "Since you probably aren't going to take me on any more missions for awhile."

Connor grinned. "Why? Because you get all dark and moody when it's all over?"

She smiled, a hint of the old impish Kate peeking through.

"No," she said, lifting her hand from his and resting it on his cheek. "Because I think I'm pregnant."

And for the first time in years, John Connor couldn't find a single thing to say.

EPILOGUE

For a long time after the sound of the helicopters faded away Orozco just stayed where he was, propped up against the remnants of the barricade that hadn't done a damn bit of good, chewing on the ration bars Kate Connor had left him and sipping from the water bottle.

From time to time he thought about being responsible and saving some of the food for later. But it all tasted good, and he was ravenous, and he really needed to build back his strength. And anyway, later might never come.

After about an hour, though, he decided he was tired of sitting. His hip was still weak and tender where the Terminator slug had grazed it, but his M16 made a reasonably good walking stick. Carefully, he levered his way back to his feet.

For a long minute he just stood there, balancing on his left leg and the M16, looking around at the wreckage of everything he'd known for the past two years. He knew he should be angry, or bitter, or at least sad. But all he felt was empty.

Maybe it was the morphine Kate had given him. Maybe once the pain came back, some emotion would, too.

But there was no point just standing around waiting for that to happen. He might as well do what he could to stay alive, if for no better reason than to keep Skynet's victory tonight from being a complete hundred percent.

The first step—literally—would be to get a little more mobile. Three of Moldering Lost Ashes' older residents had walked with crutches, and one of them had had two sets. His room had been off the north corridor, here on the ground level where he wouldn't have to deal with stairs, and there was a good chance his spare set of crutches was still there. Favoring his right leg as much as he could, Orozco began picking his way through the debris.

He had reached the north corridor and was working his way along it when he found Sibanda.

He paused there, resting on his rifle, gazing down at the body. The bodies, rather—the thin pastor still had his arms wrapped around two of the younger children. He'd probably been trying to shield them with his own body when the Terminator shot them down.

Once again, Orozco tried to feel something. Once again, he found himself unable to do so. Giving Sibanda's body a final salute, he started to walk past.

He'd gone two steps when the crucial question suddenly penetrated his mental haze.

What in the world had Sibanda been doing back here?

He turned around, frowning down at the bodies. There were no rooms nearby that Sibanda might have been trying to take refuge in. No access to the upper floors or basement, even if going to either place would have done him any good. Had the man simply panicked and started dragging the children around in circles?

And then, Orozco raised his eyes from the bodies to the wall behind them. The wall, and the empty window frame.

It was tricky getting through the window with his bad hip, but Orozco managed it. Working his way along the twisting passageway among the rubble, he finally made it to the drainage tunnel manhole cover. The cover had been sealed earlier that afternoon, just as Orozco had ordered.

Sometime in the hours after that, someone had unsealed it.

The crowbar he and Wadleigh had used to pry up the cover was still there. But Orozco was alone this time, with a bad hip and an almost useless left arm, and the cover seemed to have somehow picked up about a ton of weight.

He was working and swearing at it when the cover was suddenly pushed up from the inside and a pair of hands shoved it part way off to the side.

Dropping the crowbar, Orozco snatched his Beretta from its holster and thumbed off the safety.

"Who's there?" he demanded. "Show yourself."

"Don't shoot," a scared, quavering voice called. The hands still clutching the rim of the cover shifted to the edge of the hole near the ladder.

And to Orozco's astonishment, seventeen-year-old Candace Tomlinson rose from the shaft. The girl who, less than twenty-four hours ago, had been whining and fighting over a jar of pickles.

Though in that first instant he barely recognized her. Her face was drawn and pale, her skin swollen with the puffiness of recent crying.

"Is it over?" she asked, her eyes shifting nervously around. "Is it safe? Reverend Sibanda said that when it was safe—"

She broke off, her face screwing up as she belatedly focused on Orozco's bandages and arm sling and splatters of dried blood. She opened her mouth, and Orozco braced himself for a scream.

But the scream never came. With a visible effort, the girl dragged herself back from the edge of hysteria.

And when she finally closed her mouth again, her face had aged ten years.

"Yes, it's over," Orozco told her quietly. "But it didn't turn out very well. Are you alone in there?"

Candace swallowed hard.

"No," she murmured. Moving like a sleepwalker, she pushed the cover the rest of the way off the hole and climbed out.

"It's all right," she called softly into the shaft. "You can come up now."

A minute later, they all had. Eight of them, ranging in age from Candace's seventeen years to Rob's fifteen, all the way down to Olivia's seven.

Orozco watched them as they climbed out and lined up silently next to Candace, his heart sinking within him. Eight children, lost in a building full of their dead parents and friends.

Eight children, looking to Orozco for help.

"All right, this is how it is," he said when the last of them was out and Rob had pushed the cover halfway over the hole again. "The nine of us are all that are left. Everyone else is dead."

He watched their faces closely, waiting for explosions of disbelief, denial, or hysteria. But they all merely looked at him out of their tear-stained faces.

They'd already had their private bouts with denial and fear. And like Candace, they'd come out the other end with whatever was left of their childhood gone.

"All right, then," Orozco went on. "I know a place,

not too far away, where we can go settle in for the next day or so. After that, we'll probably have to move somewhere else. Getting out of the building won't be pleasant, though, so I want you all to promise you'll keep your eyes on me as we go through the lobby. Okay? Everyone promise?"

Hesitantly, Candace raised her hand.

"What about food and water?" she asked.

"I'm told there's some there," Orozco said. "I don't know how much. Once we're settled, I can come back here and look for more."

"But you're hurt, aren't you?" Rob asked.

"I'm not *that* hurt," Orozco said gruffly. "Come on— I want to be under cover before it starts getting light."

"There's no point in you going all that way and then having to come back," Candace said, her voice under tight control. "I know where there's some food. I'll go get it."

"That's all right," Orozco said quickly. The last thing he wanted was any of his charges wandering around among all those bodies. "We need to get to the hideout."

"We'll need clothes, too," Rob spoke up. His voice, like Candace's, was shaky but determined. "I'll go help Candace."

Orozco shook his head. "I can't let you—"

"They're all dead," Candace said, her eyes welling with tears. "We know that. We won't be...We'll go get the food, okay?"

Orozco sighed. "Okay. We'll meet you at the big pile of rock where the archway used to be. Be careful."

Candace nodded. "We will."

Walking close together, she and Rob disappeared back into the rabbit warren.

"Okay, let's go," Orozco said to the others. "Everyone

follow me."

"Do you need help?" Olivia asked timidly as Orozco got a grip on his M16. "We could try to carry you."

"Not right now, thanks," Orozco assured the girl. "Better save your strength for later, when my pain meds wear off."

Actually, the morphine was already starting to wear off, and the trip back to the building was considerably harder and slower than the trip out had been. Maneuvering his way back in through the window was minor torture, and Orozco's face and shirt were wet with sweat by the time he was once again inside Moldering Lost Ashes.

He fully expected some of the younger children to panic or scream or at least break down in sobs as they passed through the lobby. But there wasn't even a sniffle. However it was that Sibanda had chosen these particular children for a second chance at life, he'd chosen them well.

They had reached the pile of rocks when Candace and Rob returned with two canvas bags each full of food, water, and extra clothing. Over Rob's shoulders were slung a shotgun and another rifle.

Strapped to Candace's back, to Orozco's surprise, were Cap Royer's spare set of crutches.

The universe was a strange place, Orozco thought as the group worked their way over the heap of stone. He'd turned down Connor's invitation mainly because he was tired of authority and responsibility and having to do and care for others. He'd looked forward to spending some time being strictly on his own, with no one's life in his hands. Now, in a single stroke, that option was closed to him.

And what was truly strange was that he couldn't even imagine having wanted such a thing. These were his children now, his responsibility, and he would take care of them.

Because he was a Marine. And that was what Marines did.

The End

COMING SOON:

THE OFFICIAL NOVELIZATION OF THE MUCH-ANTICIPATED MOVIE TERMINATOR SALVATION, STARRING CHRISTIAN BALE.

COMING SOON:

THE ART OF TERMINATOR SALVATION
TARA BENNETT

A stunning visual chronicling of the making of *Terminator Salvation*, comprising hundreds of color illustrations, storyboards and intricately designed production art showcasing the amazing talent that has gone into creating this remarkable movie.

ISBN: 9781848560826

TERMINATOR SALVATION:
THE OFFICIAL MOVIE COMPANION
TARA BENNETT

A full-color companion takes you behind-the-scenes of the making of the brand-new movie and is packed with interviews and commentary from the cast and crew, as well as an abundance of stunning, previously unseen photos.

ISBN: 9781848560819